With

compliments

of the

publisher

HARPERVIA

An Imprint of HarperCollins*Publishers*

ALSO BY MAUD VENTURA

My Husband

A NOVEL

MAKE ME FAMOUS

MAUD VENTURA

Translated by Gretchen Schmid

HarperVia

An Imprint of HarperCollins*Publishers*

MAKE ME FAMOUS. Copyright © 2024 by L'Iconoclaste, Paris. All rights reserved. Printed in the United States of America. No part of this book may be used or reproduced in any manner whatsoever without written permission except in the case of brief quotations embodied in critical articles and reviews. For information, address HarperCollins Publishers, 195 Broadway, New York, NY 10007.

English translation copyright © 2025 by Gretchen Schmid.

HarperCollins books may be purchased for educational, business, or sales promotional use. For information, please email the Special Markets Department at SPsales@harpercollins.com.

Originally published as *Célèbre* in France in 2024 by L'Iconoclaste.

First HarperVia hardcover published in 2025

FIRST EDITION

Designed by Elina Cohen

Library of Congress Cataloging-in-Publication Data has been applied for.

ISBN 978-0-06-342751-8

$PrintCode

TO MY HUSBAND

Fame is my life. The life I knew I would have, the life I made sure to have. Was I prepared to be so successful? Of course I was. I always believed that what the future had in store for me wasn't just an existence—it was a destiny.

When people talk about fame, they think of glitz and glamour, money, devoted fans, prestige, everybody recognizing you. But they should also consider the constant feeling of superiority, the intoxicating wealth, the nonstop commentary, the vanity, the hypocrisy, the impunity. Fame is a hard drug—a ferocious monster. And I sought it out, fought tooth and nail in my pursuit of it.

Extreme notoriety unleashed in me a beast, merciless and cruel. I might as well admit it: I got my hands dirty. At my level, everyone has skeletons in the closet. Anyone who claims otherwise is a liar. Fame is a war trophy, and no one is ever ready to give it up.

At thirty-two, I'm on top of the pyramid, and I got there all by myself. I don't believe in luck. I don't believe in using connections. I don't believe in the glass ceiling. I owe my success to hard work, talent, and meritocracy. If I'd been able to be honest the last time I won an award, I would have thanked only one person during my long speech at the ceremony: myself.

There weeks on a desert island in the middle of the Pacific Ocean. A place without running water or electricity, cut off from all contact with the outside world. That's the kind of fantasy that fame can buy. When you already have everything, you have to put a little imagination into your summer vacation.

Yesterday I spent ten hours in a private jet. We landed near Tahiti, or Fiji, or maybe it was Hawaii. I climbed on board a second plane, and then a seaplane. An hour later, there it was: an atoll, nearly lost within the immensity of the ocean.

I'm walking in a postcard: Ocean as far as the eye can see, white sand, a magnificent lagoon. Flocks of seabirds are resting on the rocks. The landscape is lush; frequent rain showers, probably—the cistern is full. Coconut palms, banana trees, orange trees: I won't die of hunger. I look out toward the sea, trying to spot some other land, anything to anchor my eyes on. There's nothing.

My only shelter for the next three weeks is a little hut on the beach. It's charming, built on stilts, with a terrace that faces the ocean. The high, sloping wooden structure supports a roof covered with woven palm leaves. Inside is all one room, simply furnished with a twin bed, a dresser, a table, and two chairs. There is a large cupboard with groceries: rice, fruit, dried fish, root vegetables, canned goods, twenty-five gallons of mineral water. I open the drawers, finishing my inventory, then arrange my meager spoils on the floor: a portable stove, two canisters of gas, flippers, a scuba mask, a flashlight, a machete, a box of matches, mosquito netting, a water purifier, a fishing net, a globe, a first-aid kit, a Bible. There's nothing on the walls, no decorations whatsoever, no clock, no mirror. A bit rustic for a vacation that costs half a million dollars. But everyone knows that there's an inverse correlation between the price of your trip and the strength of your Wi-Fi. What I'm paying for is being in the middle of nowhere, inaccessible to prying eyes, cell phones, the paparazzi—and my team's incessant requests. This year I'm giving myself the best gift of all: for everyone to leave me the fuck alone.

I heard about this island for the first time six months ago. That evening I was making a highly anticipated appearance at the after-party for a music awards ceremony where I had, once again, won everything, and delivered all the acceptance speeches in a row. Trophy in hand, I had paid tribute to my fans four times, a tremolo in my voice and tears in my eyes. That's the first thing you learn: crying on command. It's the same act every time. You have to convey flushed excitement and a shy sense of triumph, explain that the only reason you make music is for your fans, give credit to all the people behind the scenes by listing a series of names that don't mean anything to anyone.

Natalie Holmes was hanging out by the bar at the after-party, champagne flute in hand. I hadn't run into her for more than a year, and that year had been eventful for me: a breakup, a betrayal, a media frenzy, drama, the triumphant release of my third album. Natalie Holmes and I had had a handful of mutual friends, but those friends had become enemies, so I was ready to bet that she would pretend she hadn't seen me, eyes cast down toward her

Jimmy Choos. But I was wrong. She came up to me with a big smile. It's funny how success can make people miraculously forget their ill will. My new assistant whispered into my ear the title of the latest film Natalie was in, the name of the director, the date it came out. I was willing to make conversation, but I needed a bit of material to go on.

Natalie began by congratulating me on my album (what an unoriginal conversation starter) and the four awards I had won that evening (another trite thing to say), then confided that she often thought about the discussions the two of us had had at John Cutler's house in Los Angeles (discussions of which I had no recollection). Her dress was giving her noticeable underarm bulge; I love bustiers, but they aren't flattering on everyone (what the fuck had her stylist been thinking?). I was clenching my jaw to keep from yawning, wishing I was anywhere other than here talking to an insipid actress. I was about to make a polite excuse and leave when the conversation took an unexpected turn. Natalie Holmes placed her hand on my wrist and started talking about her latest vacation.

"It wasn't exactly a vacation," she murmured. "More of an experience."

"What do you mean?"

"I can't say anything else, but I swear, it changed my life."

"Oh, really?"

"You can't even imagine. I wasn't expecting it to be so intense. . . . I can give you the number if you want."

"Yeah, sure."

"But I can't guarantee anything. It's all done by word of mouth, and spots are extremely limited. I heard that Selena Gomez has been waiting for months to be able to go."

If Natalie Holmes was telling the truth, then all the Hollywood A-listers were going to this top secret, ultraexclusive spot. Needless to say, that's exactly what made me want to go. No megayacht, no villa in the Bahamas, no Tuscan castle, just three weeks on a private island in the Pacific. "A *Robinson Crusoe*–style adventure," "a spiritual retreat," "an experience at the edge of the world," "a place so remote, it's as though nothing else exists." I couldn't exactly imagine Natalie Holmes spending a summer harpooning sans air-conditioning, but oh well. "It's where Christopher Nolan had the idea for *Interstellar*. . . . Taylor Swift goes there once a year to recharge and find inspiration for new songs. . . . Apparently, the island belonged to F. Scott Fitzgerald; he might have even written the first few chapters of *The Great Gatsby* there." I didn't buy this last one—to the best of my knowledge, Fitzgerald was never that rich, and his tastes were more European—but Natalie Holmes knew how to convince me; he was my favorite writer. Starry-eyed, with a meaningful smile, she added:

"The people who know about it call it 'Masterpiece Island' . . . I'm sure word will get out sometime, but for now it's still unspoiled, so this is the time to go. It's totally magical."

"Sounds like it."

I was feeling stung. Just the day before, I had run into Selena and Taylor; why hadn't they said anything? And then why did Natalie Holmes—an actress without my character or influence—know about it before me? Right before walking away, she made me promise not to say anything, as she'd signed an ironclad nondisclosure agreement. The location was top secret, there was no information about it anywhere on the internet, invitations were highly selective.

Mystery breeds desire.

One night, when I was feeling especially tired, I dialed the number Natalie had given me on a whim. I was in the middle of promoting my third album and had spent the whole day fielding requests from idiots, none of whom seemed to be able to follow my orders properly. Everyone around me was either incompetent or lazy, and the atmosphere was one of terror. They say music soothes the soul—what a joke. Speed and pressure make me unforgiving. Alone in a Las Vegas hotel room, I scrutinized myself in the mirror while waiting in vain for someone to pick up. I left a message after an enigmatic recording quoted a Bible verse.

Fine sand, turquoise water, absolute peace. I swim for a long time, slowly—breaststroke, backstroke. I contemplate the ocean currents that could sweep me out to sea, the undertow near the barrier reef, the fish whose dorsal fins contain deadly venom. The thrill is part of the pleasure.

After my swim, I untie my bathing suit under the outdoor shower, a Spartan fixture behind the hut. The rainwater is warm from the sun, and the soap lathers as it touches my skin; I let out a sigh of happiness. For once there are no paparazzi crouching behind rocks to try to snap photos of my breasts. I don't even have to suck in my stomach.

I spend the rest of my day building a sandcastle. Just like when I was a child at the beach on the Isle of Oléron, I pack down the wet sand, carve out a moat, and build up the walls of my fortress. I am calm and focused. Then I set off in search of shells to decorate the towers. It's a useless, unplanned activity, something just for me—it's such a joy to create something without trying to excel at it. Is it 2:00 p.m. or 5:00 p.m.? I have no idea. Automatically, my hand slides to my pocket to take out my phone and check. It will take me a few days to get rid of this reflex.

The day before I left, a man in a white polo had rifled through my bag ceremoniously. There was no chance of bringing a phone, computer, camera, or any other electronic device. He even confiscated my watch. The whole point was to disconnect. Be unreachable. Go off the grid completely. No calls from my assistant, no social media, no obligations. Nothing but silence and serenity.

The only exception to my self-imposed isolation: a black satellite phone with an antenna, stowed in the cupboard, next to the first aid kit. I bet some celebrities sign up for this crazy experience and then break down after forty-eight hours, use this very phone to call to the outside world. Many of them probably ask to leave early, terrorized by a nasty spider or bored to death. I'm sure that these three weeks won't be easy. Solitude is a different kind of hell.

But for the moment, I'm in paradise. For several months now, what I've been pining for is not another prize but a break. My team has noticed that I've become irritable and impatient, that I'm always in a bad mood. They don't understand what my life is like. No one can. The only way I can come close to describing it is that I'm in a washing machine, and the cycle has been going on for seven years.

I will never admit it publicly, but I'm exhausted. I was prepared for all the wars I had to fight to become famous, but I didn't know that they were never going to end. I have to fight just as hard to stay at the top as I did to get here in the first place.

It is my first evening on the island, and the sun is setting over the ocean. My suitcase is open at the foot of my bed, and the fire that I lit with some deadwood crackles on the beach. Guitar on my knees and notebook within reach, I sound out the first words of a verse. This retreat in paradise has to give me the material for my fourth album—I've isolated myself on an island, not taken a vow of silence. At nightfall, the sea gives way to the sky, and I see thousands of constellations whose shapes I don't recognize. I'm somewhere in the Southern Hemisphere.

The flames cast saw-toothed shadows on the sand. Shivering, I give the globe I found in the hut a light spin. It's from the second half of the twentieth century; there are nations on it that no longer exist, acronyms from another time, present-day borders that are missing. I run my finger along the latitudinal and longitudinal lines, trying to figure out where I am. In all likelihood, the island isn't even on it. I'm just one small dot in the immense Pacific, but where? Outlines of countries appear before my eyes. The nearest continental coast is probably more than two thousand miles from here, somewhere in South America or Oceania.

What am I doing here? For that matter, how did I even get here? My head is swimming. To calm myself, I stroke the scars on my thighs, my head, my hands, my arms, my ankles—scars that trace the journey I've taken in my life so far, the milestones on the road to glory.

There's a price to pay for fame, and it has to be paid every day.

PART ONE

Faith

My name is Cléo Louvent Johnson. My mother is a French statistician, my father an American Egyptologist; I can toggle seamlessly between French and English, feel equally at home with hieroglyphs and numbers. I grew up in an apartment filled with books in a quiet corner of Paris's fourteenth arrondissement. My father, who tenderly nicknamed me Cleopatra, pinned up my drawings of sphinxes and pyramids in our kitchen. On Saturdays my mother would take me to visit the neighborhood library; on the way back, we would stop to stay hello to the ash-gray herons in Parc Montsouris.

My favorite books were the ones that my father would liven up with his own commentary. As an Egyptologist who was passionate about all of antiquity and its lore, he would tell me about the misfortunes of Isis and Osiris and their battle against Seth, but also about Odysseus's wayward journey home and the childish antics of the Olympians; I drank in his words as he narrated the exploits of Ramesses II, Pericles, or Alexander the Great. Each story we read was merely the pretext for a detour through history's tallest tales, which teemed with characters on extraordinary quests and fantastical creatures.

One night, when I was four, my father was tucking me in after one such story and was about to turn off the light when he sensed that I was preoccupied with something. He asked several times what was on my mind, and finally, I confided in him: "Dad, I would like to be as famous as Céline Dion."

I don't have any memory of it, but for a long time, my parents loved to remind me of this story, which they found very funny. I can imagine a sort of tenderness mixed with surprise: *Where on earth did she come up with that?*

My parents lived in a bubble of academic research, publications, conferences. They had no idea who popular celebrities were—they would be incapable of recognizing even those from their own time if they saw them on the street. Red carpets, power couples, Hollywood, private jets, tabloids: all of that belonged to another exotic world, one in which they had no desire to spend their vacations.

When they dropped me off at school, my parents seemed older than other parents. My mother had explained to me that her pregnancy hadn't lasted nine months; it had lasted nine years. I was their only child. Their struggle with infertility wasn't a secret; my Wikipedia page says that I was conceived via in vitro fertilization. For some reason, this fact adds to the mythos of my birth: Did science have to intervene for such an exceptional person to be created?

I was a well-behaved, solitary girl with short hair who would slip plane-tree leaves into the pockets of her coat to make into salad for her dolls. My parents would hear me talking to myself in my room and noticed that I always kept the door closed when playing.

They never suspected that their darling child was spending her afternoons filling up notebook after notebook with different variations of her own autograph in an attempt to find one that looked starworthy. At seven years old, I practiced doing signings as fast as possible. The next year, I did my first interviews. The questions came to me naturally, and I answered them methodically, in both

French and English. At my feet, several stuffed animals—a hedge-hog, a whale, a ladybug, a squirrel—listened attentively. My world-class menagerie formed a captive audience, the best I could have dreamed of.

I also sang along with my favorite pop stars, whose music I played on the CD player that sat on the floor next to my desk. I learned all the lyrics by heart, sitting cross-legged on my light-blue rug and studying the jewel case booklets. Later, as a teenager, I would graduate to lyrics websites, spending hours online capti-vated by their repertoires of thousands of songs.

So many times I've explained to journalists how I got here. So many times I've told my story in interviews. So many times I've played this dangerous game without understanding its seriousness.

I've lightly fictionalized my life, embellishing my answers to make me seem better, more impressive. I've cut out of my story any part of my past that doesn't cast me in the right light, and little by little, I've started to forget about those parts altogether. I've fab-ricated a new version of myself with false memories. In search of juicy details and poignant anecdotes, I've dug into other people's pasts and borrowed from novels and films, to the point where I'm no longer sure which are my own.

Memories are fragile. You only have to tell a story three or four times before the past begins to reshape itself. Carefully, you change the lighting, you erase certain details, you dial up the drama to get the audience hooked. You transform the past into a story, and over the course of many retellings, the original memory is ruined. There are stories that I've told so many times that I no longer know if they're true or false.

There were plenty of early indicators of my future success: the precocious interviews with my stuffed animals, my exceptional mezzo-soprano voice, my fascination with song lyrics, my perfect pitch, my gift for the piano, my guitar teacher's words of encouragement, the ease with which I learned to read music, my advanced grasp of music theory, my passion for choir. But it's a whole lot simpler to follow the path in reverse.

I started music lessons when I was seven, but that doesn't really mean anything. Where I come from, all good students take music lessons after school. My parents weren't trying to make me famous by getting me to learn an instrument—we weren't in Los Angeles. Music was a bourgeois reflex, not a way of encouraging me to become an international pop star.

My desire for fame didn't come from my family; it came from my own flaws. For my whole life, I've sought out the admiration of millions of strangers, forced anyone who's ever crossed my path to respect me. I have only one goal: for all of them—the baker, the pharmacist, my kindergarten teacher, the neighbor on the fourth floor—to recognize my superiority.

People often talk about the mental health problems that celebrities have. How many of them become alcoholics, suffer from other forms of addiction, fall into a depression, commit suicide? Fame makes you crazy—and you have to be crazy to chase fame. The ones who hear the siren call of being a public figure are the narcissists, the sociopaths, the degenerates. Well-adjusted people don't need to feed on love to such an extreme.

I think back to the little four-year-old girl confiding in her father about how she was sad not to be famous. In that thirst for admiration, compliments, and applause was a degree of need that had long surpassed the norm.

When I met Cléo Louvent for the first time, I knew right away that she was going to be famous one day." In articles about me, there's always a quote like this from some former teacher or classmate claiming that my potential was obvious to everyone. But in reality, no one would have thought I'd be anything special. I was a regular kid, shy, not particularly pretty.

My first report cards were excellent, but they always included encouragements for me to speak up more in class. I hid behind my good grades, which I owed to my anxious perfectionism. As soon as I made a mistake in my notebook, I would tear out the page and start over again.

At eight years old, I skipped a grade and found myself sitting next to the beautiful Juliette Marchand. My new best friend was completely the opposite of me: popular, chatty, loud. I was impressed by how at ease she seemed. My mother thought Juliette had an unfortunate tendency to show off; my father disliked people who had big personalities or who sought the spotlight. If I had behaved like Juliette at home, they would have reprimanded me curtly: *Stop trying to be the center of attention.*

Juliette divided her affections among Lydia, Clémentine, and me. We were her royal entourage, and at every recess, I feared no longer being the favorite. When Juliette held forth about the importance of kissing a boy before middle school, I would stand behind her and nod my agreement. She started calling me Cléou, changing the pronunciation of my name from "Clay-oh" to "Clay-ooh"; I hated it, but once again said nothing.

A couple of years into our friendship, one Monday in October, Juliette decided to organize a fashion show with several girls from our class. It would take place at her house on Sunday, in front of an audience of her parents and their friends. We spent the whole week talking about it in the courtyard. At ten years old, I was sure nothing was more important.

The day arrived and my father dropped me off at Juliette's, my backpack stuffed with all my nicest clothes. To secure my place in the show, I'd told everyone that I had a pair of bell-bottoms; once I arrived, I pretended I'd forgotten them at home. In the bathroom, I caught Lydia saying that I was a dirty little liar and that there never were any bell-bottoms. Clémentine agreed with her and added that I had a deep voice, like a boy's, and hairy thighs. Juliette defended me firmly: The queen always protected her favorites and reinstated peace. I choked back my tears on the other side of the door.

Juliette orchestrated the whole event, chose the order in which we appeared, started the music. In her bedroom, which served as our dressing room, we changed quickly; we were each given four turns to walk the runway. She went first, wearing a flounced skirt and an orange tank top, her blond hair hanging loose down her back. Half an hour later, when she closed the show wearing a midnight-blue dress with spaghetti straps, I was so jealous, I couldn't breathe. Juliette walked confidently to the sound of the audience's applause, spun around, winked at the captivated adults. The next day at recess, I stole her snack and spat in her schoolbag.

To become famous, you have to accumulate a sufficient amount of resentment, boil with frustration for months, stew for decades. The years I spent in the shadow of my best friend gave me the endurance I needed for the later years in the spotlight. It's not by chance that I decided to dye my hair blond, like Juliette's, right as I was beginning to become famous. I was ready for revenge, and not just the hair-related kind.

At night, in my bed, I resented my parents for giving me such a short and ridiculous name. Why Cléo? I would have preferred to be called Juliette, or Mathilde, or Émeline, or Éléonore. A girly name—elegant, significant (at least three syllables). I was jealous and petty and hoped that no one would come to Juliette's birthday party. Or better yet, that she would tell me that her mother was dead. And then I imagined my retribution; I could have almost tasted it. Once I reached the top, I wouldn't show any mercy to those who had underestimated me. I'd no longer be satisfied with spitting in their bags; instead, I would spit in their faces, reduce them to ashes.

I wish my parents had explained this to me earlier: The children who get all the attention don't usually end up with the most dazzling adult lives, the closest-knit families, the most impressive careers. The elementary-school star never becomes the global superstar. By now I've observed it dozens of times. Fame isn't a victory. It's a vengeance.

I still have very clear memories from the summer when I was fourteen: riding my bike through the pines with my cousins, picnics on the beach, a roller-skating race. I accompanied my aunt when she went to buy oysters at the market, I took sailing lessons, I plucked my eyebrows in secret. My diary was hidden in my underwear drawer; I suspected that my cousin Violette read it when I was in the shower and that she took sadistic pleasure in quoting from it during our conversations. I'd look at her suspiciously, and she would gloat. Or, at least, that's what I thought she was doing.

My mother's sister had a vacation home on the Isle of Oléron, off the west coast of France, and I had always spent part of my summers there. The rest of the time, I'd stay with my grandparents in Aix-en-Provence, or camp in Auvergne with my cousins and uncle, or even fly to Boston to visit my father's side of the family. That summer my father joined us in Oléron for a week. One afternoon, when he was watching the Olympics on TV, I grew curious and settled down next to him on the couch.

As I stared at the screen, I was seized by a burning realization, almost violent in its intensity: I hated team sports. Handball, volleyball, basketball—the idea of having to rely on someone else for victory seemed insane. Wouldn't you want to burn your teammate alive if they performed badly?

Swimming seemed to be a much more reasonable endeavor (with

the exception of relays, obviously). The day before, a seventeen-year-old French girl had surprised everyone by winning the four-hundred-meter freestyle. Our new national star was only three years older than me, and that morning she had been all over the front pages of the newspapers. Fascinated, I learned from her interviews about all her years of sacrifice—waking up at dawn, swimming sixteen kilometers a day, the chlorine smell that clung to her skin to the point of nausea, the relentless work it took to get one-hundredth of a second faster. It all made sense: her strength of character, her tolerance for pain, her need to win. In this I recognized the jagged contours of my own ambition.

I too had something to prove. I too was determined to do ten times more than other people. I too was ready to fight. I too was a perfectionist with a tremendous work ethic. I too wanted to live in a world where the best person won. It wasn't for nothing that I was always first in my class, had never ceded my rank to anyone else; I was also the most gifted music student, the best in my piano lessons, my guitar lessons, my singing lessons. If the goal were ten, I'd achieve a hundred. An overachiever, my father said. Outperform or bust.

And yet I couldn't explain this eccentricity of mine. Why was I dying to be famous? Was it so that I could feel special, powerful, loved? Of course I felt different from other people—out of sync, misunderstood—but wasn't that one of the most universal feelings people had as they were growing up? So how else could I interpret this rage? Hadn't my parents given me enough attention? Or could it be the opposite, the result of them projecting their ambitions onto a long-awaited and pampered only child? Was my thirst for fame the consequence of an innate personality trait? Or something I'd experienced? An inheritance? Harassment? Neglect? I didn't know. I had no cause to attribute it to, nothing psychological, familial, sociological, astrological, mystical, existential. I couldn't explain it, and yet I was burning up inside. I had grown up in a nice residential neighborhood in Paris; I was born to be a poodle, but instead I was a pit bull.

"Swimming is a dog-eat-dog kind of sport," my father declared, fittingly, as the starting beep sounded for the hundred-meter backstroke.

A minute later, the French girl won her second gold medal.

"Dad, do you think she knew she was going to win?"

"Of course. You have to dream big to be big."

In September of that year, I decorated my bedroom walls with pictures of my new idols: female swimmers, boxers, fencers, a tribe of determined and disciplined women who resembled me in some way. Céline Dion didn't make the cut for a role model, and anyway, Juliette thought she was cringey. I still wanted to become a singer, but I didn't relate to my favorite artists. Creatives were more likely to lead dissolute lives of passion and inspiration, whereas I wanted to be a star because I wanted to be a machine. My body would be part of my rise to the top.

In addition to my music lessons, I signed up for tennis with Juliette and for dance classes. I learned to love movement, rehearsal, performance. At night I would do abdominal exercises; in the morning, I'd get on the scale. I weighed all my food scrupulously, counted calories and grams of protein. Every week I added my weight to a line graph. Whenever I gained half a kilogram, I'd run until I collapsed.

Even top athletes need to rest, so on Friday nights, I allowed myself to play games on my computer. My favorite was *The Sims*.

Charlotte, my new avatar, played guitar and piano. She had a social life, a fiancé, and a Dalmatian. One day her house was burgled. Later that evening, she repaired a leak in her bathroom. To develop more charisma, Charlotte spent hours talking to herself in the mirror. I also made her go to the gym, improved her diet, and gave her frequent makeovers. I wasn't just forging ahead blindly for free, for the fun of it. I had a goal in mind: make her a star. If she wanted to have any hope of getting there, she had to make friends with other famous people and remain in a good mood at all times.

Charlotte worked hard, running from auditions to concerts to photo shoots. I could have chosen another career for her: Her friends included an acrobat, a bank robber, a dog trainer, a secret agent, and a fighter pilot. But I wouldn't be satisfied until Charlotte was finally famous. I wanted a limousine to come to her house to pick her up, for strangers to ask for her autograph in town. Only once that happened would I buy her a more comfortable bed, masterpieces to hang on her walls, a shower with brand-new silicone caulk, a stove with all the latest features.

As long as I remained first in my class, my parents didn't prevent me from spending so much time on the computer, but that's not to say they approved of it. "Wouldn't you rather read a book?"

The game lasted several weeks. Despite all my efforts, my Sim didn't become famous. Failure wasn't an option. It would never be an option. I led her into the garden and built four walls around her. She would die like a medieval recluse: walled up alive.

Juliette had been in the bathroom arguing with her boyfriend for an hour. That night we were celebrating my birthday in her father's apartment on rue Princesse. Everyone in our high school knew that my best friend threw the best parties. Earlier that day, we had made a chocolate cake and asked her older brother to buy us some alcohol.

While Juliette was dealing with her romantic problems, I was talking to Nathan, a friend of her brother's who went to the prestigious high school Henri-IV. He was shy and blushed easily; this was the first time we'd exchanged more than three sentences.

"'Nathan' is short for 'Nathanaël,' which means 'God's gift' in Hebrew," he informed me. "Do you know where your name comes from?"

No one had ever used etymology as a pickup line on me before—clearly, we were in Saint-Germain-des-Prés. While he was talking, I was smiling to myself, because Nathan made me think of a stork. He had long, thin legs and a tiny little head.

"'Cléo' is a nod to 'Cleopatra.'"

"Oh yeah, your father is an Egyptologist, right?"

"Yes, he wanted to name me Cleopatra, but my mother wouldn't let him, so they agreed on Cléo. He calls me Cleopatra all the time, anyway."

"Cleopatra is a pretty name. It must mean something?"

"Yes, I think it means 'father's pride,' or, at least, that's what my father always tells me. *'Patros'* means 'father' in Greek."

"But then 'Cléo' must mean something too? Pride?"

"I've never looked it up."

I took out my phone to Google it, but the reception was bad, so we continued chatting as the page loaded. Nathan refilled my drink, vodka with orange juice. At the same time, Juliette came out of the bathroom, her eyes red; passing by the door, I'd overheard insults and tears. How could she waste so much time on that guy? Didn't she have anything better to do?

In the living room, girls were dancing to the latest hit song. Their bodies were warm and unclothed, and whenever the chorus came on, everyone shouted the lyrics in unison. In my line of vision: discussions taking place in dark corners, dirty glasses piling up in the sink, crumbs on the herringbone parquet floor, Nathan's gray eyes. When the answer to Nathan's question finally appeared on my phone screen, I had to put my hand on his shoulder so that I didn't fall over from disbelief. "Cléo" came from the Greek *"kléos,"* which meant "glory." Renown. Fame.

Clearly, my life was an adventure film: On the evening of her fifteenth birthday, the heroine discovers the secret of her origins. *Your name means "fame" because your destiny is to become an international superstar.* Here I had grown up hating my name, without realizing that it contained a prophecy. This discovery made me realize, with all due modesty, that I had been chosen.

For a long time, I had felt that I was different from other people, without being able to explain my strange intuition. That evening everything became clear. It was not just that I admired fame, or that I fantasized about it like any awkward teenager; it was that I was going to be famous. *Holy shit, I was actually going to be famous.*

Fame wasn't just a childhood dream; a glorious future awaited me. I visualized myself spinning the wheel of fortune and winning the jackpot, stepping up onto the top of the podium, collecting every award with a laurel wreath on my head. I had been born in the wrong place, in the wrong body, in the wrong life. And soon it would be up to me to set things right.

Without thinking, I seized Nathan's face and kissed him. I finished my drink in one gulp and banged the empty cup on the table before taking Nathan by the hand and leading him to the bathroom. I locked the door, unzipped his fly, and slid his pants down his thighs before kneeling in front of him. I was going to become famous. There was no way I was going to remain passive; I wasn't the good little girl who kept her mouth shut anymore. This time I would open it wide.

I really wanted him to take care of me in return, but the douchebag didn't lift a finger. What a doofus. Dipstick. Ding-dong. I finished him off and went back to dancing.

I took my place in the middle of the dance floor in a halo of glory—the absolute monarch. Eyes closed, I swayed my hips and torso to the beat, the center of the universe; as I danced, magnetic and imperial, I could feel everyone looking at me. I was their queen bee.

Without saying goodbye to anyone, I left the party. It wasn't even midnight yet, and I hadn't blown out my candles; they would continue to celebrate my arrival on this earth without me. Certainty. Certainty. Feeling. Joy. Peace. This was my Night of Fire, and how brilliant it was! Tipsiness had intensified my ecstasy; the icy wind was burning my face. I biked up boulevard Saint-Michel, pedaling through the night, standing up to climb the hill. I passed alongside the Luxembourg Garden and continued straight until the avenue de l'Observatoire, my heart fluttering with happiness; my birthday should be a national holiday. From my headphones came pure joy, the world-famous World Cup victory anthem "Samba de Janeiro"—no need to understand Portuguese to understand euphoria or the drumbeat that throbbed through my body. I ran a red light and then a second one, zigzagged among the cars around Place Denfert-Rochereau, closed my eyes, took one hand off the handlebars and then the other, lifted my arms so that I was flying like a bird. I ignored the cars honking at me. You don't kill the main character at the beginning of a movie. Into the frozen night I shouted, louder and louder, the four premonitory letters that spelled out my destiny: *C-L-É-O.*

When I got home, I spat onto the sidewalk the remainder of the semen that had lingered on my gums. My phone was ringing; Nathan was asking me where I'd gone. I wasn't surprised. He was already in love with me. I didn't respond to him. What was the point? We couldn't be together—it would be too complicated once I was famous.

The apartment was quiet and my parents already in bed, but all the same, I had returned before my curfew. In the kitchen, I drank a glass of water and assembled a plate of food. The night was going to be long.

At age fifteen, I had just received irrefutable proof that I would become famous. Now it was time to figure out how. I opened a notebook filled with graph paper. My writing was rushed, peppered with arrows, underlined words, sentences in all caps, numbered lists of ideas. Half-drunk, I launched into my first skills assessment.

1. My precision, my perfectionism, my need to be the best, my
disdain for laziness and platitudes: They all made sense. I would
be an *A-list* celebrity, not some cheap starlet. I didn't want to be

merely a singer; I wanted to go down in history. Like Cleopatra herself, I was going to make a mark. Tutankhamun, Homer, Plato, Aristotle, Alexander the Great, Caesar, Charlemagne, Shakespeare, Napoléon . . . the list didn't include many women, but I was ready to volunteer!

2. I had a spectacular voice. Everyone knew it—I'd get compliments as soon as I opened my mouth to sing. And I wasn't just another soprano with a smooth, high-pitched voice like a nightingale. My voice was deep, husky, gravelly; it was hoarse, complex, distinct—it would be easy for the public to recognize. Everyone was going to love me.

3. I had a keen interest in poetry, was an excellent student of literature, and was capable of writing songs in both French and English, which would ensure that I could make it big internationally. You can find a pretty voice anywhere, but I was worth more than that. I wouldn't just sing other people's songs; I would become famous by writing and singing my own.

4. Puberty is rarely a gift, but for me, it was a blessing. The features on my heart-shaped face were softening, my breasts were growing, and exercise was sculpting my body. The awkward little girl was turning into someone with the slender, sleek silhouette of a star. There was still work to be done: get a different haircut, find the right shade of lipstick, buy new clothes. But with all of that, I would be posterworthy, and close-ups of my face would be tacked onto bedroom walls all around the world.

The proof was there; now what I needed to do was not procrastinate. My plan of action was to compose the song that would make me famous, starting right away. I searched for a melody quietly, murmuring so as not to wake my parents in the next room. As I tackled the chorus, I thought of Céline Dion: Her mother and brother had written her first song for her when she was twelve years old. Unfortunately, I couldn't ask my family for help. There was no way they could write lyrics, nor could they help me get my foot in the door. I wished my mother were a director, my father an actor. How could they be content with such small lives? No one knew of them, no one would remember their name—and you don't become a millionaire by slaving away on your research. My parents were simple people, nerds, losers. They weren't invited to launch parties or previews on Saturday nights; instead, they would watch documentaries about abstract expressionism or Turkish ambitions in the Mediterranean and read on the couch in the living room before going to bed at 11:00 p.m. I loved my parents, but they were of no use to me. And yet I refused to think like a victim. There were always more reasons to fail than to succeed. I immersed myself once again in my song. If Thérèse and Jacques Dion had done it, so could I.

I spent the next several hours refining and polishing my song. Inspired and determined, I had written an elaborate story of impossible love. I was high on the feeling of knowing exactly what I wanted and plotting my coup d'etat, composing my masterpiece in my bedroom. Everyone would be amazed when they heard this miraculous piece of music for the first time. *You wrote this all by yourself? I didn't know that there was a genius among us! This song is incredible; I'm sending it right now to my aunt who works in television. She'll definitely find you a producer!*

The first rays of sunshine signaled the end of my Night of Fire. There were footsteps in the hallway, the jangling of keys, the metallic clang of the apartment door closing. My father was going down to the bakery to buy croissants like he did every Sunday morning. Meanwhile, my mother was getting ready in the bathroom while listening to the radio. She was humming in the shower. I had finished my song.

I've said that I started writing songs at eight years old so many times that I ended up believing my own lies. The truth is more banal: I wrote my very first song at the age of fifteen. And while I may have been struck by inspiration, the result was pathetic.

When you've received a 19.75 out of 20 average on your baccalauréat exam and you're the top student in your class at the famous Sciences Po, you dream of a prestigious career in public administration, not being on TV and signing autographs. At twenty years old, I had everything going for me, I had the face of an angel, the future was beckoning, and yet I felt blocked and bitter, with the acute sensation that I was living a life that wasn't my own. I resented the whole world. Everyone was telling me how well I was doing, but I didn't feel like a success. At the end of the semester, I was sure of one thing: I was putting far too much of myself into this degree.

Obviously, I wasn't planning on putting my brilliant studies on pause just so that I could be the opening act at shitty bars. I deserved much better than playing at tacky venues, going to auditions, becoming a backup singer. But my stint as a perfect student took up a ton of time, sucking me dry without giving me any creative oxygen. When I tried to write songs at night after spending the day grinding away, they always turned out flat and prosaic, without any substance to them. They were exactly what I refused to be: mediocre.

So I stayed in the shadows, preparing my grand entrance. I wasn't immobile but rather paralyzed. I was waiting for the right idea, I was waiting to write better songs, I was waiting until my piano playing improved, I was waiting until I could buy a new guitar, I was waiting to get my degree, I was waiting until I found an internship, I was waiting for advice from my singing teacher, I was waiting until I was thinner, I was waiting until I treated myself to a corduroy jacket, I was waiting for pigs to fly, for the first of never, for hell to freeze over. For the moment, I didn't need anyone to try to keep me from getting famous. I was doing it all by myself.

"*Could you please* keep it down? We're in the library."

First warning. I delivered this request sharply before turning back to studying, unlocking my computer with the password I've used for years: Make_Me_Famous75!.

But my intervention had no effect on the group of four idiots sitting at my table. I'd come here to surround myself with others who were concentrating, not losers who were playing on their phones instead of studying. Second warning. I shot insistent glares at them to get them to quiet down. Unfortunately, my dear companions continued to chat.

I knew these kinds of people well. General laziness, a lack of discipline, unwillingness to work. They all came from the same litter: a family of slackers. Soon they would return home, satisfied with having spent three hours in the library (actual working time: 17 minutes). I stared at the guy with greasy hair and dirty glasses, sure that he was the type to be content with a 13 out of 20. Passable, but not great. The underbelly of the class. I had nothing but disdain for them—average people who were distracted and confused, who chewed gum, snacked between meals, and sniffled, who didn't exercise and who did arts and crafts for fun, who were always late and never gave things their all, who went wherever the wind took them, enrolling in a university for a liberal arts degree because they wanted to do whatever their high-school friends were doing. Their lack of ambition nauseated me.

One of the girls opened a pack of cookies, and I stared at her double chin to signal to her that she didn't need the extra 30 grams of sugar. *Sweetie, put down the chocolate-covered cookie. You already look like an overstuffed turkey.*

An hour later, they went outside for their third smoke break (total break time since they'd arrived: 47 minutes). As soon as they disappeared from view, I got up and very calmly went over to their things. Computers, books, notebooks, pouches, calculators. I slid everything that would fit into my bag before walking away. They weren't going to do anything with them, anyway.

With the money I'd found in their wallets, I bought myself a pair of suede leather booties. Paltry compensation for the afternoon of studying that they'd spoiled. I threw the rest of their things into a trash can on the rue de Rivoli.

At the end of the day, Juliette met up with me for a drink. As soon as she saw me, my childhood friend jumped into my arms and kissed me on the cheek, as clingy and affectionate as a Labrador. Friendships are never fixed entities. For us the rules changed every five years. Juliette still called me Cléou, but I was no longer her obedient sidekick, and she had long since stopped trying to throw her weight around.

Juliette was in her second year of medical school. She dreamed of being an emergency physician, could already imagine herself rushing out in an ambulance to rescue car-crash victims. I applauded her career choice; there was no way for her to outshine me from the breakdown lane. Plus, I had finally become the more beautiful one out of the two of us. Golden-brown hair, hazel eyes, perfect skin, defined eyebrows, long eyelashes, plump lips. And the miracle that would change everything: bangs.

I had become aware of my undeniable beauty due to the way other people looked at me. At parties, people now approached me first, not Juliette. To compensate, I kept my distance from all her romantic interests—past, present, future, potential. This didn't bother me at all. I was cultivating an air of detachment and coolness, a girl who was both sublime and indifferent, all the more so for not realizing it (a sexist trope but a truthful one).

We took a seat on the terrace outside. Juliette was telling me about her love life; she was currently transitioning from Nicolas to Antoine. I had never known her to be single. She had been a serial monogamist since kindergarten, one of those people who were always in some kind of serious and complicated relationship. The complete opposite of me. I was trying to listen to her explain to me why this time would be different from the others (false), but the idiot to our left was distracting me.

"Can we switch tables? This guy keeps blowing his smoke into my face."

"You smoke too," Juliette pointed out.

"Yes, but it's different when it's not my smoke."

"You're such a tyrant."

We moved to a table a little farther away before ordering a second round.

At 9:00 p.m., Juliette dragged me to a party in the eleventh arrondissement, and I reapplied my poppy-red lipstick on the stairs leading up to her friend's apartment. I had no desire to go, but it was Saturday night and I was twenty years old, and this was the kind of social life students were supposed to have. My problem was that I never felt like I worked hard enough to deserve a break.

Her med-student friends chatted and leaned out the windows

to smoke, beers in hand. There were boys there, attractive ones, even, but I only had eyes for the beautiful brunet with mahogany highlights in a corner of the living room, near the library—I swear the Yamaha was winking at me. It was still early and no one was dancing, so I seized my moment, asking the host politely if I could play the piano.

As an opener, I sang "Only You" by The Flying Pickets, softly. The conversations drew to a close, and a silent group gathered around me. Next I played John Lennon's "Jealous Guy," then Claude François's "Le chanteur malheureux." An overly sensitive girl was crying before the first chorus.

"Oh, sorry, I didn't want to kill the mood!" I said, with false modesty.

"No, no, don't stop! Do you know any other songs?"

"Sure, if you'd like. Is there a guitar here?"

Someone brought one over to me, and I continued with Elton John and Kiki Dee's "Don't Go Breaking My Heart" before carefully choosing my last song: "You Can't Hurry Love." Several people were looking up the lyrics on their phones so that they could sing along with me. Perfect. I'd always dreamed of having backup singers.

My impromptu concert ended with applause. Everyone kept telling me, ten times, thirty times, one hundred times, that I had a phenomenal voice. I played it down.

"I took music lessons at the conservatory for a while."

They insisted, with open admiration. I accepted their compliments with feigned humility.

"Well, you're a great singer, Cléo. What do you do otherwise? Oh, you study political science? Where?"

Despite my powerful voice, no one, not even Juliette, thought that my real aspiration was to be a world-famous singer. Who could blame her? In high school, she had two volleyball practices a week and games every weekend, but it wasn't like she was planning to be a professional athlete.

"You should do a show every once in a while, Cléou, you're so talented. There's a bar in Pigalle with open mic nights every first Saturday of the month. You could . . ."

I burst out laughing, as though what Juliette had said was ridiculous, then rolled my eyes before replying, "I'll remind you that I've got midterms to study for and an internship to find."

On the way home, I let Juliette, who was walking ahead of me briskly so as not to miss the last subway, carry the conversation. She was cheerful and bouncy, unleashing a running commentary about the party and the guests, voluble even after midnight. I, on the other hand, said nothing in order to hide my bitterness. Why hadn't I sung my own songs? I should have tried them out—I had written three new ones the month before. But most of all, I should have been open about my dream of becoming a singer instead of just shrugging disdainfully; one of the guests might have been the daughter of an executive at Universal, or the nephew of a musical theater producer. If I never told anyone who I really was, I would never be discovered. And, anyway, being brilliant at covers was easy. It was a waste of time to sing other people's songs. The only thing I was good at was showing off in low-stakes situations. I was a piece of shit. A coward. A failure. A karaoke singer.

I lit a cigarette and took three deep puffs. It was time for me to roll up my sleeves. One, two, three. I stubbed out my cigarette on my arm and kept it there for three seconds to make sure the lesson would stick, gritting my teeth so that I wouldn't cry out. Juliette didn't turn around.

I kept a close eye on the competition. During my Monday-morning public-law class, deep in concentration behind my computer screen, one earbud surreptitiously in my ear, I created a document listing the strategic branding for all the female singers who were currently popular.

1. The pop star shattered by a very public on-and-off relationship

2. The rebellious former Disney star

3. The prolific lyricist and musical genius

4. The born performer and dancer

5. The glamorous diva with the big voice

I also noted down the ages at which each of them had stepped into the limelight: seven, nine, thirteen, nineteen, twenty-three. I had to hurry up. At twenty-one, it would soon be too late for me.

The law professor had been staring at me for five long seconds. Clearly he had just asked me a question. Laughter was rippling through the room, and everyone else had turned to look at me too. Lifting my eyes from my computer, I apologized humbly. All the same, I had no need of learning anything about how French institutions worked. I was the institution.

As soon as the professor moved on, I turned back to my task. For the biggest singers I noted down their best-known songs, their awards, their collaborations with other artists, and the number of years between each of their albums. I dissected their written interviews, watched their TV appearances, listened to their radio segments—part of my research was about their PR strategies. And finally, I created a spreadsheet grading each one on a scale of one to five in the following categories: charisma, creativity, physical attractiveness, clothing style, oral expression, sense of humor, cardiovascular endurance.

This initial overview was essential for figuring out exactly whom I aspired to be. Adele or Selena Gomez? Britney Spears or Lady Gaga? Shakira or Rihanna? They were all different targets that required distinct positioning. I often asked myself, and others, this very question: "Who do you want to be?" To my left, Emma was taking handwritten notes about the role of the Constitutional Council, carefully color-coding dates, laws, and definitions; she had been talking about her dream of becoming a political journalist since the first day of class. I leaned toward her and whispered, "Do you want to be Léa Salamé, Élise Lucet, or Edwy Plenel?" She stared at me uncomprehendingly. But she should have known the answer. They weren't the same reading materials, the same shoes, the same internships, the same arrondissements in Paris. At some point you have to know where you're going.

My study of the musical landscape confirmed that there was a place for me as a celebrity who was also intellectual. I could play the good-student card in Hollywood like Natalie Portman, who spoke six languages and had a degree from Harvard. On a whim, I looked for other celebrities whose parents were academics and

found that Kanye West and Reese Witherspoon had set a prece-
dent. I was relieved. Anyway, it was decided: I would be the sexy-
but-intelligent-singer-who-was-starting-a-book-club. I would be
known especially for the genius of my lyrics and my powerful voice.
My spot awaited me, somewhere nice and cozy, between Taylor
Swift and Miley Cyrus.

For my direct competitors I produced an even more exhaustive
analysis, filling out a four-part matrix with their strengths, weak-
nesses, opportunities, and threats. I wasn't inventing this—the
SWOT matrix had been used in the business world for years and
had been proven to help the largest businesses define their strategies. I was fascinated by successful entrepreneurs, whose inspirational videos I watched on repeat. I should have gone to business
school.

I filled out the same matrix for three other singers whose careers I had studied in detail. With each one I was left with the same
feeling: I was not intimidated by the competition. If I were them,
my voice would be more controlled, my songs more successful, my
live performances more impressive, my interviews more convincing. To put it simply: I could have done that. And frankly, I would
have been even better.

All I was missing was an album. Since I didn't have class that
afternoon, I took advantage of the opportunity to go home and sit
down at the piano to search for a hook, a chorus, a good idea. The
window was open, and noise from the street filtered in: A father
was picking up his daughter from preschool downstairs, middle
schoolers were chatting and drinking cans of soda, a couple of
tourists were strolling along the sidewalk, a woman was locking
her bike to a fence. I let myself be distracted.

JANE CABELLO

Strengths

Famous since she was a kid, America's sweetheart

Many devoted fans

Extremely public relationship with Harry Miller

Sensuality, sex appeal

Distinctive personal style, fashion icon

WEAKNESSES

Voice is smooth but "weak," criticized for not being able to sing

Catastrophic performance at the last MTV Video Music Awards went viral

Most recent album didn't do well (no Grammy nominations, disappointing Billboard ranking)

OPPORTUNITIES

Her role in the latest Almodóvar film: diversifying as an actress?

Her Cuban origins—an album entirely in Spanish?

Launch a clothing line?

THREATS

Alexa Rodriguez, the singer who looks like her but is younger and has a more powerful voice

Recent breakup with Harry Miller

What is intelligence? It is the power of analysis. *Come on, Cléo, it's time to put your big brain to work on your songs.* I abandoned the piano; maybe the guitar was the better instrument for composing. My graph notebook was open at my feet, the first song I'd ever written, the night I turned fifteen, still in it; it made me feel ashamed, and the subsequent songs were no better. Ten, twenty, thirty mediocre attempts: an accumulation of inane, stilted, clumsy songs with no personality whatsoever. On the other hand, in the margins, next to my meaningless lyrics, was a succession of encouraging mantras I'd written to myself, full of fervor and in all caps:

YOU ARE AWESOME, CLÉO
DO IT FOR REAL OR DON'T DO IT AT ALL
YOU ARE A WAR MACHINE
IN THE TOP 1%
YOU'RE GOING TO FUCKING CRUSH IT

Apparently, all my efforts had gone into rallying the troops. In the last pages of the notebook, I had also drawn up a list of songs that I wished I could have written, including "That Don't Impress Me Much" by Shania Twain and "I Will" by the Beatles. I had not only copied out all the lyrics but also improved them—deleting a repetition, developing a verse, tweaking a rhyme, editing a chorus, adding a bridge. Basically, I was helping Paul McCartney out.

Seated on the rug in my bedroom, I began to work out a new song on my guitar, determined and confident.

Two hours later: My attempt was pathetic. Why weren't my songs as great as I was? Five chords, a lifeless melody, insipid lyrics. I leafed through the pages of my notebook. All my songs were alike, and none of them bore any resemblance to the masterpieces I'd imagined. I was famous and brilliant only in my own head—and meanwhile, the path was wide open for my rivals.

I lay on the ground, my arms crossed over my chest like an Egyptian mummy, and stared at the ceiling, furious, immobile, crying tears of rage. Then I sat up suddenly and dragged a razor blade along the inside of my thigh to punish myself for not being at Jane Cabello's level. A failure, a penalty. With each wrong step I would administer a proportionate retribution. That would teach me.

I didn't write a new song for three months. My inaction only increased my frustration, a sickening feeling that became a monster that I kept well-fed with the fresh meat of the successful singers I continued to list on my computer. I was jealous, horrible, anxious. The more they resembled me, the more furious I became. And like the Minotaur, my frustration hid in the labyrinth of my fears; it devoured me from the inside.

One night I awoke with a start, soaked in sweat and disoriented. I had had a nightmare about a young artist who had just burst onto the music scene. She had the same first name as me. And then I realized, horrified, that we had the same last name too. Which one would be more devastating for my career? There was space for multiple famous Jennifers, but not for multiple famous Cléos. The same went for my last name, Louvent—there were no famous Louvents, and this was something I was grateful for every day. It was even the reason I had chosen to use my mother's name and not my father's. "Johnson" was too common; it was already used up, ruined. And I took the expression "make a name for oneself" very seriously.

Ten years later, in Cannes, I would meet an actress named Mélanie, who had been overshadowed by a more famous namesake. One night, at a private party on la Croisette, she confided in me how painful it was to be constantly mixed up with her rival: "If only my name were Sabrina or Capucine."

It was four in the morning, and I reached for my phone in the dark. I checked the internet: No other Cléo had broken out overnight.

decided to move to New York after graduation. I had to veer off route, the way one might divert a train. It was about time.

Paris was too limited, almost provincial. Its music scene wasn't up to my level. And everyone said that you had to leave home to succeed. If I stayed hidden in my mother's skirts and subject to my father's opinions, I would get stuck and die.

My parents didn't understand why their darling little girl wanted to go to the United States. I could continue my studies in Paris, prepare for the competitive examinations for senior civil service, pass the bar, and become a lawyer, go to journalism school. I resisted their suggestions. For the first time in my life, I was going to swim against the current.

I moved into an apartment in Manhattan on 106th Street between Amsterdam and Columbus, rented from an unpleasant Columbia student who was subletting their room for a year. The Saturday after I arrived, I took a free ferry to go to the IKEA in Brooklyn. On the way there, I took a photo of the Statue of Liberty to send to my parents; on the way back, I was caught in a summer downpour, a clothes rack in my arms and a pillow in my backpack.

My dual citizenship allowed me to work in the United States legally; all I had to do was figure out where to start. The logical choice was a job in the music industry on the lowest rung of the ladder, as an entry-level production assistant, to get my foot in the door. A week after I interviewed with a prestigious New York label, my cell phone rang. Immediately afterward, I received a message of congratulations: The job was mine. I was finally going to enter the world of studios, stars, glitz. But I didn't respond.

The team tried to reach me again early that evening. The screen of my phone, which was on the edge of the sink, lit up, displaying their number. I got out of the shower, soaked and shivering. As the phone vibrated in my hand, my instincts screamed at me to stay away, and I saw my future flash before my eyes. I was going to be serving coffee to musicians who were less talented than me (first ring), spend my best years reserving plane tickets (second ring), waste my intelligence working for artists I despised (third ring), become a frustrated producer (fourth ring), kill myself at age thirty because I had failed my life (fifth ring). I stared at the phone without answering it. I was going to be a star, not the assistant to a star.

Everyone talks about imposter syndrome: living with the feeling that you don't deserve your success, that you've been lucky, slipped through somehow, that you've taken the place of someone more deserving. But I had to battle the opposite and inadmissible kind of anguish: I believed that I was incredibly talented and wondered when the rest of the world would finally see it. Having my genius go unnoticed would be the ultimate injustice. I was exceptional, but I feared that I would never be able to prove it.

I hadn't yet accomplished anything, but nevertheless I was at the height of my arrogance. Was it clear-sightedness or an excess of pride? Where did healthy self-confidence stop and hubris begin? Did I recognize my own value, or was I in the midst of an episode of megalomania? Over the course of my career, I have met star journalists, successful actors and singers, brilliant entrepreneurs. None of them have ever apologized for being where they are.

When I arrived in New York, I was torn between two existences: the life I was currently living and the life I aspired to live. Or, rather, the life I believed I had the right to live. In English they say "entitled," which means something like "what rightfully belongs to me." I liked that word; it reassured me, and I clung to it. I would be famous because I was entitled to be: I deserved the spotlight, it belonged to me. It was owed to me, even. However, there was a significant gap between the vastness of my aspirations (to become a global celebrity) and the smallness of my daily life (I was one of many twenty-two-year-old young women).

After several weeks of cover letters and interviews, I found a job in a bookstore in Midtown. My strategy: to keep my distance from music rather than orbiting its periphery. This was intended to be a way of limiting frustration, ruminations, and anxiety; it was also a promise that I would enter through the front door, not a side one. I would go directly from being an unknown to being a superstar. I would pass everyone from the right lane. One day it would be my chance, and no one would have seen it coming.

Meanwhile, it was time for me to act like an American. My aunt and uncle came from Boston to visit me at Thanksgiving; I either biked to the bookstore or took the subway, depending on the weather; I bought bananas for $1.25 apiece at Whole Foods; I discovered bagels with cream cheese at Absolute Bagels—which I burned off by running the loop of Central Park, six miles of changing views and steep hills.

After my days at the bookstore, I would give private piano lessons to rich families on the Upper East Side. Some of my students attended the Lycée Français, and others were the children of ambassadors. Seventy dollars an hour, given to me three times a week in white envelopes. And my parents sent me money every month.

I spent it all on recording equipment, a turntable, vinyl records, concert tickets, a new guitar, a keyboard, a gym membership, fresh fruits and vegetables, a scale that measured my body fat percentage. I also treated myself to a vintage Jean Paul Gaultier pareo dress that tied around the neck and was worn without a bra. The orange-and-green pattern made me think of neon psychedelia.

My parents grumbled and worried—they thought I was throwing my money away. It was actually the opposite: I was investing. I had to bet on myself because nobody else was going to do it. As with any financial investment, I was motivated by the prospect of a future return and calculated that these expenditures would be quickly paid off by my record sales. When she was a waitress, Lady Gaga didn't deposit her earnings into a savings account. She bought herself a Gucci purse.

Living alone for the first time, I learned what it meant to have no one to answer to. Outside of my work hours, I was as free as a bird. No one was waiting for me for dinner, so I could have a bowl of cereal for lunch, lounge around in my underwear until noon, or go out without explanation—no one would notice whether I came back at midnight or at 5:00 a.m.

I liked to describe myself as a determined and ambitious young woman, but truthfully, I still wasn't doing much of anything. In Paris, I immersed myself in my studies, but what was my excuse in New York? This was the time to become famous, to launch my career, to kick down doors. But instead, I spent my free time removing body hair while listening to records. I heard music better when my hands were occupied, so I would sit down on the carpeting in my bedroom in a ray of sunlight and mangle my calves with a pair of tweezers. A 1980s gold digger, I discovered "Under Pressure" by Queen and David Bowie, and "(I Just) Died In Your Arms" by Cutting Crew. And then, in the middle of waxing my thighs, I fell in love with the song "Vienna" by Billy Joel, without suspecting that, in two years, its chorus would upend my destiny.

Once I was burning from the removal of all my body hair, I would prepare myself for a run. This time I would go twice as far, two loops of the park—twelve miles, with the goal of returning before sunset. My endorphin addiction was just as intense as before, but in New York my obsession with my body wasn't that different from everyone else's. Here no one was surprised when I explained that I went to the gym every morning before the bookstore. What could be more normal? I may have still weighed all my food, but I was no longer plotting my weight on graph paper; a phone app took care of that for me now.

After my run, I watched *Notting Hill* in bed. I knew it by heart, so I recited Julia Roberts and Hugh Grant's lines alongside them, surprised by the sound of my own voice; I hadn't spoken to anyone since that morning. The movie has everything I like: a Hollywood actress named Anna Scott walks by chance one day into a small travel bookstore in West London, where she meets its awkward, divorced owner, William. The two are total opposites, but they fall in love. My favorite part is the dinner scene, when the film star meets some of her beloved bookstore owner's friends and family. "Good lord, you're the spitting image of . . ." Will's best friend doesn't think it's really her at first, because what would Anna Scott be doing in her living room? As for Will's little sister, she is completely overcome with love and admiration: "Oh, holy fuck. I absolutely, totally, and utterly adore you, and I just think you are the most beautiful woman in the world." Then there's the struggling banker friend who takes an interest in what he sees as a fledgling talent: "What do you do? I've always imagined it's a pretty tough job, though, acting. . . . I mean, the wages are a scandal, aren't they?" Anna replies by telling him that she earned fifteen million dollars for her last film.

Each of their reactions to Anna Scott's fame is delicious. In the scene, Julia Roberts's hair is pulled back into a braided updo, and she wears jeans, a belt, a green camisole, and a flowered jacket with a mandarin collar. I roamed the streets of New York wearing the same hairstyle and visited thrift store after thrift store in Brooklyn in search of a similar outfit.

Before going to sleep, I'd drink an herbal tea or some broth, and read biographies of famous people while touching myself. Nothing turns me on as much as success stories.

My memories are fading as time takes me further and further away from the bygone days in which I wasn't yet a star. But here on the desert island, some recollections are resurfacing. Thinking back on my life before I became famous makes me feel a strange mix of emotions. Anonymity seems to belong to a faraway world of obsolete habits, implausible movements, archaic objects, a mythical city that's been swallowed by the waves. Deep down, I haven't forgotten those years in limbo. I was so young, my face didn't mean anything to anyone, I celebrated my twenty-third birthday by making out with strangers in a club in Brooklyn, I washed my clothes at the laundromat on the corner, I took the subway, I hadn't yet experienced the pleasure of a silk kimono. On the other hand, I could walk around without inciting a riot, go for a run without a bodyguard, use my real name to reserve a table at a restaurant, leave the house in pajama pants, give a random guy a blow job without everyone knowing about it. I had no idea that one day I'd be willing to spend millions of dollars just to relive a single day of that life.

I let myself fall back into the time when I ambled around my living room in my underwear, listened to vinyl records, tweezed, watched movies, ran, shopped, read, worked at the bookstore, tutored. I didn't know it yet, but those hours weren't idle, as I'd thought at the time. They were blessed, defining, instructive—lucrative, even. To create something, it's just as important to take your time as to waste it. Without knowing it, I was gathering my strength and building my character, taking advantage of a world that was destined to soon disappear.

I hadn't responded to the latest two letters from Juliette. They were lying on my desk, between my song notebooks, my books, and some tubes of lotion. As far back as I could remember, Juliette had loved written correspondence. She explained to me once that it was because of the joy of finding a little surprise in your mailbox.

But I could at least manage the time for a phone call. Juliette picked up on the first ring; she was returning home from a shift at the hospital. I let her talk while I got ready, muting myself while I brushed my teeth and blow-dried my hair. From what I was able to gather from snippets here and there, her monologue was more about her newest love interest than about her clinical rotation. The lucky fellow was named Michael, and he was replacing Tim, or maybe it was Florent? I didn't quite catch it.

A few dabs of concealer, some Guerlain powder on my cheeks, a swipe of mascara, a red lip for the evening. I spritzed some perfume from a cone-shaped bottle onto my clavicle, allowing the clean violet scent to mingle with my own scent of honey soap. Inspecting my reflection in the entryway mirror, I let down my hair and slid my keys into my purse. Juliette stopped speaking abruptly. Apparently it was my turn.

While walking to the subway I updated her on my daily life in

New York. The bookstore, my colleagues, my nights out, my workouts, news from my parents.

"Where are you going?"

"To a friend's house."

"Liar. You're going to meet up with a guy."

"No, I'm not."

Yes, I was. I checked out my reflection in the windows of the
cars parked along the sidewalk. Each time was the same excellent
surprise: I looked absolutely sublime.

"Okay, I'm here. I'll let you go now."

"Did you call me to talk, or did you call me so that I could keep
you company on your walk?"

"Why does it matter? The important thing is that we talked,
right?"

Chad looked just like his photos on the dating app: square
shoulders, square jawline, square glasses. He had asked me to come
over late to show me that he had a very important job at which he
made $650,000 a year (not including bonus). "Fridays are more
chill at the office and I leave early. We could meet up at eleven p.m.
if that works?" I laughed when reading his message before realizing
that he had written it without a trace of irony.

We had met on a high-end, ultraselective app for "trendy
creatives." Everyone said that Raya was what celebrities used; in
reality, there were more investment bankers on there than singers. But I didn't use Tinder—I wasn't just anybody—and I was
fine with paying for a platform that would get me dates with
rich, well-positioned, well-connected men.

I wore bloodred wedge heels, jeans, and my Julia Roberts

flowered jacket. It was the second time I'd been asked out to the same rooftop to drink thirty-seven-dollar cocktails. Maybe they were spreading the word at Goldman Sachs?

Chad's voice was so deep that it sounded like he was about to vomit every time he opened his mouth. Had he been repressing gastric reflux since the beginning of our conversation, or was that his real voice? On the weekends, Chad borrowed the family helicopter to go to the Hamptons. He described his house in Montauk to me—the number of rooms, the renovation they'd done in 2014, the southeastern exposure, the nearby amenities (why was he spewing all this information at me? I wasn't a real estate agent; I had no intention of estimating the value of his property at the end of our conversation). He got excited when I told him that my father had also gone to Yale, but for the first thirty minutes, he didn't ask me a single question; he was too busy talking about himself and checking out my breasts.

"So, Julia, you said you were a bookseller, right?" he finally asked, in his deep, guttural voice.

"No, actually, I lied!"

"Oh really? So what do you actually do?"

"I'm a singer."

"Cool. Are you well-known?"

"In France I am. I'm only in New York for a few days. I live in Paris."

"Oh yeah? Say something in French!"

"Bonjour, je voudrais un pain au chocolat."

"You really are French! How is it that you can speak English without an accent?"

"My father is American, my mother is French."

"Oh, that's right, you told me. What's your last name? I'm going to Google you."

"I'm not going to tell you. It's so nice not to be recognized. I can chill out here. I'm enjoying it."

"Julia, you're really something."

"And obviously, Julia isn't my real name."

Chad was pretending to be an interesting and complex person, while I was pretending to be a star. Which of us was fabricating more? Technically my fame wasn't a lie; it just wasn't true *yet*. I was anticipating it.

I told him about my life in France in the spotlight, the pressure of fans awaiting my new album, and my last relationship, which was all over the media, creating for him a reality that was worthy of me. Was I a pathological liar, or had I just mastered the law of attraction? It's been proven that you have to manifest what you want in order to make it come true. Really what I was doing was practicing visualization five years before it became a thing.

I didn't know if Chad believed my story. At any rate, my self-proclaimed fame didn't stop him from suggesting that we go back to his place and have anal sex on his couch. I declined this charming proposition in favor of the more conventional missionary.

Chad accelerated his thrusts, his eyebrows furrowed, his lips pursed, deep in concentration. Sex wasn't my favorite thing to do, but I made sure to get it done at least once a month. It was routine, almost a hygienic practice, so that I didn't get rusty—if you have a beautiful car, you don't hide it away in the garage. On the television screen in front of us was a paused football video game (had Chad actually been at the office before our date, or had he just been occupied with his PlayStation?). The screen was prompting him to choose players for his team, who were ranked according to six levels: beginner, amateur, semipro, professional, champion, and legend. While Chad was writhing around on top of me, I reflected on how I didn't want to be an amateur or a semipro in the world of music—I would be at least a champion. And as Chad emptied himself inside me, I imagined him choking on his deep voice and his vomit when he discovered my real identity a few years from now. *Oh, sweetie. You had no idea that you were fucking a future legend.*

There was a room opening up in Brooklyn that checked all the boxes: desirable neighborhood, spacious apartment, reasonable rent. I learned about it thanks to a coworker at the bookstore. The stars were aligning: I would have to give back my studio in a month.

I secured the room after what was essentially a job interview. The competition was fierce, with about thirty applicants; I had to convince Aria and Celeste, the two current roommates, to choose me. When I went to meet them, I put on a show, flaunting my nicest personality, my best clothes, my excellent guarantors. I even played the guitar and sang a song for them to earn bonus points—I was about ready to start juggling. In the end, I was the lucky chosen one because I was "so French." Celeste loved France and was already excited about the idea of drinking a coffee with me at Café de Flore in Saint-Germain-des-Prés and adding me to her long list of cosmopolitan friends.

The apartment was bursting with life, parties, people. The week I moved in, two of Aria's friends were visiting New York. They slept graciously on our couch and spent a little too much time in the shower, if you asked me.

Celeste was a mountain lake. Every morning when she stepped out of her bedroom, it was like a serene landscape had appeared before us, calm and unchanging. She was even-tempered, gentle, considerate, and a good listener, and had been in a relationship with a charming guy named Tom for forever. Her nails were always lightly glossed with clear polish, she dressed in white and beige, and her clothing was never stained or wrinkled, which I couldn't understand, as I never saw her use an iron. Celeste took care of her skin, went to sleep early, made her bed in the mornings, ate fruit, and wore exquisite lingerie. Whenever we got ready to go out together, she'd assemble her things meticulously. I'd watch her diligently put each object in its place—her cell phone in the side pocket, her wallet in the interior one. She wasn't packing a bag; she was stringing pearls. The process always made me simmer with impatience, so I preferred to wait for her outside with a cigarette. But her slowness was also gracefulness. The way she held herself was regal, with her hair swept up into a bun at the nape of her neck—in my whole life, I've never seen someone with such perfect posture.

Celeste worked at a contemporary art gallery in Chelsea, but her real passion was baking. I watched her in the kitchen with astonishment; her desserts required a precision that I would never have. I was much too impatient to make a Saint Honoré. Meanwhile, Celeste would hold the sides of her chair tightly when she saw me making crêpes for breakfast. I never bothered to measure out the flour or milk before mixing them with the eggs.

Aria, my other roommate, was from a completely different planet. Only one word was needed to describe her: chaotic. She was always late—she had problems with the subway, or her purse was stolen, or she forgot her suitcase or lost her driver's license. She left her things scattered around the bathroom, dropped her keys in the street. The other day, she'd missed her flight to Chicago: She arrived at the airport on time but then got distracted by testing perfumes and lotions at the duty-free shop. Aria was insanely charming and had massive black eyes; to this day, I've never seen such big eyes on a human face. The girl looked like a very pretty owl. Aria laughed too loud and cried as intensely as she laughed, vacillating incessantly from one to the other. She'd get changed in the middle of the living room, or walk out of her room in a thong to brew coffee in the kitchen. She was also a bombshell. How did she manage to be so magnetic? She had major sex appeal, whereas I didn't have quite enough. I envied her sensuality, wanted to feel it, absorb it, copy it; I made a mental note of every intoxicating perfume she wore, every bit of lace or flash of skin she revealed. But I would have to study her voluptuousness even more closely, get to the root of the desire: Maybe I'd spend the night with her, why not?

Where Celeste was reserved and contained, Aria was a tireless social butterfly who flitted around from group to group, drinking nectar from a thousand different friends. Aria knew all the right bars, brunch spots, clubs, restaurants, and galleries; she was always the one to choose where to go. And all her friends were good-looking and well-dressed. Most of them were actors, like her, or artists.

Sitting on her bed, Aria confided in me about her dreams of the theater and cinema. She'd graduated from Juilliard and was desperate to act and be seen. Dreaming of Broadway and Hollywood Boulevard, she went from audition to audition and was always looking for a better agent. Her fate was even more painful than mine: Until someone gave her a chance, there was nothing she could accomplish on her own. She could only wait for the phone to ring, at the mercy of a producer or casting director's whim. So she took shitty TV jobs, playing a receptionist, a waitress, a crime-scene cleaner. As she waited for her breakout role, she worked at a cocktail bar. She also walked dogs four times a week, sometimes accompanied by Celeste. The two would chat while strolling around the neighborhood. Stella, Daisy, Philipp, and Robinson Crusoe would scamper ahead joyously, pulling on their leashes.

A room in Williamsburg for only $1,700 a month: There had to be a catch—and there was. The apartment was one of many properties owned by Celeste's family. Her parents had lived there for a few years before moving to the West Coast; they had held on to it because "everyone knows that you don't resell New York real estate." It took me several weeks to appreciate the trendy Brooklyn neighborhood. I felt like I had moved to the eleventh arrondissement in Paris; the vibes were very similar.

During the first few days, I had to ask Aria to stop taking my cereal. Same request for my conditioner, which finally I just hid in a drawer. One night I came out of my bedroom in a chemise, livid, my jaw tensed with anger, to ask: "Can you be quiet? I'm trying to sleep."

But we settled into a rhythm. Celeste and Aria had been friends since childhood and their bond was obvious, and yet they made space for me in their duo. I liked them, and living together had its perks. I stole silk underwear from Celeste when she wasn't there, went into the bathroom while Aria was showering so that I could sneak a peek. Celeste helped me repaint my bedroom walls white, Aria kept me supplied with coke on Saturday nights. With them, I actually enjoyed going out. Aided by drugs, the three of us would dance until the early morning before staggering back to the apartment. As the sun was rising behind us, the comedown would hit, and I'd look forward to getting into bed. Alongside Celeste and Aria, I felt at home in New York for the first time.

I may have had an American father, and I had lived in New

York for more than a year at that point, but I'd grown up in France, and no one was fooled. It was the same as for anyone with dual nationalities: In the United States, I was the French girl; in France, I was the American girl. It's true that, with the exception of my gym addiction, I didn't exactly blend into the scenery. I spoke at a reasonable volume, I waited until I was back in Paris to visit the dentist, I still thought in kilograms and kilometers, I didn't drink protein shakes, I didn't go to Starbucks every morning, I didn't walk down the street holding a giant three-liter bottle of water as though I were hiking in the desert, I didn't snack between meals, I didn't slather myself in self-tanner, I applied makeup sparingly, I didn't curl or straighten my hair. I didn't change clothes to go out either, unlike my roommates, who would slip into shorter dresses, higher heels, shinier jackets. My daytime clothes were just fine.

A month after I moved in, Celeste and Aria threw a party to celebrate my arrival. I met Lauren, Ellen, Margarita, Matt, Darius, Yasmin, Brent, and Aaron; their friends quickly became my friends too. *Did I like living in New York? What book did I recommend the most? Did I read all the latest releases? Did I dream of opening my own bookstore?* Their eyes lit up at the thought of such an exciting prospect of a person. It's true that a literary career could make for a nice life, if that were what I wanted. But my need for fame left me feeling indifferent to what I had. Only Aria seemed to notice my distress.

"Cléo is definitely hiding something from us."

"What? I'm not hiding anything."

"She's a very secretive person," Aria added knowingly.

"I'm not at all."

Aria talked a lot, but that didn't keep her from observing things. She was right: I shared everything with them except what was most important. I wrote songs in my bedroom almost every evening, full of ambition that was swallowing me whole.

To change the subject, I grabbed my guitar. "Why don't we choose a theme song for the apartment?"

As I strummed the first chords of "Make Your Own Kind of Music," an awestruck circle formed around me, and everyone joined in to sing the chorus together. When you want to keep a secret safe, the best way is to hide it in plain sight.

Every person you meet teaches you a lesson. Celeste taught me a major one: *You have to be hungry to accomplish big things.*

Celeste was born into a unique set of circumstances: She would never need to work in order to live. Her great-grandfather had made a fortune in newspapers, and since the money had been wisely invested, her whole family would be able to live for another three thousand years at this pace.

Celeste was bustling around in the kitchen, carefully brushing egg yolk onto puff pastry dough. I watched her in silence, amused. What was it like to be free from work for your entire life? Did she regularly bubble over with joy at the thought of being so incredibly rich? How had her status as an heiress affected her perception of time, of freedom, of the world?

The previous evening, we had gone out for Mexican food at a restaurant in the neighborhood—who could resist a sudden craving for quesadillas? Menu in hand, Celeste hadn't hesitated for a second when the waiter came around. I could see in her eyes the carefree attitude of the rich, the indulgence of a sugary beverage, the certainty that the future would always be bright: She ordered a Coke. In three seconds, my friend had increased the total cost of the bill by 20 percent without even thinking about it. You can tell exactly what someone's relationship to money is by whether they treat themself to a soda along with their meal.

At any rate, the amount of money Celeste spent was not correlated with the amount of money she earned. The two had nothing to do with each other. In fact, her paychecks were now being deposited into her father's bank account. Celeste had changed banks without notifying her employer of her new account number. What was the point? The revenue from the gallery was a drop in the ocean compared to her inheritance. Usually, she used the family credit card without even thinking, just as she'd been taught, in accordance with her lifestyle.

"I don't think I refrigerated the croissants for long enough before putting them in the oven. If the butter's too soft, it melts while they're baking and ruins them," Celeste said, pulling me out of my reveries about economic capital and the value of labor. For two weeks now, she'd been on a quest to make the perfect croissant: crisp but not dry, buttery but not greasy. She tried again and again, noting where she needed to improve and then starting over. I tasted them reluctantly, as each mouthful represented a dangerous percentage of my daily caloric allotment.

"Pastry making is all about chemistry. I definitely can't have them doubling in size in the oven," she continued.

In a month or two, after dozens of adjustments, Celeste would set herself a new challenge, abandoning croissants in favor of brioche, mille-feuille, or macarons.

"Hey, did you call Damien Dujean?"

"No, not yet," Celeste answered, wiping her floury hands on her apron.

The previous week, I had given her the telephone number of a famous French pastry chef who lived in New York. Damien Dujean was an acquaintance of Juliette's parents; I had sent him an excessively polite email to give him a heads-up that a friend of mine would be getting in touch.

"I didn't have time," she added. "We were celebrating my dad's birthday this weekend." She took the croissants out of the oven, carefully inspecting their reddish-brown sheen. Gleaming but not glistening. "Anyway, there would be no point in me contacting him now, since I'm leaving for Costa Rica soon. I'll call him in September."

It was there, surrounded by the smells of butter and dough, that I understood. Why would you travel across New York to meet a successful pastry chef when you already had so much? What was the use of monetizing your passion when you were all set financially for life? Celeste loved baking for free, on her own terms, without any goal other than achieving the perfect croissant.

A few weeks before, she had had a moment of fame on social media: A raspberry dessert she'd made had gone viral, gaining her thousands of followers thanks to an algorithm that was suddenly and inexplicably pushing photos of clafoutis. I encouraged her to post some new recipes to capitalize on her sudden popularity, but she didn't take my advice. For days I kept wondering what she was planning to do with her flash success. Finally I had my answer: nothing.

The only thing that drives major success is frustration. To be truly hungry, you need to feel a certain degree of discomfort, of dissatisfaction with the status quo. Of course you need a solid dose of privilege to get you off on the right foot, but not too high of a dose. Celeste would never be tormented by the need to be the best that I felt deep in my guts.

The key to understanding Celeste was that exercising her privilege kept her busy. There were the weekends on the private island in the Bahamas. The house in Notting Hill where her brother lived. The apartment in the center of Milan that her sister had just moved into. Her grandparents' vineyard in Napa Valley. The family got together for not just every birthday but also Christmas, Thanksgiving, Mother's Day, Father's Day, and the Fourth of July, not to mention winter, spring, and summer vacation. In total, forty-three days each year were already booked—and Celeste's presence at each of these events was not optional.

I, on the other hand, didn't have to give up any trips to Costa Rica to shut myself in my room and write songs. And most importantly, I was the only one who could ensure my ascension to a certain lifestyle. My family had money, but I would have to pay for my villa in California by myself.

Nonetheless, it would be unfair of me to reduce Celeste to this single observation. She was also the most generous person I knew—with money, with time, with affection. Celeste lived with roommates by choice, not necessity: She liked to be surrounded by people, though she was never the center of attention. Several years later, she would be the one with whom I'd celebrate every victory. "Oh, that's awesome, Cléo!" It's not always easy to rejoice in other people's success; I've never considered it a common gift. Jealousy is a more natural inclination. But Celeste would revel in my success without any malice whatsoever. I'll always be grateful to her for it. "Congratulations, I'm so happy for you!" When you're not starving to death, it's easier to let others eat.

The smells of milk and melted chocolate were wafting through the apartment. Celeste turned off the oven, swept up the eggshells that were on the countertop, and wiped down the table. Aria was sitting next to her, her expression defeated, her eyes swollen.

"It's horrible."

". . ."

"I didn't get the part."

". . ."

"I'm going crazy."

". . ."

"Why bother giving me a callback if you're just going to give the part to another girl two days later?"

". . ."

"I can't take this shitty industry anymore."

Aria threw her head back, her hand on her forehead and her face streaming with tears, as though she were the persecuted heroine of a melodrama. Sarah Bernhardt, my national treasure, would have to watch out.

Frankly, she was giving me secondhand embarrassment. Crying in public is vulgar—such shamelessness. If I had to shed a tear, I did it silently in the shower, like everyone else. An image came into my head, and I suppressed a smile: Aria was a puddle. A tiny little pond, stagnant and shapeless. And across from her, Celeste was the mop that absorbed her sorrows.

As Aria unspooled her laments, Celeste reassured her, promising that her time would come: "It's going to be okay." I would have rather told her to *stop being such a drama queen. Have a little self-respect. What is your problem? Did your mother not hold you enough when you were a baby? Why are you so needy and fragile?*

Despite Celeste's reassurances, Aria continued to moan theatrically. If we were in a cartoon, her tears would have been spurting out sideways. I was on the verge of laughter. I had always had trouble empathizing with others' suffering; earlier Celeste had cut herself when cooking, and when she stifled a cry, my reflex had been to assume that she was pretending.

"It's because of my shitty agent."

"..."

"The whole system is corrupt."

"..."

"I'll never make it."

"..."

"I suck."

Honestly, Aria wasn't that talented. She had rehearsed the previous week in the middle of our living room, and her performance had been awful. *No, you haven't just learned that your lover has died from tuberculosis, your character doesn't need to roll around on the floor in grief.* It all rang false, overly exaggerated, when the script called—in my opinion—for a bit of restraint. I didn't say anything at the time, but I'd been right, since Aria wasn't ultimately picked.

She didn't know it, but Aria and her demons made me feel more secure in my decision to write my own songs. I found the passivity of actors repellent: There was no way I was going to just wait around to be chosen, to be a mere interpreter. And I'd rather die than find myself in a situation where my friends were rubbing my back and calling me "poor thing." I didn't want them to console me, or to encourage me either. I aspired to a dazzling career, to become famous from one day to the next, without struggle or setbacks—and without whining.

I helped Celeste clean up the kitchen, still watching the grand consolation scene from a distance. Aria reassured me without overshadowing me because our dreams were similar without being in competition. I learned from her experiences, her mistakes, her choices; I learned and I took, but I gave nothing in return. I was a parasite: I analyzed her failures without revealing my own to her. I was a vampire: I witnessed the power of the desire for fame take effect on her.

At the end of the evening, I shut myself up in my room to jot down some notes in my notebook.

STAY DESIRABLE

MAINTAIN YOUR DIGNITY

DON'T TELL OTHER PEOPLE ABOUT YOUR FAILURES

DON'T BE A DISGUSTING VICTIM LIKE ARIA

hated to see Aria cry, but God knows I wanted to see her come. The jingling of her bracelets on her wrist had been mesmerizing me the entire evening. I had watched her chatting with her boyfriend on the couch, ordering something to eat, dipping a spoon into a carton of ice cream. She laughed, she cried, she got emotional, she batted her eyelashes, she changed the subject, she raised her voice, she lost her temper, she calmed down. The girl was a tempest.

That night she was more beautiful than ever. More sensual, especially. Her brown hair was tumbling over her shoulders; she wore a black cotton tank top and a pair of shorts. I had spent the evening looking at her, but she hadn't seen, so I let my gaze drop to the small of her back and linger on her curves. When I lifted my eyes again, Aria was staring at me. Had she just realized that I wanted to touch her? She put her hand over mine and continued talking as though nothing had happened. I didn't dare move, incredulous.

When Aria and her boyfriend slipped away into her bedroom, I got the sense that they were encouraging me to follow them. I stood up cautiously. They were kissing on the bed, and I watched them for a moment, hesitating by the door that they'd left open, feeling both ill at ease and mad with desire.

Aria turned her head, taunting me with her big black eyes. Her boyfriend's face was buried in her neck, and he slipped the strap of her tank top off her shoulder.

"Are you coming?"

I wasn't delusional. Aria was inviting me in.

Her ass was rocking back and forth on top of her boyfriend's cock, her lower back tensing with each thrust. Aria was intense, extreme, an actress. Ecstasy was written all over her face; her mouth was contorted. I realized that I had never experienced pleasure like that. The men who had slept with me must have thought I was an icicle. Noted for the next time: fake it ten times as hard. I tried to burn the image of hypersexual Aria into my memory so that I could call it to mind later, when I was shooting a music video or sleeping with someone famous.

Kneeling on the bed, I stroked her hair and her hips, wrapped myself behind her so that I could kiss her neck. Holding my palm to her forehead, I tested her temperature. She was feverish. I took hold of her small, bouncing breasts, one in each hand, in wonderment; I didn't dare lick them, but I desperately wanted to. Her skin was soft, its texture velvety, like that of an apricot. Her body seemed fragile on top of her boyfriend's hard, sturdy one.

What this was, more than anything, was incredible anthropological research. A couple was making love right next to me. I wasn't watching them through a screen, like in a porno; they were right before my eyes. I couldn't get over the fact that this age-old spectacle was taking place mere inches away.

Her boyfriend grabbed her waist and lifted her up to free her, then positioned her sitting up on the end of the bed before he descended between her legs. His tongue flickered over her clit. Pressing my cheek to his, I extended my own tongue, our saliva mixing together; Aria moved her hips forward, straining to get closer to our mouths. What a pleasure it was to learn how she tasted. Then I touched her with my index finger, feeling her clit harden, and looked her right in the eyes. She grew pale as I once again plunged my tongue into her melting pussy. When I couldn't take it anymore, I slid on top of her, rubbing myself against her thigh before coming, hard, with a deep cry that took me by surprise. This time I wasn't pretending.

Silently, I got up and left the room. Aria closed the door behind me. For a long time, I would hope that she would reopen it.

I had a whole life ahead of me, and yet I had already screwed it up. At twenty-five, I'd never felt so old.

"Everything okay, Cleopatra?"

"Yes, everything's fine, Dad. I'm happy to see you."

The evening of my birthday, I was eating dinner at a restaurant with my parents, who had come to New York just for the occasion. I smiled to please them, but my spark was gone. I was neither rich nor famous; how could I possibly feel happy? Musical geniuses just two years older than me had already had the time to lead brilliant careers and die of overdoses. I promised myself that I would jump out a window if I still wasn't famous at thirty.

Eyes closed, fists clenched as hard as I could at my sides, I leaned over my cake and made a wish. It was always the same one. For every birthday, shooting star, and wishing well, as far back as I could remember. *To become famous.* But that evening my wish seemed far-off. An illusion, a mirage, a chimera. My father rubbed my shoulder before leaning over to whisper in my ear: "Sweetheart, be careful what you wish for." I blew out my candles without heart or conviction.

Tears welled up in my eyes as I pushed my spoon into the chocolate lava cake, though I didn't say anything to my parents about my sadness. They probably imagined I was going through a breakup or a quarter-life crisis. They had also noticed that my job at the bookstore wasn't fulfilling, and carefully suggested that I go back to school to figure out what I wanted to do. And why didn't I come back to France? They didn't understand my choices. I couldn't hold it against them; I hadn't given them any way to understand. In front of my dessert, from which I'd barely managed to take more than two bites, I was about to tell them the truth: That over the last few months, I'd written dozens of songs. Nothing great, but someday I would be a star. But I was afraid that they'd tell me that music was a passion, not a career. That they wouldn't understand that I was different from other people. I would have rather died than see disappointment, embarrassment, or pity in their eyes. *Great, our daughter's gotten it into her head that she's going to become a singer.*

My father handed me my present, wrapped in tissue paper: a crew-neck beige cashmere sweater. I recognized my mother's elegance and the label of a Parisian boutique she often visited. Even today the sweater is one of the items of clothing I'm most attached to; I love how the fabric feels against my skin, the way it holds my scent, its color somewhere between cream and sand. I take good care of it, just like I cherish all the presents that I received before I became famous. Giving a gift to a celebrity is a trial by fire. What can you possibly give someone who has everything?

I returned to Brooklyn on the subway, leaving my parents to walk back to their hotel. My favorite song at the time was playing in my headphones, telling the oldest story in the world: that of time passing. "Time Go" was the ideal soundtrack to a depressing birthday evening. I had discovered the song, which was from an LA-based indie rock group, thanks to my constant reconnaissance. To develop my ear, I listened to everything, all the time—old songs and new releases, the hits of the summer, complicated experimental pieces, songs with high production value, Latin American commercial successes, whatever was trending in South Korea or anywhere else. . . . I planned to spend the next few hours drinking herbal tea and listening to the comprehensive playlist I'd created of the very best sad songs from around the world.

But then I opened the door to the apartment: lights, camera flash, applause! All my friends were there. Aria and Celeste had organized a surprise party, and my parents had been in on it. A moment later, the festivities were in full swing. I poured myself a glass of wine, then a second one; a true moment of joy after all. I hugged my coworkers from the bookstore.

"It's so nice to have you all here!"

"Did you guess?"

"Not at all!"

Celeste and Aria were talking and drinking beer in the kitchen. Matt, Ellen, and Margarita, who all worked in finance, were discussing their year-end bonuses. In the hallway, Yasmin threw her arms around me: She was pregnant! The day before, Juliette had called me from Paris to say that she was getting married.

All around me, my friends were busy crafting their futures: They were at the starts of promising careers, they were getting promoted, they were in serious relationships, they had bought real estate. Soon I would be invited to my first bachelorette parties, I'd attend baby showers—and even if I didn't really want any of that, it would still make me feel like I had ruined my life.

I leaned out the window to smoke. Aria turned the music up, and Aaron and Lauren danced around her. I thought back to a decade earlier, on rue Princesse in Paris. I was celebrating my fifteenth birthday, sure of my destiny, the heroine of my own adventure film. What had I accomplished since? Nothing. In ten years, I hadn't moved forward an inch, and my paralysis was a fatal choice.

Should I give up my childhood dreams, resign myself to my lack of fame, build something new? Was it time to change jobs, take on more responsibilities, find a boyfriend? In front of me, bodies drew closer, guided by the music, and I watched them, impassible, turning around to blow cigarette smoke into the icy January air.

I stubbed out my cigarette butt before shutting myself in my room. On the other side of the wall, the party was going on without me. I would give myself a minute. Sixty seconds to mentally run through the last ten years. The memories flashed by: I had a dream, but I wasn't doing anything to make it come true. The piano and the guitar, for nothing. My golden voice, for nothing. My studies, for nothing. New York, for nothing. All those years were lost. A ten-year void. I rummaged through my closet, found a leather belt. I sank to my knees and used the belt to flog my thighs. Ten lashes. Ten cracks of the whip for the ten years I had wasted. There was no time to whine: I had punished myself, and now I would return. I wiped up the blood with a cotton round before putting on an ivory long-sleeved dress—flowing, voluminous, filmy. Looking like a vestal virgin, I walked back out to the dance floor, as magnetic and majestic as I had been ten years earlier.

All the remaining furniture had been pushed against the wall, and everyone was dancing and sweaty. The song that was playing brought everyone together. No one needed to know the name of the artist to scream the chorus—it was a masterpiece of international pop. I swayed, regal and flamboyant, mouthing the lyrics as though the song were my own. Around my thighs, my dress was stained with miniscule drops of blood.

Celeste and Aria hugged and kissed me, and I knew that I had to hold steady. More than ever, I had to cling to my faith. To believe when there was no longer any reason to do so. If you remind a believer of the data, facts, and statistics, they will continue to believe, beyond all logic. I would be that exception. I would be the one person out of ten million. My conviction was not rational; it was intuition. I visualized celebrities parading down the red carpet, receiving awards, giving interviews, appearing on television: I knew that I would be one of them.

In the kitchen, I poured myself a glass of gin, and then a second, and then, finally, I drank straight from the bottle in giant gulps. Screw all of them. There was something bigger than a promotion, a house, a husband, or a child waiting for me.

Cell phone to my ear, I was walking quickly to change from one subway line to another; the bookstore would open in half an hour. I don't remember exactly what my mother said, but I understood that I had to return to Paris immediately. My father was in the hospital: He had had an accident on his way to the university.

At the airport, my mother offered to buy me a coffee. I must have been exhausted from the jet lag, she said. Was she making fun of me? Her hands were trembling, and she wouldn't look me in the eye. Why wasn't she in a hurry to get back to my father's bedside? Why wasn't she telling me about the visiting hours, doctors, operations, side effects, months of rehabilitation? Why wasn't she running toward the car? Why were we wasting forty-two minutes making our way down to an underground parking lot on the other side of the airport?

I could hardly breathe in the elevator. By the time we reached Basement Level 3, the classical music was giving me a headache, I was too hot, I was suffocating; I took off my coat, and all of a sudden, the truth hit me; I needed air, I dropped my suitcase on the concrete floor, causing my mother to stop short, and took off running, snaking my way among the cars, the pain chasing me down each of the numbered aisles; the sorrow wasn't external, it was part of me, I couldn't escape it; I vomited on the back tire of a Mercedes with a Swiss license plate.

Had my mother not had the courage to tell me the truth on the phone, or had my mind tried to protect me by not allowing me to understand? 2:45 p.m., rue Dante. My father had been hit by a car and died instantly.

Why are we programmed to think that the people we love will live forever? I hadn't responded to the last message from my dad, in which he'd told me he hoped I would have a nice day. I had told myself I would do it later. We always think we have the time.

There was no sign of the tragedy in the apartment where I'd grown up. My father's shoes were lined up in the rack in the entryway, and everything was in its place—his red umbrella, his plaid scarf, a letter from the revenue service on top of a pile of magazines, a grocery list scribbled on the back of an envelope. On his desk was his computer, asleep, and several pages of handwritten notes that he'd clearly intended to return to later; in the margins, my father had sketched a horse carrying a mouse on its back. I looked for hints of his impending death but didn't see any. I found nothing but life, everywhere—pulsing, mundane, sweet, funny, waiting.

As I rifled around in his things, I stumbled upon his coin purse, a rigid leather semicircle that had fascinated me when I was a little girl and my father would drop his coins into it at the bakery. Without saying anything, I slid the childhood memory into my bag. I also stole four ID photos from a drawer, some pens, and his shaving cream, as though everything that had belonged to him was doomed to disappear at the same time he did, just as quickly.

In my room, the bed was unmade. My mother hadn't had the courage to sleep in her own the previous night. After dinner we lay down next to each other. There were glow-in-the-dark stars stuck on the ceiling. Around 3:00 a.m., I reached for my mother's hand under the covers. We cried for a long time, without saying anything to each other, without letting each other go.

Four days later, an asshole wearing loafers spoiled the ceremony. Twenty-two years old, medium-length brown rich-guy hair, navy-blue Hugo Boss suit, an air of self-satisfaction. Did he understand that he was at a funeral? I was reading a tribute to my father when the son of a bitch started shaking his right leg nervously, as though he were keeping time with his foot. *I'm supposed to live without my father, and you're out there jiggling your thigh? What are you trying to say? That you're bored? Or that your body is so powerful, so strong, so alive, that you can't stand sitting still for more than twenty minutes? Because you can leave—be my guest. I think we'll all survive if my mother's cousin's son doesn't make it until the end.* When he crossed the aisle later at the end of the ceremony, I slid my bag across the floor, and the idiot tripped and fell. As he lay there on the ground, I was dying to beat him up. Two kicks to the ribs, one to the stomach.

I returned to New York in a daze. My grief manifested itself first in compulsive shopping at the airport: several Dior lipsticks, some Estée Lauder moisturizer, a pair of too-big sneakers, a bottle of men's cologne. On the plane, I treated myself to a glass of champagne—one for me, one for each of the passengers in my row.

Hundreds of euros, because my father would never be there again, because he would never see me grow old, because my twenty-fifth birthday was the last memory I would ever have with him. Then a thought occurred to me that was even more painful. How could I admit it? I was devastated to realize that my father would never see me succeed. He had spent his life calling me Cleopatra, and yet he would never witness me become a queen. "Father's pride"—how sad that etymology was, given that he would never have a reason to be proud of me. He would never listen to my songs, he would never come to one of my concerts, he would never attend my coronation. I would never give him a new golf bag, pieds-à-terre in Rome and Cairo, or Egyptian antiquities (would he have preferred a collection of amulets or the bust of a goddess?).

I got up to ask a flight attendant for a blanket and saw that a man in first class was crying. It couldn't be heartbreak or fear of turbulence. Handing him a tissue, I asked whether he had lost his father or his mother. He looked at me incredulously and didn't say anything in response. For the rest of my life, whenever I saw a stranger crying, I would automatically assume they were an orphan. I would call that instinctive pain attribution.

Ever since the funeral, Juliette had been writing to me every day. She encouraged me to express my sadness, while I was doing exactly the opposite: burying it deep down. I deleted her messages without responding. We would leave the grief in the Old World.

On the way to the bookstore, music playing in my headphones, I scrolled through songs in search of one that would keep me from crying. I couldn't find one upbeat enough and was growing increasingly desperate, skipping from track to track faster and faster. As I exited the subway, I stumbled on a Britney Spears song. No one had ever cried to "Gimme More." No one. I turned up the volume and walked along the sidewalk to the beat, started to bop my head; my tears stopped, and I slid my left foot to the side. In the music video, Britney danced around a pole wearing a brown wig. I didn't think about onlookers' judgment—no one else existed apart from Britney and me—so I started to gyrate around an imaginary pole myself. At the chorus, I crouched down, stood up, held my arm above my head. I performed each step of the choreography in the middle of the street, lofty and loose-limbed—a loon. It was a miracle. I hadn't cried for four minutes, and I was almost at the store.

My father's death was a wake-up call. A brutal one. I paced around the apartment like a madwoman, devising incomprehensible plans. Celeste and Aria asked me what I was talking about; it was the first time they'd heard me talk to myself in French. "Cléo Louvent, il faut que tu te secoues le cocotier." Cléo Louvent, you'd better shake that coconut tree.

Alone in my room, I spent hours rereading the lyrics I had written over the past few months, organizing my songs into folders on my computer, sorting through my voice notes containing embryos of melodies. I was relying on my academic instincts.

At the same time, I was tackling two new songs. The ideas came to me at night, when I was in bed; inspiration struck when I was in a meditative state, on the cusp of sleep. I would slide my hand under my pillow to grab my phone and whisper into the recorder.

Three months of rigorous work led to an astounding result: My creations were just as bad as ever. My faith wavered. If I were as gifted as I thought, why had I still not managed to compose a masterpiece? I was brilliant, erudite, intuitive: Why didn't that come through in my music? I couldn't be wrong. It wasn't possible. Otherwise, everything would collapse.

I gave myself a slap. Followed by a second one, more violent. Then I grabbed my straightening iron, brought it to the sole of my foot—whimpering until I was begging for mercy. The punishment was severe, in proportion to the intensity of my disappointment in myself. At the time, I was incapable of seeing that the essentials were already there: In all my songs there was a hook, a chorus, two or three verses, a bridge. The bones were good. But in the absence of clarity, I at least realized this one thing: I needed help.

Unsteady, I left my room to enlist my roommates, who were eating dinner. The question I was about to ask them required superhuman courage—it was a hundred times more painful than the burn under my foot, and I would have rather yanked my own tooth out with pliers than ask for their opinions—but I went for it:

"Girls, would you do me a favor and listen to one of my songs?"

"You write songs?"

Celeste and Aria settled themselves on the couch, and I sat on a stool with my guitar, facing them.

"Your voice . . . We already knew your voice was hypnotizing," breathed Celeste when I finished.

"But I'm not asking you about my voice, I'm asking you about my song."

After a long silence, Aria delivered the verdict:

"It's great . . . but it's not you."

I had always preferred occurrences that confirmed my genius to those that denied it. I wondered if that wasn't my greatest strength: always concentrating on my successes, and legitimately forgetting my failures. I had just made an idiot of myself in front of my roommates, but the next morning, I swallowed my shame and sorrow. After breakfast I went back to composing.

We'd turned it into a weekly appointment. Every Sunday evening, I made them listen to a song. Even if I wasn't satisfied. Even if my chorus wasn't finished. Even if a verse was missing. *Cléo*

Louvent, now we are going to sit our ass down on that stool and we are going to sing them our songs.

In their eyes I could see fascination for my voice, but also the same incomprehensible distance when it came to my songs. Something wasn't working, but I couldn't figure out the mechanisms of the resistance. Celeste was encouraging, while Aria relayed to me recommendations from her drama teacher: "You have to make yourself ugly, get dirty, roll around in the mud, put yourself in danger, expose yourself. Art isn't about presenting an idealized version of yourself; it's about showing everyone your worst side." I wrestled with their advice, stubborn and determined. I wandered around my room topless, wearing only underwear, thinking about my most inadmissible faults. I started a song that I called "Entitled," my favorite word, which in eight letters summed up my uncontrollable feeling of superiority coupled with my burning intuition that I was too good for my current existence. The chorus was brutally honest: "I deserve much better than this shitty little life." Each lyric was a piece of me—one I'd never dared expose to anyone.

The same week in April, I wrote two other songs. A clear sign that I had found an effective hook: I would get horrible diarrhea. My fingers on the keyboard, I would play the first notes, reel off the first words. If my guts twisted and I had to run to the bathroom, I knew I was going in the right direction.

My second song was about my inability to love. Why write devastating love songs when my heart had never stirred? Why invent romantic suffering when I had never been in a relationship? Might as well tell the truth: "I Feel Nothing." I had a cold heart incapable of feeling, impervious to empathy; ever since I was a teenager, I had looked on the internet for proof that I was a sociopath. I'd recognized some of my own behaviors and symptoms on psychiatry forums. So I dove right in, starting with the first verse: "Most of the time, I feel absolutely nothing."

My song was coming to life, and I devoted hours to it, spurred on by a feeling of urgency. Writing a song is always a race against the clock. The emotional anesthesia I was talking about was a fairly common truth—I had to be the first one to write about it. I didn't want to just *add* something to a topic; I wanted to be the one to point it out first, to announce to the world, *This is the topic* that we are now going to talk about.

My third song was about success. Again, I preferred to be honest: "You aren't here anymore, and the worst part is knowing that you will never see me win." No one needed to know that I was talking about my father, so I kept the details vague. In "Entitled," I had done the same, evoking my pride without revealing the exact reasons for my frustration: I wasn't going to say that I was irritated to be working in a bookstore when I should have been on a worldwide tour, or that I was furious not to have been invited to the royal wedding in England that was going to be taking place in a month.

I had two compasses: my guts and my roommates. Sitting on the couch, Aria and Celeste were in agreement about which melody was the most effective, which chorus was still muddled. Despite my efforts, my songs improved at an infinitesimal pace, as though I had to pass through all the stages and make every possible mistake, without taking even the tiniest of shortcuts. I worked on my songs fervently for five months, modifying each verse 1,457 times. Still, my memories of this period are happy ones. Creation has been a delight ever since I started putting my honest feelings into my work.

Then, finally, the miracle occurred: Those three songs sounded like my favorite songs. They could have been written by someone else.

"*I wrote this* song in ten minutes while sitting on my bedroom floor. The words just flowed out of me." Who could believe such bullshit? And yet that's what I said in interviews, nonchalant and brilliant, obsessed with giving the public good reasons to admire me. It's one of the best-kept secrets about me: I'm a drudge. Sometimes I wonder if I even have any talent. Nothing has come to me easily. At best, a few rare flashes of inspiration in a sea of labor.

Everyone knows how I became famous. One June night, between 2:00 and 3:00 a.m., I filmed myself singing a ballad on the piano by candlelight. A verse, a chorus: forty-one seconds. Around me was an assortment of twenty or so mismatched candlestick holders, thrifted by Celeste, who collected them; they included one in the shape of a fish with a gaping mouth, several that looked like metallic fruit sculptures, and a ceramic lantern made to resemble a half-timbered house. In several hours, my cover of "Vienna" by Billy Joel went viral. I had TikTok—the social network where music was front and center—to thank.

People often credit the start of my rise to a favorable algorithm. But they forget that videos go viral every week, and three days later, no one's talking about them. They forget that a popular song on the internet isn't the golden ticket to the paradise of the musical industry. They forget that at that point, the most decisive battle is finding a competent manager and the right people to surround yourself with.

Over the weeks that followed my moment of glory on social media, I rode the wave of my success, approaching its crest and then paddling with all my strength. Several mediocre artistic directors sent me enthusiastic messages, but if they were coming to me, I wasn't interested. I wanted only those who were at the top of their game. I sent my three original songs to people who mattered, targeting the managers of the biggest stars in the country, the best booking agents, the three most influential record labels. I paid $40 on illegal Russian sites to get the email addresses of the label directors. Just because I was an artist didn't mean I was disorganized and aimless. I sent 197 emails in 17 days and carefully recorded all my outreach in an Excel spreadsheet. Response rate: 11%.

I installed software on my computer to track when my emails were opened, how many times, and at what times. When someone didn't respond to me or when I received a rejection—even a polite one—I highlighted the name of the guilty party in red on my grid. I would remember them.

After I was done working at the bookstore for the day, I would cross Manhattan to go get coffees with young producers who accepted my invitations to meet up. ("Music is a very competitive world, it's hard to break through without knowing the right people"—thanks for this analysis, Kevin, very helpful.) That summer, in the hopes of being discovered, I went to my first open mic nights in sticky bars because, apparently, some important Sony scouts went there regularly. I also hung out in the trendy clubs where all the failing artists in New York went drinking, in search of contacts; for example, I found the address of the restaurant where all the former contestants on *The Voice* met up (it was dingy and the fries were disgusting). Most of all, I worked diligently on my social media content, making sure to post every day so that engagement wouldn't drop off. I even bought some fake followers to artificially boost the momentum—just a few thousand to give me some credibility and a head start.

To what did I owe my success? To the good fortune of an unexpected breakthrough on the internet? To a musical cover that I happened to post at the right time? To my beauty in the video, to the privilege of being a pretty white girl? To Celeste's astonishing collection of candlestick holders, which elicited thousands of comments that boosted the algorithm and visibility of the video? To my three original songs that I had just finished in my room and that would soon make my name known around the world? To my father's death having opened my eyes? To Celeste and Aria's astute advice? To Andrew, the first manager to believe in me? To my ten years of music lessons, to my mastery of music theory, the guitar, the piano? To my innate talent for singing? To my unforgettable raspy voice, a genetic gift for which I could thank my parents?

The answer was that my success didn't have a single origin but ten thousand—all of which converged at one point: me.

If it were 2400 years ago, I would have crossed the Egyptian desert to reach one of the most remote oases; I would have climbed two hundred miles of dunes and set up camp between the palm groves and salt lakes before setting off again toward the sanctuary at Siwa. Then, like Alexander the Great, like a great Macedonian queen, I would have consulted the Oracle of Amun to learn my future. So: What was going to happen?

Instead, I looked for answers on my way to the bookstore. At the street corner, if the light was green, I would have a career in music. But if there was a walk sign, I wouldn't make it. I had a system of predictions for my phone too, which I consulted at random: If the time was a round number (9:00, 9:05, 9:10, 9:15, 9:20, 9:25, 9:30), I would soon be a global celebrity. I searched everywhere for confirmation.

All of a sudden, the morning of August 15th, my surroundings began to send me signs. In my field of vision was a brown leather couch with rolled arms in the shape of a letter "s." The handle of my mug formed the same letter, as did the waves of my coworker's ponytail. A client approached me to ask a question, and when I asked her name, she told me it was Sarah. The two books she was looking for were by Salinger and Steinbeck, and she had always wanted to read Stendhal. . . . I felt dizzy. "S's" were everywhere. It was unnatural, and there was only one explanation: it was "s" for "success." Stunned, I asked my coworker to cover for me for a few minutes; I needed some air. Everyone in the street was smiling at me; they all recognized me—no, wait, that couldn't be right, I wasn't famous yet. . . . But I swear that one couple was smiling at me. I was almost there.

I remember the day, I remember the time, I remember the open boxes in the storage room, I remember the pile of books waiting to be put away, I remember the wooden step stool we used to reach the higher shelves, I remember my mug of tea on the counter, I remember the smell of vanilla and spices, I remember the creamy texture of my lipstick, I remember my forest-green skirt, I remember the sound of my heeled sandals on the parquet. A ray of sunlight was streaming in through the window when my phone vibrated in my back pocket. It was an unknown caller.

Soon I would say that it took me ten years to become an overnight success.

My first week on the island is both wonderful and terrible. Lying in total darkness, I am faced with primal fears—I haven't slept without security close by in years. Curled up under a blanket, I flinch at every little noise. I imagine that pirates have landed and are coming to rape and murder me. Or that some lunatic has figured out that I'm here and is preparing to kidnap me. Maybe poachers in search of protected species will stumble upon me by accident and decide to force me into slavery or sell my organs. Another horrifying scenario: A storm will unearth two skeletons buried in the sand next to the hut. My night terrors are also populated with ravens that peck out my eyes, pythons that wrap themselves around my neck, anacondas under my bed, rats that gnaw on my bones, tarantulas, scorpions. Trembling with fear and soaked with sweat, I don't dare turn on the flashlight that I clutch against my chest. I comfort myself the best I can: The satellite telephone is there for a reason. The area must be closely monitored. You wouldn't send a celebrity out to risk their life. There's always a safety net.

The fourth day, it rains incessantly. The wind is blowing so hard, I don't dare venture outside. There will be plenty of water for my showers and my tea, but I have to wonder: Where should I seek shelter if there's a hurricane? My hut offers only modest shelter. In the fairy tale "The Three Little Pigs," their houses are built of straw, wood, and brick, respectively. The moral of the story is unequivocal: It's better to count on something solid.

I can't imagine Natalie Holmes here. The island is so wild, so inhospitable. That said, a lot of people would have trouble believing that I'm as resourceful as I am. Ever since my arrival, I've been digging up memories of sleeping outside in Auvergne with my cousins and my uncle, the long-forgotten summer-vacation rituals of lighting and maintaining a fire, gathering bark and pine needles, keeping the wood dry. I compile a rigorous inventory of my food stores and draw water from the tank to boil for my rice so that I can save my bottles of mineral water. Was Natalie Holmes as quick-witted, or did she forget to mention to me that she was accompanied by her assistant, personal chef, and bodyguard? What about the other celebrities who have come here? Did Christopher Nolan go hungry? Did he relieve himself in a hole? Did Taylor Swift?

It's hard for me to imagine these global superstars playing at being adventurous travelers and bathing themselves in rainwater. Natalie Holmes lied to me. She herself can't have lasted the full three weeks; it's just not possible. She made it only three days. What's for sure is that I am not going to cave. Out of pride, out of curiosity, out of desire—I vow to myself that I will last to the end. Three weeks and not one day less.

For despite the fear and the discomfort, my daily life here is also, in many respects, the nicest it's been in years. The possibility of danger may keep me from sleeping soundly at night, but in the afternoon, I take long naps in the hammock. Breeze wafting over my face, eyelids heavy with sleep, soothed by the lapping of the waves, I wrap myself in solitude as though it were a duvet. I'm more rested than I am after a week in one of the most luxurious spas in Paris or Los Angeles.

Every day I go swimming in the warm, shallow water of the

lagoon. I read novels, I do crossword puzzles, I build sandcastles. I go to sleep at the same time as the sun and awaken with the dawn. I take care of my body with planks, push-ups, and yoga. Island life is the best fitness regimen: I can see myself getting thinner and more toned.

It really is satisfying to lead a simple existence, reduced to one suitcase and ten objects. Tranquility is sometimes found in what is taken away rather than what is added. I even relish the slowness and idleness—maybe by next summer, I'll be ready to take a donkey ride. Who would have believed it? Productivity is not my only objective. I'm no longer optimizing every second; I'm tasting the pleasures of simplicity. The machine has been paused.

Not talking to anyone, not giving orders to subordinates, organizing my time as I see fit . . . I'm not looking for my cell phone in my pocket anymore. I've forgotten it exists.

Cléo Louvent, what would you bring with you to a desert island?" People ask me that a lot in interviews. My response is always the same: "Definitely my guitar or my piano. I can't live without music!" It's a safe answer, publicist-approved, but it's also one of my only truthful ones.

Every day I sing covers and accompany myself on the guitar. A melancholy version of "Freed from Desire" by the fire, a spirited version of "Celui qui chante" in the hammock. Even more than the comfort of a bathroom or the expertise of my private chef, what I miss the most is listening to music. I could use a hi-fi system under the coconut palms.

Just like I was told, this place is perfect for composing music. I don't have any recording equipment, so I have to meticulously note down every chord so that I don't forget the melodies I'm creating. I've started working on several songs inspired by my childhood, New York, and my daily life before I was famous. The solitude revives old memories, intact and ambiguous: the raw material for all the best songs. My music is stripped to the bone. More poetic, more direct, more effective. I don't need anyone else's confirmation to know that I'm at the height of my artistic powers.

All the same, I don't allow myself to work more than a few hours every day. I absolutely cannot throw myself headlong into the next project, the next battle. More than anything else, I'm here to rest, so instead of falling into a creative frenzy, I give myself the freedom to appreciate the scenery—and, for the first time in many years, to look backward.

Ever since my arrival, no planes have flown over the island, no cargo ship has twinkled in the distance, and the satellite phone hasn't rung. The Earth could have stopped turning and I would have no idea. A nuclear war, a sudden and violent pandemic, a bacteriological catastrophe, a massive terrorist attack, a total reversal of the world order—how would I know about any of it? And what if everyone died except me?

Natalie Holmes was right about one thing: I'm not on vacation, I'm having an experience. Getting back to nature is definitely testing my strength. I've lost all notion of time. I'm scared every night. I toss and turn. My brain spins in circles. I marvel at the most beautiful starry skies I've ever seen. You have to have the right psychological armor to face solitude without hanging yourself with a belt or a sheet after two days. The idea has crossed my mind several times.

The isolation. The dizzying vastness. The anxiety. The introspection. How did I get here? In six months, my perfect life had spiraled. I was exceedingly proud, the leader of the pack, so sure I would win in every way, and I nearly lost everything. It all comes back to me in a blood-soaked flash.

No one isolates themself on a desert island voluntarily if they don't have serious issues to work out.

PART TWO

Ascension

"Cléo Louvent, do you know that your life is going to change?"

The elevator doors opened, and the record label director herself stepped forward to greet me with this sentence I would never forget. Was it a promise or a warning?

I took a second to think before responding, weighing each word carefully before looking her straight in the eye and saying, without a trace of embarrassment, "No, you don't understand. I'm the one who's going to change your life."

Nikki burst out laughing and put her hand on my bare shoulder to guide me toward the room at the end of the hall. I was wearing my Jean Paul Gaultier vintage dress. I had an investment to recoup.

Fifteen people were waiting for me around a glass table on the forty-seventh floor of a skyscraper. I wanted a team that would match my own ambition, so I had chosen the massive promotional machine. Andrew, my manager, leaned toward me and whispered, "So, are you happy now?"

I smiled, biting my lips with pleasure. Over the last few weeks, we had gone to meeting after meeting with record companies to create a frenzy, concluding our mad dash at the top: International Records. My online presence had continued to blow up, assuring me that my audience was engaged and growing. But it wasn't Tik-Tok that had opened the doors of one of the biggest labels in the country for me: It was the three songs that I had written. They proved that I wasn't just a passing fad, an empty product of social media.

Nikki showered me with compliments, but I wasn't fooled. International Records was taking a moderate risk with me: They were signing me to make sure that one of their competitors didn't do it first. They must have seen hundreds of fresh-faced girls just like me who never made it, knockoff starlets who'd do anything to succeed. How many other singers thirsty for success had been invited to sit at this exact table? International Records was investing in me the same way they were investing in ten other talents simultaneously: *To see what happens.* In industry parlance, I was a "developing artist." The label's plan was to have me release a few songs so they could test the waters; my streaming and viewership results would determine what was next. It would be up to me to prove to them that they had pulled off the deal of the century by signing me.

The terms of my contract were clear: I was giving them all the rights to my music. None of it would belong to me any longer. It was a standard major label deal: International Records would take care of me every step of the way, and in exchange, they would be the owners of my catalogue. At this stage, my earnings were pathetic. I would see so little of the money that my songs brought in that it was almost laughable. Essentially, I was the little mermaid making a Faustian bargain with the sea witch. I had to choke back a laugh because Nikki actually did resemble Ursula. She was imposing, with short white hair, a lavender blouse, a beauty mark above her lip, red nail polish, and sky-blue eyeshadow. I checked under the table: no black tentacles, no purple suckers. While she was capable of stealing my voice and locking it inside her seashell necklace, I was, in return, making my dreams come true. Unlike Ariel, I was taking responsibility for my choice.

Today I could choose to be shocked by the conditions of the

agreement. I could take offense at the hegemony of the major labels, denounce the giants who control most music catalogues. I
could sympathize with the hundreds of thousands of artists who
have been ground down by this industry. But that wouldn't be
honest, because that day, I knew exactly why I was signing. I wasn't
fighting the system; I was taking advantage of it.

My career moved forward more in one hour of discussion than
in ten years. Since then, I've realized that time isn't linear. Since
then, I've lived years that have been richer than whole decades.

Next to me, Andrew was taking notes on his tablet. My manager wore a T-shirt, a wedding ring, and a baseball cap, no matter
what season it was. A fortysomething who loved music passionately, he had recently opened his own artist management business
after years of working at a record label; I was in good hands, expert
ones. With him I was able to spare myself from the cliché of the ag-
ing manager, past his prime, who had worked with boy bands in the
nineties—the has-been who wasn't above stealing from the pro-
verbial till (the envelopes of cash floating around during concerts
weren't fooling anyone). And, most importantly, Andrew hadn't
bestowed upon me the kind of idiotic advice I'd been hearing left
and right over the previous few weeks: "First of all, you definitely
have to lie about your age. Say you're twenty-two, not twenty-five.
And you should adopt a different first name, like Giselle or Rose.
Or go by Cléo Eiffel, Cléo Montmartre, or Cléo Baguette. No one
knows how to pronounce 'Louvent.'" (It was only two syllables,
"Loo" and "Von," but okay.) Andrew wasn't a stupid asshole, and
he seemed relatively honest. When his phone lit up, as it did regularly, I could see that the lock screen was a photo of his Dalmatian
in a yellow windbreaker and rain boots.

I observed each person at the table, noticing every detail—their
clothes, their ways of talking. It was incredible to see my life taking

shape. Like any good leader, Nikki talked the biggest game. If my music took off, she said, they would invest millions of dollars in marketing and merch, and hire the best producers on the planet to work with me. She talked about boosting the algorithms on streaming platforms, ambitious tours, an unbeatable legal team. The conversation turned to exclusivity, earnings, attorneys, agents, albums . . . but I heard only one thing: *We are going to make you famous.*

looked for the book on the shelf, handed it to the customer, rang it up, printed the receipt, asked whether they wanted it gift wrapped. It was the last time. I knew I wouldn't be coming back.

My new life began that evening, when I left the bookstore after giving my set of keys back to my coworkers. The moment was solemn: It marked a chronological milestone, the end of a chapter of my existence. And I couldn't wait for what was to come.

For my roommates, it was like any other night. Aria was continuing to flounder. She had just come back from rehearsal for a play that was in search of funding; it was an unpaid part, so that she could meet people, expand her network, position herself strategically. Maybe the director would break out in a few years, and he would think of her for a role. Or maybe one of the 170 casting directors that she had invited to the premiere would actually decide to show up. Who knew? This modest Off-Off-Broadway production could be the missing piece of the puzzle, the roll of the dice that would jump-start her career for good because a famous producer happened to see it on a whim. I knew all of Aria's dreams by heart; they often came close to delusion. Celeste sent me a text; she had just finished up at the gallery and was on her way to the restaurant, where she'd made a reservation for 8:00 p.m.

I walked up Park Avenue, letting my mind wander. It isn't like in Paris, where you have to pay attention to keep track of where you are and sometimes look at a map on your phone. New York is like a checkerboard. Every street is numbered, and you just have to set off in the right direction, then count the blocks until you reach your destination. The street numbers get higher as you go uptown and lower as you go downtown. Manhattan is the only place in the world where I know at all times whether I'm going north or south. At Eighty-Second Street, I turned left. I didn't spare a glance for the people passing by, the shop windows, the view; I wasn't moved by the light after the September thunderstorm, or the double rainbow threading through the buildings and yellow cabs. Life was elsewhere. What was far more interesting was inside my head—my successes to come, the stories I was telling myself, hypothetical thrills, new ideas to develop. The most stimulating conversations had always been the ones I'd had with myself.

Celeste and Aria were sitting outside the restaurant across the street. Aria was animated, gesticulating wildly as she spoke, intense and passionate. I imagined she was telling Celeste about her rehearsal, the other actors, her hopes and dreams. Celeste was listening to her while sipping an Aperol spritz.

I lit a cigarette while continuing to watch my friends from afar. Celeste was wearing a white silk blouse that would remain white even as she ate spaghetti with tomato sauce. Aria's hair was loose, and wavy from the humidity; she wore too much makeup on her big black eyes. My sweet friends.

I smiled so wide that I had trouble inhaling the smoke and letting it slide down my throat. I had signed with a label. I had a manager. I was going to record my songs. I had no guarantee of future success—in fact, I had every reason to panic. The stakes of the game were high enough to make anyone dizzy, suffocated by the pressure. And yet I had never felt so calm.

I took my phone out of my jacket pocket to take a picture of my friends. They were beautiful, effusive, absorbed by their conversation. Then I switched to the front-facing camera and, squinting with joy, captured my euphoria, promising myself that I would remember this moment forever. I was at the foot of the mountain, just about to begin my ascent. I still had everything to prove, but I couldn't be happier than I was right then, on the threshold.

The previous year, Celeste's boyfriend, who worked in diplomacy, had gone back to school to study book conservation. To everybody else, it was an incomprehensible decision: Was dusting each page of a Bible from 1478 one by one really more satisfying than dissecting international relations? But now Tom woke up in the mornings excited for each day to begin. I remembered how astonished Celeste was. His salary was a third of what it had been previously, and yet she had never seen him so radiant.

So many people aren't where they are supposed to be. They've chosen the wrong career, the wrong partner, the wrong place to live. And then they change course, and suddenly everything makes sense. No more compromises, no more exhaustion; working feels effortless, nothing seems like a sacrifice. Everything fits together— natural, easy, joyous.

I hope that everyone in the world will one day experience the miracle of being in the right place.

didn't find it at all tiring to rerecord the third phrase of the second verse 149 times to change a single breath. As long as my song could be improved, I would continue to work on it in the studio. I had waited for this moment too long to take a coffee break.

I wanted to deliver a perfect recording, to check all the boxes, but I was afraid of stressing out my collaborators with my extremely high standards. I wanted to come across as kind and humble, not a bitchy diva who was impossible to satisfy. It was crucial that I be liked, so I did everything I could to make those around me happy and unite everyone as a team.

My charm offensive began with my producer, Justin Tedder. This wasn't his first rodeo. He'd already created hits, launched careers, demonstrated his skill. He knew what was on trend and how to calibrate a song so that it would be played on the radio, go viral on social media, do well on streaming services. I brought him "I Feel Nothing" on a platter, and he worked efficiently on the sound, the voice, the instruments, the effects, the tempo. His job: to transform the demo that I'd composed alone in my room with my guitar into an international hit—basically, to take it from artisanal to factory produced.

Nikki kept saying that the guy was a genius. If the director of my label thought that Justin was amazing, I would agree with her, laying my flattery on thick: How lucky I was to have the honor of working with Justin! What an ear! What talent! Nikki's love for her new artists wasn't unconditional. I needed her = I would do anything to please her. The equation was simple to understand.

I eventually learned that International Records had paid a fortune to get Justin to work with them exclusively. Justin was, in fact, a good producer—I had two or three techniques to learn from him—but to put it frankly: He drained my energy. Today he walked into the studio fifteen minutes late, and I was ready to bet a million dollars (which I didn't yet have) that the first thing out of his mouth would be negative.

"Unfortunately, I didn't have time to go home before coming here. . . . I didn't sleep well, so this day will be rough. But that's the way it is. Let's get started."

What could I say? The man really brightened my day.

Looking preoccupied, he drank his coffee, which would cause us to lose five more precious minutes. I was dying with impatience to get to work—since the previous night, I had come up with 509 new suggestions for changes to make to my chorus—but I held myself back from saying anything. His phone vibrated on the table.

"Who's texting me now?" he grumbled.

He was in classic form. "Today's going to be crazy; let me tell you, it's going to be tough." "We're really going to feel it this week." "Well, as you can guess, we had some issues with the mix. God knows it can never be straightforward." You had to admire Justin: Building such an impressive career when you whine so much is a challenge, especially in New York. We weren't in Paris.

The grievances continued throughout the afternoon. "I'm going to tackle the part I'm dreading the most." "I know for a fact that this stage is going to be hell." "It's going to take me forever to start this all over from the beginning." Whenever any piece of information passed through the paper shredder of his brain, it was transformed into bad news, no matter how innocuous it was to start. Discouragement, fatalism, resignation: *There you have it, that's how it always is, totally typical, it's no one's fault, things never turn out the way you want them to.* Justin could win the lottery and still find reasons to complain: The process for claiming the money was too complicated, he didn't know what to do with it, the whole thing was just a hassle, he wished he'd never picked the winning number in the first place.

His bad mood annoyed me all the more because he was lukewarm about my work. Nikki had hired him to produce my song, but he would have preferred to be somewhere else. I knew exactly what he thought: He felt like he was wasting his time with me, that I would have no future after the social media buzz died down, that I was too old to break out (it was true that at twenty-five, I was basically a prehistoric creature in the jungle of the music industry). The less enthusiasm he displayed, the more determined I became. I did everything I could to show that I was legitimate, a step above the others—the very picture of perfection, hardworking and talented, with a voice that transcended the rest. I ignored both his complaints and his reservations. At any rate, I had another objective: I wanted to convince him to start my song a cappella. Just my voice, raw, without instrumentation or artifice, for the first five measures. I had a gut sense that it would be effective on streaming platforms, where it was crucial that listeners be hooked in the first few seconds. The future would prove me right, but at the time, I was navigating by feel.

Justin shot it down right away. "I see where you're coming from, but no. It's a bad idea."

I was sure that the risk was worth taking, and insisted diplomatically. Finally, he gave in. In return, I agreed to be accompanied by a string quartet, even though I had dreamed of a guitar-piano ballad. I didn't sulk when the cellist showed up, and I even offered a drink to the violinists and violist. The end of the song sounded like majestic mush, as though it were part of the *Jurassic Park* soundtrack. You win some, you lose some. Everything became a tug-of-war, with each side trying to wrest back creative control. I was learning to choose my battles—a major lesson.

At the end of the day, I thanked every member of the team, down to the sound engineer's assistant's assistant's assistant. "Thanks for all you've done, Talia." "Everything was great today, Larissa." "Perfect, Claudia, you're such a gem." "Have a good night, Mattias. See you tomorrow." "So nice to work with you, Gavin." Damn, I deserved a medal. It required superhuman effort on my part to remember all their names.

I collected my tea mug and empty bottles of water, dragged the chairs back to where they belonged, put away my microphone and headset, and waved goodbye to the receptionist as I left. I didn't have a choice; you have to reach a certain level of fame before you're allowed to be rude. I understood the order of magnitude: You can start to be difficult if you've sold at least two million records. Below that, you have to say goodbye and thank you. This applies to every domain: People with exceptional physiques can be nasty in a way that ordinary mortals can't; the same goes for billionaires and successful entrepreneurs. During my ascension, I took care to be nice to everyone, conciliatory and charming. The next day, I would bring homemade cookies for everyone in the studio.

I finally got undressed, exhausted from the day of recording and drained from having shown so much kindness and tact. Justin's defeatist attitude had devoured my energy. *Stop criticizing everything*, I wanted to tell him. *Drink a glass of water, smoke some weed, go for a walk in the woods.* Before going to sleep, I still had to write to him, but after drafting the message, I froze, unable to make a decision. A shower would give me a chance to think.

The question was thorny, existential, nearly unfathomable. Pyrrhonian, I suspended judgment while washing my hair. I had to weigh the pros and cons carefully; it wasn't something to take lightly.

In the message I was going to send to Justin, should I add emojis, and if so, how many?

I aspired to become a singer who was known and respected worldwide; it would be ridiculous for me to throw in a flower or a sun. I had to prove that I had the substance and the class to be an international star, and therefore couldn't allow myself to send a flurry of multicolored hearts, animals, plants, and shooting stars. At the same time, I didn't want to seem cold and overly sure of myself, so it was out of the question to end the message with a period. Should I just go with a smiley face? I combed my conditioner through to the ends of my hair and let it sit for four minutes before rinsing it out with lukewarm water.

Ever since my arrival in the studio, I'd been walking on a tightrope. I was afraid of asserting myself too much; I was afraid of not asserting myself enough. I wanted to be taken seriously; I wanted to be appreciated. I intended to assume my duties with authority; I intended to show that I knew how to work as a team. I was totally rigorous in my approach; I was terrified at the thought of getting a bad reputation in the industry when I'd only just gotten my foot in the door. Setting my sights on perfection was crazy, yet I couldn't be content with less. My goals were all mixed up, and I was having trouble finding an equilibrium.

Soon I wouldn't have to burden myself with these considerations any longer. The work I was doing would invert the power dynamics—no more trying to please, no more politeness; no more complaints, no more cookies, no more compromises.

I blow-dried my hair and then sent the text to Justin. I added a smiley face, but no flames and no exclamation points.

I was a genius. A melody had come to me in the dark, just as I was about to fall asleep, my eyes heavy with fatigue. I turned on the lamp on my bedside table and recorded the hook, whispering into my phone as though it were a secret. The beginning of this song was amazing.

It was 11:00 p.m. and I was buzzing, incapable of going to sleep after such a breakthrough. I might as well get up and start working. I started the timer: In an hour, I wanted to have the first verse and the chorus.

I took out my guitar, my notebook, and my keyboard, poised to attack. I had a big dream, but I wasn't a dreamer. I was a war machine, a fighter jet, an atomic strike, a nuclear submarine, a tank, an attack helicopter. This song was going to make its way around the world. I visualized the dozens of awards, the fans shouting out the lyrics they knew by heart, the millions of dollars in royalties. The next morning in the studio, I would test my verse with brass, a tambourine, a double bass, a clarinet, maracas. Only thirteen more minutes. I wasn't there yet. I added an hour to the timer. Then two, then three. And then I stopped counting.

At 8:00 a.m. my song was magnificent. I had been touched by grace. Listening to the chorus again, I experienced full-on Stendhal syndrome, overwhelmed by emotion at the beauty of my own composition. Pure talent. It was well-envisioned, well-put, clever, sensitive. Effective without being academic. Ambitious without being needlessly complicated. In a word: incredible. I was full of energy—trembling hands, hot flashes, stomach butterflies, heart beating at full speed. My vision blurred, and I felt like I was walking through cotton. I chugged my fourth bottle of water, skipped breakfast. After an ice-cold shower, I burst into hysterical laughter while brushing my teeth.

By 11:00 a.m. my song had become the worst creation in the history of music. Justin was trying to be nice, but I could see it in his eyes the minute I started singing: It sucked. Why was I surprised? I had never known how to compose. I had ten years of failures in my past to remind me. What an idiot. The verse was unoriginal, the tune boring, the chorus annoying. My chest seized up in anxiety, tears sprang to my eyes, I held them back, I was having trouble breathing. I was falling out of a 149th-story window.

"Is everything okay, Cléo?" asked Justin.

"Yes, everything's great, why?"

"Well, anyway, good work. Keep going and see where the song takes you."

"Yes, great. I'll keep you posted."

I'd rather die. No part of it was worth saving. I would never make it. I might as well start over from zero. I might as well put a bullet in my head.

The next morning, twelve hours of sleep and a meaningless compliment from Justin had changed my perspective. It takes only the tiniest thing—a grain of sand, an adjective, a breeze, an ant, a piece of string—to reverse a trend. My songs were once again promising. My future debut album would be fabulous. Celeste kept telling me that she believed in me; of course my friend was right, how could I have doubted myself? I returned to the studio as though I were entering the Colosseum: a gladiatrix with a trident, determined to battle the lion in the arena, galvanized and sure of my forthcoming victory.

I was making progress on my composition, but the sea was choppy; I swayed back and forth, astounded by the height of the waves. The higher I went, the more vertiginous the fall. I was on a roller coaster, looping over and over without being able to get off. Creation happened between two extremes: There were no intermediary levels between nothing and everything. I either thought I was brilliant, or I thought I was abysmal. I was an angel, or I was a monster. I was a virtuoso, or I was inept. My songs were sublime, or they were forgettable. And every one of these oscillations between utter trash and utter genius was deeply, violently painful.

Does Cléo Louvent write her own songs? I can say this without prevaricating: *Yes, every word.* I've always refused to have a writer set foot in my studio, and I've never given in on that point. It's not a question of talent, it's a question of control.

I hate the idea of my success depending on someone else—even for a single chord, even for a single rhyme. I'm the only captain at the helm of my ship, and I dream of being free, sailing around the world without stops or assistance. Above all, I'm conscious of the fact that if I write everything myself, I'll be more difficult to replace.

At that time, I already sensed that it was easy to be dispossessed of your own music. There are already so many concessions you have to make in the studio; the last thing I want to do is add more cooks to the kitchen than are strictly necessary. If I wasn't vigilant, in two minutes, I would find myself with three lyricists and five producers who made all the decisions on my behalf, and I'd be condemned to singing songs I hadn't written a word of myself (not to mention sharing the rights).

So I tried to tactfully maintain control, especially because once the songs were finished, I barely had any say at all. I wrote them, but I didn't decide when they would come out, the order of the singles, the strategy for the next fourteen months, or the promotional budgets. My first three songs were a powerful starting point; I finished recording them in December. After that I needed a repertoire, so I continued composing without any break. The process of winnowing them down was intense. I worked on forty or so titles, of which we finalized thirty in the studio; only the seven best ones would make it onto my EP. Success rate: 17.5%. Every track had to be signed off on by a series of producers, managers, directors, publicists. Each song had to work its way up from the bottom to the top, where it had to convince the decision-makers before proving itself to the public.

I dreamed of sailing the seas alone, but being at a label as powerful as mine was more like being on an enormous cruise ship with two hundred crew members.

want to tell you guys about my day in the studio today. I'm having a hard time tonight. I've poured my heart into these songs for you, and I can't wait for you to listen to them. But at the same time, I'm terrified. I'm afraid of not being good enough. If you knew just how much I'm doubting myself . . . I actually lose sleep over it. I'm having trouble eating. . . . You can't tell I'm struggling from the pretty photos on Instagram, but it's the truth, and I'm sick of pretending otherwise. Mental health is something we don't talk about enough, but it deserves to be at the forefront of every conversation, especially in the music industry."

I was speaking directly to the camera on my phone, looking drawn and tired, wearing no makeup. Behind me was a chair piled with clothes, an unpacked suitcase, and a sleeve of mass-produced cookies, peanut-butter-flavored Oreos. I'd never touched that junk in my life, and my room was always perfectly clean, but my intuition told me that the backdrop would make me seem relatable and human.

Every Friday for the last month, I'd been baring my soul on social media. People wanted to know what was going on behind the scenes, and I was happy to tell them. My label liked this initiative, and the comments under my last video had been unanimous in their approval. "Love her humility, something you don't find often in this industry." "A woman who's both talented and down-to-

earth!" "Bravo, this is truly French classiness, she's not pretentious
at all, totally natural, we love to see it." "This girl is so elegant and
intelligent. Thanks for showing us the other side of the story."

Only Juliette teased me gently, asking, "Who forced you to record this?" She wasn't yet used to seeing me act the part. That day
on the phone, she had admitted that she was having trouble with
the idea of having to share her Cléou with hundreds of thousands
of strangers.

On Sunday at 3:00 p.m., the light was perfect, with rays of winter
sun glinting off the floor. I sat down to film myself singing a cover
at the piano; I hadn't forgotten that this was the setup that had first
caused my audience to fall in love with me. Mascara, winged black
eyeliner, golden-brown hair, slightly mussed straight bangs, nude lips.
My eyes lowered, my expression serious, and my hands on the keys, I
began the first verse of "Seras-tu là"—I'd always had a weakness for
Michel Berger. I alternated my covers: four in English, one in French.

When I finished filming, I looked back at my posts for the
week. Outfit-of-the-day pictures, unhinged selfies, photos in which
I was making a face but still looked amazing. If I posted something
sexy, I balanced it out with a second image of myself in a goofy
pose. My socials had to create the illusion that I was giving my
followers access to my personal life, so I tried hard to hide what
the accounts actually were: self-promotion. To that end, I posted
an endless stream of dispatches from daily life: a badly composed
photo of a sunset, a blurry group shot from a birthday party, a fit of
laughter with a full mouth at a restaurant, screenshots of hilarious
WhatsApp conversations, a night in bed watching *Notting Hill* in
leggings. You couldn't post sterilized and aloof images. You had
to post inside jokes, ideally ones that included a pet with a funny
name. Since I didn't like animals, I opted instead for recurring
photos of Rocky, the neighbor's bulldog.

The peak of my audience's engagement on Instagram occurred at 6:00 p.m.; I'd set a reminder on my Google Calendar to tell me when it was time to post. Unlike major celebrities, I still had the passwords to my social media accounts. After someone reached a certain level of fame, their team would change the passwords so that the person wouldn't post drunken polemics. I too couldn't wait until I could hand off my online communications to someone else. It wasn't my favorite thing to do. But for now the responsibility was mine, so I did my best. I scrolled through the photos I'd taken on my phone the past few days, the camera roll forming a mosaic before my eyes, then selected the tiny pieces I wanted to share with the world. Post by post, I shaped and refined my public persona. *Presenting Cléo Louvent.*

In the studio next to mine, an artist was laboriously recording a boring song. I had listened to Kyle Havens's first album during my run in Central Park on Sunday, and it confirmed my theory. *Kyle, it's not because your label didn't invest enough in you; stop telling everyone that. If it didn't work, it's because your songs suck.*

Kyle intercepted me in the hallway, a human trap closing in. When he started talking, it was impossible to stop him. The guy wasn't looking for a conversation partner: He wanted an audience. He had grown up on a ranch in Utah, and described to me the woodstove in his childhood house, the mountains he could see from the kitchen window, the American flag on the porch, the cattle and the horses, the snowmobile in the winter. Kyle spared me no detail: This paradise was located in the Kamas Valley in Summit County, facing the wonderful Wasatch Mountains, at the western edge of the Rockies. Had I ever been to Salt Lake City?

My sexy cowboy was loquacious. I didn't know how to extricate myself.

"Cléo, would you want to listen to my new song?"

"Of course, I'd love to."

I'd rather puncture my own eardrums. But did I have a choice? Kyle was explaining to me how he came up with the idea for this musical epic about the giddying euphoria of being in a wide-open space. *Just because you had an idea doesn't mean it's a good one. No one cares.*

"So, what do you think?" he asked after he finished the song.

"I love it! It's so powerful."

It sucks. He was writing the music that he wanted to sing, not what the public wanted to hear. He was offended that his first album hadn't been as successful as he'd thought it would be, but even he wouldn't listen to his own songs. How could someone separate the art they made from the art they consumed to such an extent? Where had this quasi-pathological dissociation come from? Obviously, I could show him several ways to improve the song—an ingenious suggestion for the verse, catchier lyrics for the chorus—but I refrained from letting him benefit from my instincts. It wasn't impossible for him to suddenly become great after meeting me.

"I had my girlfriend listen to it too. She thought it was incredible."

I let this go. *If you think your song is good because your girlfriend told you she liked it, you really are an idiot.*

"Thank you so much, Kyle. I'm really touched that you let me hear what you're working on for your album."

False: I had wasted my time. And I was continuing to waste it, so I tried to edge away so that I could return to work, but he kept talking. This time he decided to explain to me how the music industry worked. I would have preferred more of the tour of his family's ranch.

"It's overcrowded. Everyone wants to be a singer now."

Bullshit. The problem is that people like you are allowed to make albums. The problem was that people who would make perfectly good artisanal bakers got it into their heads that they should make music. The industry wasn't oversaturated. In fact, it was quite the opposite: It wasn't selective enough. The proof was that Kyle was in the middle of recording a second album. When I said that I wanted everyone to experience the feeling of being in the right place, I should have added an important qualifier: For some people, that place is onstage, and for others, it's in the back kitchen. There's a hierarchy of beings and skills; let's leave the spotlight to those who actually have talent. Like me, for example.

"It's hard to break through with a first album. It's tough to make a living from it for the first few years," he continued.

That depends on who you're talking about, sweetie. I didn't know anything about American football, so let's take French soccer. You've got someone from Ligue 1 and someone from National 1: Sure, they both played soccer. But how could you compare an athlete who earned several million in Paris with an athlete who earned 30,000 euros in Dijon? It's the same thing for a Hollywood actress and someone trying to make a living acting part-time in Cincinnati. *Same thing for you and me.*

"Just because you signed a contract doesn't mean your album will come out. Your label doesn't owe you anything." He was still talking.

"..."

"Did you know that nine out of ten artists who have signed with a label won't end up releasing an album?"

"..."

"But everything you create belongs to them!"

No kidding. Another killjoy to remind me that nothing was guaranteed, as though I didn't understand that already. I couldn't stand his condescension, and I really couldn't stand being underestimated. Clearly, we were not meant to get along. And how could I explain to him that I took advice only from people whose work I respected—which disqualified him immediately? What success made him feel like he could pontificate and preach? Didn't he realize that he wasn't talented enough to be so pedantic? I smiled silently, but I was dying to spit my tea in his face.

"Anyway, you'll see. Everything depends on whether your label decides to invest in you or not. Who'd you sign with, again?"

"International Records."

"Oh wow. Well, they're the ones who will decide. If I were you, I would have stayed at the bookstore long enough to find out."

"Don't worry about me. I'm planning to sign an exclusive three-million-dollar contract with Chanel before my first album comes out."

As soon as the words left my mouth, I hated myself for saying them. Luckily, Kyle burst out laughing.

My plan was to be beautiful, rich, and famous. Making a fortune was always part of it. Being a starving artist whose work became known only after their death wasn't for me. My music was an emotional commodity worth millions of dollars.

My music was commercial. It was mouthwatering. It was enticing. It was a turn-on. It made you want to click, to buy a T-shirt with my face on it, to see me live, to go to a nightclub, to dance, to fuck. It wasn't an accident that the titles of my songs sounded like the names of lipstick or nail polish shades.

My music was an asset. The rights to my music constituted in themselves a business entity requiring complex financial arrangements. One day my catalogue would be sold to an investment fund for a nine-figure sum.

My music was a cult of my personality. I embodied my songs with my beautiful face, my bangs, and my ass; my smile was fetishized and plastered onto tons of merch. *Cléo, Cléo, Cléo.* Soon hundreds of thousands of newborns would be named after me in America, my rare first name on everyone's lips—the symbol of a generation.

My music was for everyone. The more you listened to it, the more you liked it. You didn't need a doctorate in musicology to appreciate it.

But popular didn't mean meaningless and badly written. Simplicity is the boldest path you can take. There is actually nothing more demanding than producing commercial music. Kyle could only dream of it. It wasn't that he *wanted* to write songs for a niche audience. He wasn't a snob, he was incompetent.

To anyone who thinks that pop stars are superficial and that they have nothing to say: You haven't understood at all. How many car rides, nights out dancing, vacation memories, and lovemaking sessions have been set to pop soundtracks? Can you imagine having that kind of platform? If you have a message you want to send to the rest of the world, you'd be much better off putting it in a pop song than in a long speech. Pop is and will always be the most extraordinary Trojan horse.

Oversized steel industrial windows, eighteen-foot ceiling, unobstructed view of the Hudson, marble kitchen, minimalist lightwood furniture, collection of objets d'art: This Greenwich Village loft gave me the sense that picking out clothes for celebrities was a lucrative activity.

The most sought-after stylist right now was named Petra Mackay. Fifty-five years old, just over five feet tall, a former high-level ice-skater and editor for *Vogue* whose tenure lasted ten years, polyglot, socialite, and faux bohemian, with a silk scarf in her hair. She circled around me, sizing up the merchandise inquisitively. I was in my underwear and bra in the middle of her living room. Petra inspected my breasts, buttocks, and legs, analyzing my body as neutrally as a geometrician, breaking it down into segments and lines, shapes and curves. After a long silence, she listed my assets out loud: forearms, face, chest, toes.

Next to her, Stefani, my new manager, was nodding her agreement. I'd dumped Andrew after six months of good and loyal service. He had tried to protest, to guilt-trip me—"After all I've done for you! I thought we were a team!"—except that to form the best team, you need the best players. Stefani was better known, more experienced, more dreaded. She was interested in me, and *this was a very good sign*. My star was rising; I could tell because of the sharks that were starting to circle around me.

Stefani Angelina Messina had grown up on the Upper West Side in a middle-class Italian family. The thirty-six-year-old fake blond was as sweet as a cream puff, a vanilla ice cream, a caramel—she paid close attention to anything you showed her and remembered names and dates. "How was your evening with Celeste yesterday? Were you able to rest a bit afterward?" "I listened to the Kyle Havens album you were telling me about, and you're totally right!" "Happy birthday, gorgeous. I'm taking you out to eat to celebrate." But that wasn't why I had chosen her. Beneath the layers of powdered sugar, Stefani was a real fighter. A formidable woman with a big smile: exactly the kind of person I wanted around me. Her first mission was to renegotiate my contract with my label. "This is the time to rob the bank. I'll make sure you're paid like a rock star," she told me. I'd chosen my side: the side of the powerful. Earlier that day, she'd come to pick me up in a Bentley—not a Honda.

While I tried on a terra-cotta wrap dress, Petra gave Stefani a rundown of the outfits seen yesterday on the red carpet in Los Angeles. "Did you notice what they made their new ambassador wear? Frankly, it looked like a slutty schoolgirl costume!" "Obviously she wasn't able to choose her own clothes. . . . Her jacket looked like a duvet cover." "Ever since I stopped dressing her, it's been a parade of tackiness. That skirt embroidered with gold swirls was pathetic—she looked like a giant Ferrero Rocher." I appreciated her approach to relationships: sarcastic, frank, laid-back. Petra was a subtle mix of fishwife and aristocrat.

Victory was far from assured, but I noted that my label was ready to pay the best stylist in New York to create a starworthy wardrobe for me. Again, *this was a very good sign*. Petra knew all the brands; she spent her life drinking champagne in showrooms with publicists. Her famous clients paid her handsomely to have taste on their behalf. She went through clothing racks mercilessly, pushing the hangers aside one by one: "Yes, no, yes, no." She had firm opinions on pale pink, tulle, mother-of-pearl, overstitching. And I needed her to call a spade a spade: Was this piece edgy or hideous?

Today I was the one being evaluated as she walked barefoot around me on her Berber rug, rubbing her clavicle in thought. My clothes didn't need to become a new kind of tyranny, but each out-fit would determine the artist I aspired to be—a sexy pop singer, a diva with a big voice, an extravagant fashionista, the girl next door. Every element would be scrutinized: the length of the dress, how much cleavage the neckline exposed, the sheerness of the fabric.

After a few laps, Petra disappeared into one of her mezzanines in search of three new eveningwear gowns for me to try on. As she came back down, her arms piled with colorful finds, she continued questioning Stefani: "What story do you want to tell with her?"

After some thought, Petra opted for French and Italian design-ers, but mainstream ones. Parisian elegance without elitism. For the time being, I didn't have any exclusivity contracts, so Petra sug-gested the following distribution: Chanel (30%), Versace (20%), Prada (20%), Valentino (20%), miscellaneous (10%). There would be no more improvising, not even for a pair of sunglasses or socks.

One detail after the next, inch by inch, I was changing. My red nails—the shade was called "Firefighter"—became my trade-mark ($100); a reshaping of my eyebrows, along with micropig-mentation, added to the depth of my gaze ($200); a lash lift and keratin treatments gave me doe eyes ($300); a buccal massage sculpted my jaw ($400); a traditional Japanese technique known as a kobido massage rejuvenated my face ($500); a radiofrequency skin-tightening treatment firmed up my butt ($600); whitening my teeth gave me a dazzling smile ($700); invisible aligners fixed my overlapping canines ($8,000); a keratotherapist created custom moisturizers perfectly adapted to my skin type ($4,000); ten laser hair-removal sessions left my legs smooth forever ($10,000). In addition to these were various medical fees and expenses from cosmetic surgery ($32,000). Like everything else, beauty could be bought (total cost: $56,800).

One February evening, I left the hairdresser's. In a few hours, snow had covered the cars, the benches, the bikes. It was dark in New York, and I was blond. I slid my phone into my Chanel purse and carefully caressed the strap, chain woven with leather. I had received it earlier that day by messenger, and it marked my first foray into the intoxicating world of freebies: brands dressed me, and the label paid for everything else. I no longer had to spend a dime from my own pocket. In fact, they had just sent a car to drive me home, and I looked for it at the red light. Suddenly I recognized the Italian restaurant across from me as the one where I had eaten dinner with Aria and Celeste after my last day at the bookstore. It hadn't been so long ago that I'd been standing on this same sidewalk, cigarette in hand, tipsy with joy and fulfillment, taking a selfie and promising myself I would never forget that moment. It was six months ago; it was a lifetime ago. That evening, if I had seen myself in the snow, my hair dyed, a luxury handbag on my arm, getting into a town car, I wouldn't have been surprised—but I wouldn't have recognized myself.

I was lying on a bed wearing only underwear and a white tank top. In the background was a miniature alarm clock, a pocket watch, two vintage armchairs, and pastel-colored walls. Torn from a deep slumber, the sleeping beauty opened one eye, looking lost and wild. The camera zoomed in on my face, and I rubbed my eyes before lip-syncing while caressing the floral sheets.

I repeated the lyrics to "I Feel Nothing" one, ten, thirty times. I hadn't consumed anything for twelve hours other than some vegetable juice; they'd asked me to fast beforehand so that my stomach would be flat. Posing seductively, I rolled around in the blankets, put a hand over my head, and grabbed a pillow that I hugged to myself before turning over. You could see the outline of my breasts as I moved, which was the whole point of the sequence.

Now I was supposed to get on the rug on all fours. For someone who felt nothing, I found the whole setup oddly sexual. Had the director of this music video even listened to the lyrics of the song? I complied, with the thirty-person film crew all watching.

"Okay, we're going to need you to meow."

"What do you mean?"

The director urged me to be less cold and more instinctual. "A virgin, but a slut, you know what I'm saying?" So I closed my eyes and thought about Aria—her sex drive, her hair tumbling down her back, her breasts. I did what I could to get into the right head-space: It wasn't a music video; it was soft-core porn.

After a lunch break, during which I still wasn't allowed to eat solid food, they changed the set so that we could film the shower scene—obligatory for the genre, apparently; were people concerned about pop stars' hygiene? The director kept saying, "Don't worry, you're going to look stunning." What I heard was "Don't worry, you're going to be Photoshopped."

I spent three hours in a fake bathroom, my hair coated in gel from roots to ends to create the impression that it was wet. I was sticky and gross, my mouth was dry, my stomach was growling. Stefani, who was watching over me from the set, asked for a five-minute break.

"You poor thing, you must be exhausted."

"No, it's all good. I could have kept going, no worries."

I was drained, starving, and freezing, but I would have rather died than admit it. I wasn't fragile. My manager wrapped a towel around me to warm me up.

"I'm naked from start to finish. Is that really necessary?" I asked her.

"Yes, it's fantastic," Stefani replied enthusiastically.

"I'm going to get a lot of flak for this. It's not 2015 anymore."

"No, you won't. We're showing that you're a free and independent woman who chooses what she does with her own body."

"I find it completely tasteless."

"It's not tasteless, it's feminist."

I was completely nude, I was seducing my audience, and what's more, it was a political stance. I was winning on all fronts. My label knew what they were doing; they'd chosen a trendy director, a young, artsy prodigy who represented a wide range of female bodies in her work. So, yes, you could see my breasts, but the background was colorful and futurist.

I didn't complain. The label had shelled out for my first music video. They wouldn't have bothered with all this for a second-rate singer no one was betting on. I stayed loyal to my mantra: *This is a very good sign.*

The next morning we filmed the last sequence of the video. The script: I was driving away with another girl in a convertible. Translation: Two friends were defying convention and fleeing the scene, with vibes reminiscent of the film *Thelma & Louise.* I thought Ridley Scott was very chic, but still didn't see how it related to my song.

I wore pants for the first time since we'd started filming (first miracle). One of the most in-demand models was playing the role of my copilot (second miracle). Hailey Bowen hugged me. Brunette, tanned, perfect; low-rise jeans with a whale tail, tinted sunglasses (the return of 2000s fashion was very confusing to me). She was facing me, ready to film for an hour in order to appear in my video for twenty seconds. Miracles did exist; you had to know how to make them happen.

A month earlier, Stefani had told me, "I've just gotten a call from the agent of a girl named Aria Sadler. He tried to persuade me that it would be nice to cast her in your music video since the two of you are friends. What do you think?"

I stiffened. Aria had actually floated the idea to me the week before, then followed up several times: "So, what are you thinking for your video?" I had sidestepped the question and she had stopped asking, but clearly she hadn't dropped the idea, since she had suggested it to her agent. I was furious. Why did Aria feel like she had the right to say that she knew me? I hadn't needed anyone else to succeed. Not a soul.

"So?" Stefani pressed. "What do you think?"

"Tell him that we've already found an actress for the role."

"What do you mean?"

"Tell him it's not possible."

"Did you have someone else in mind?"

"Yes, actually. Since you know so many people . . . Could you get me Hailey Bowen?"

I wasn't high enough to pull Aria up with me. I needed to surround myself with people who were more successful than me, not less. In my video, I wanted a famous model, not a failed actress.

Apparently, some birds exhibit unusual behavior before an earthquake. It's thought that they can feel it coming thanks to vibrations in the ground or changes in the Earth's magnetic field.

In the same way, you had to pay attention to weak signals to pick up on my growing fame. The quality of an interaction, the response times to my texts, the warmth of a smile: It was in these tiny variations that I first sensed a major shift was occurring.

Since signing with my label, I'd filmed five videos and released the same number of songs on an EP, and opened for a few singers who were moderately talented, albeit excessively famous. Organic growth, driven by the success of "Entitled" and "I Feel Nothing." TikTok was continuing to blow wind into my sails: People were using my songs to create their own videos, propelling my music up the rankings and into the ears of the entire world. It was all systems go; I was breezing through each checkpoint, with ten new things to celebrate every week. I was the new pop sensation, the French American phenom everyone was talking about. A warm-up before my album came out in November.

But these early wins wouldn't have meant anything without a good dose of emotional appeal. People were moved by me. I was the singer with the husky voice, the young girl who had lost her dad too young in a terrible accident. When I sang, especially when solo at a piano, something happened. And it was something that couldn't be controlled.

Ever since I'd set foot in the studio, my music was being refined and clarified at the speed of light. Unlike most other *developing* artists, I wasn't spending years trying to find myself—those years were behind me. I wasn't fumbling around in the dark: I was charging straight ahead, knowing exactly where I wanted to go. I alternated between catchy pop songs with hints of disco and funk, and hypnotic tracks with moody synth, aware that the greatest strength of my music was my lyrics. I really *wrote* them; they were poetic and cryptic, with sophisticated phrases that packed a punch. The themes that emerged were the fantasy of revenge—revanchist dance anthems—but also ballads on self-hatred, solitude, beauty. And then there was my voice, immediately recognizable; I'd fought fiercely to keep the succession of producers by my side in the studio (Justin had been followed by Benny, Jack, and Katy—equally interchangeable) from smoothing out my voice too much with editing tools. I insisted on hearing the breathing, the texture, the background noise, a little bit of saliva—usually producers erased all flaws, but my intuition told me to highlight them. Again, there was only one way to go: against the current.

The first song from my first album came out Friday at noon, New York time. At 12:01 p.m., "Revenge" was already climbing the rankings. I refreshed the YouTube page for the music video every three minutes; the number of views and comments was increasing like crazy. I kept track with dozens of screenshots on my phone, watching for the signs of my sudden ascension alone in my room.

The gears of my acceleration were digital. My label spent a phenomenal amount of money to make my song go viral on listening platforms—I was now their priority, and they were betting it all on me. I even suspected them of artificially inflating the numbers with fake listens, but we were too polite to address it; Nikki didn't confirm my suspicions, and I pretended I didn't have them. It used to be that record labels would buy boxes of CDs the day they came out to get their artist into the Top 50; now they'd buy clicks from Malaysia. Becoming a star was different now from how it was in the 1990s, but the recipe was the same: You had to pay up to break out.

At the record label, it felt like people in the hallways were talking about me, whispering my name, admiring my clothes. But I still thought it was all in my head. Everyone there was used to seeing artists who were a hundred times more famous than me.

At 8:00 p.m. Nikki invited the team to dinner—a first. Leather booths, purple carpeting, lounge music, hushed atmosphere, candles on the tables. I thought of my father, who would have said, "Turn on the light; you'll ruin your eyes."

At the table were Justin; Stefani; Nikki's associate, Sabrina, and assistant, Brandon; several producers; and some other people from the label whose names and job titles I'd forgotten—weeks earlier I'd stopped trying to memorizing the employee directory. Confidently, Nikki ordered three bottles of champagne; it was so good that I felt like I was drinking unicorn blood. She congratulated me, praised me, toasted to my success. Nikki thought of me as her best racehorse, and she was right. *I told you, Nikki, you're going to win big with me.* Within the label I had already passed the other pop singers of my ilk who were in the same stage of their career as I was. There was only one spot available for a cool, young female singer, and it was mine. In her black bustier dress, Nikki still made me think of the sea witch, but this didn't bother me: She had no time or money to waste, and neither did I. Another formidable woman with a smile on my team.

After the drinks arrived, I started telling a story to Stefani, who was seated to my right. Nothing thrilling, nothing groundbreaking: In the studio, a musician and I had both found something hilarious. Suddenly, all twelve people around the table stopped their own conversations and turned toward me to hear what I had to say. I would never forget that second of silence.

I launched into my speech, worried that it wouldn't be up to the level of attention I was being given. But when I finished, everyone laughed, nodded, chimed in. I hadn't changed, and yet everything had changed. I hadn't become more interesting, nor had my stories improved; nonetheless, I was giving off a different kind of light. The charisma of a singer on the rise. An aura.

The waiter arrived to take our orders. I had no way of being sure, but it appeared that several of the team members waited to see what I was having before requesting the same for themselves.

In a helicopter flying over Manhattan toward the airport, my hands were clammy. My album was going to come out in a week; it was unthinkable for me to die right now. When I was eight, I'd written in my diary: FAME OR DEATH. I was about to attain the first—I simply could not be bumped off now by the second.

On the basis of miles traveled, how many helicopter accidents were there compared to car or bike accidents? Unlike a plane, a helicopter had no wings; it couldn't glide to a landing if the engine failed. Or what would happen if the rotor fell off? I wasn't an aeronautical engineer, but I knew that without it, we'd fall. And those were just the technical failures; what about human ones? Our pilot looked like he was about fourteen years old. If only we'd been able to go to the airport by ferry or pedal boat.

"Is everything okay? Are you scared of heights?" Stefani asked me.

"No, not at all. The view of the Hudson is incredible."

"You've got to get used to seeing the world from above," she answered, laughing.

While I was at it, I also had to get used to turning a blind eye to my carbon footprint. I had big things to accomplish on this planet, so if anyone was allowed to pollute, it was me. And it was for a good cause. That morning I was taking a helicopter and then a plane so that I could make a four-hour appearance in Los Angeles;

I'd been invited to a preview of Margot Robbie's latest movie, and I couldn't miss that.

We landed after fifteen minutes of torture, and I was able to breathe again. During the flight, I'd gotten a text from my mother—as someone who loved Daniel Balavoine, she'd be delighted to learn that I hadn't also died in a helicopter accident. The day before, I'd told her about several pieces of good news related to my album; I was trying, awkwardly, to prepare her for the forthcoming tidal wave of publicity. My mother's entire response, just three words, fit in the message preview on my screen: "Congrats love mom." *Congrats love mom.* I'd gotten the same text when I told her that I'd been hired at the bookstore. My mother didn't grasp the significance of what was happening. Or maybe she was refusing to see it.

For a while now, I'd gotten the sense that she felt she'd been overtaken by her own creature. She thought: *I am a normal mother who has brought forth an abnormal daughter.* As a rigorous scientist, she thought of life in terms of probabilities, and from that standpoint, my fame was a statistical anomaly. Applied mathematics didn't prepare you for a child who was a superstar. What had my chances of releasing an album been? One in a million? One in ten million? And yet my mother should have known that I didn't give a damn about statistics. My uncle had been killed in an elevator accident; my great-grandmother had been crushed to death by a drawbridge. Fuck statistics.

I called my mother before boarding the plane to LA. She needed help getting on to Instagram.

"I wanted to listen to your cover of Ben Mazué's song '25 ans.' A colleague told me about it, but I can't find it."

It took me ten seconds to realize that my mother was talking about a video posted six months earlier—and, more importantly, that she didn't have an Instagram account (I didn't think she was quite ready for TikTok yet). We brainstormed a username for her together; she chose her middle name followed by her wedding anniversary, Sophie0607. She was signing up for Instagram ten years after everyone else, and mine was the only account she followed. For years among the thousands—the millions—of notifications that I received on social media every day, I would find myself looking for likes from my mom.

The album was coming out the next day. I'd planned to go running in Central Park, had put my hair up in a ponytail and tied the laces of my sneakers. But when the elevator doors opened, I didn't move. After a few seconds, they closed again. That morning I had found my phone in the fridge and my lipstick in the microwave; I was too distracted, too agitated, too restless. I was at risk of being hit by a car while crossing the street, or someone could follow me. I refused to be kidnapped, held hostage, raped, or killed today. Not now. Not when I was so close to my goal. I turned around and went back to my room.

As I stepped out of the shower, I took special care not to slip on the bathroom tile. I dried my feet, wiped down the floor, and put on a pair of nonslip, grippy socks. I wasn't scared of death, but I wanted to at least live until the next day. Oh yes: I wanted to see what would happen the next day.

Success isn't abstract. It can be measured. It's a numerical data point, a number of streams on listening platforms, a ranking on the Billboard charts, album sales figures, radio airtime, television appearances, social media engagement statistics, festival lineups, nominations for prestigious awards, concerts that sell out one after another.

There's no circle more virtuous than that of success. Each of my wins led to the next: Fortune smiled upon me, people wanted me, I was in demand everywhere. I blew even the most optimistic predictions out of the water, and my team celebrated every victory in wonderment. What had they expected? Of course I was the goose that laid the golden eggs. Nikki called me seventeen times a day to tell me that I was the best, the prettiest, the greatest. All of a sudden, I had no problem getting in touch with the director of my label. Nikki was very, very available.

My friends and relatives started reaching out; I received enthusiastic messages from distant cousins I hadn't spoken to in ten years. My loyal supporter Celeste sent me streams of emojis—rockets and clapping hands. It isn't during the bad times that you realize who your real friends are. It's when you're succeeding. It's easier to take out the tissues than it is to pop a bottle of champagne. Aria didn't send me any texts to say congratulations; she merely pointed out that it was thanks to her advice that I'd managed to write the songs that had gotten me off the ground.

I talked to myself in front of the mirror, repeating the same sentences. *I knew it. I was sure of it. I told you.* My success was proving me right. The validation was both the best and the worst thing that could happen to a narcissist.

"Congratulations! What's happening is incredible!" exclaimed Juliette. Yes and no. First of all, I'd known it would happen. Second of all, I couldn't think of an alternative scenario in which I didn't succeed. It's similar to how a rich person isn't likely to feel moved by their own wealth every time they wake up in the morning: It's wonderful, but it's my life, and it's the only one I know.

Like money, success doesn't make you as happy as you might think. There are limits to human emotions: lower limits and upper limits. We tend to overestimate happiness just as we overestimate unhappiness. My first album was a triumph. Of course I was over the moon. I was excited, enthusiastic, sometimes even euphoric. But I didn't sing my own songs in the shower every morning; I didn't scream with joy for six months straight; I didn't jump up and down; I didn't do cartwheels; I didn't shake my ass dancing the night away, nor, for that matter, did I shake it all about dancing the Hokey Pokey; I didn't don party hats; I didn't have a box of confetti under my bed, or streamers, party favors, or a bubble machine.

For years afterward, I would stumble upon photos of myself that I had no memory of taking. Most of them were from this period. I wouldn't recognize my outfit, and I wouldn't know where the picture had been taken, as though a body double had taken my place. For example, there's one of me in front of a gray marble fireplace holding a big tabby cat. Was the background created by computer-generated imagery? Had the colors of my clothes been edited later? I would have remembered posing in a town house with a red cap and a yellow sweater. And I'm allergic to cats.

I have no memory of that particular photography session, but this isn't that surprising. My ascension was a blur of meetings, round trips in a car with tinted windows, and early-morning wake-ups. On average I met about fifty new people per day. It was impossible to remember a single name or face.

If sudden fame were a drink, it wouldn't be a glass of champagne, bubbly and festive. Fame was violent and brutal, like ten shots of tequila, each accompanied by a pinch of salt (the critics) and a slice of lime (the money). I downed shot after shot. My head spun, I grew nauseated, and, above all, my thoughts stopped being clear. From then on, everything became blurry.

The host began by asking me to react to Angelina Jolie's comments: The actress had said she listened to my album on repeat. I responded, focused, playful, and charming, my hands resting on my knees so that I wouldn't gesticulate. I didn't know when the camera was aimed at me versus the host, so I didn't stop smiling, just in case. My loose hair was held back by a black velvet headband; my legs were crossed, and my black dress was riding up to the tops of my thighs—one more inch and you'd see my butt. I pretended nothing was wrong, and no one seemed to be bothered by the fact that it looked like I was wearing a baby-doll nightgown: satin fabric, thin straps, a little ribbon bow in the middle.

I won't shock anyone by revealing that the interview was scripted, conceived as a short play that cycled in thirteen minutes through the following registers: laughter (four minutes), deep emotion (four minutes), promotion (five minutes). The mechanical magic of talk shows. My team had decided two weeks in advance whether I would greet the host with a handshake or a kiss on the cheek, and adjusted the angle of my seat by ten degrees to be more flattering. There wasn't the slightest element of surprise; I recited the words I'd learned by heart after a week of rehearsal. It was too bad—I would have been even better if they'd allowed me to retain an ounce of spontaneity. And anyway, the show wasn't even live.

Filming took place at 5:00 p.m., and it aired at 11:30. It was nighttime in New York when I turned on the television to find myself there, beglammed and bejeweled. I was perfect: a true performer, completely at ease in an environment whose codes I had quickly assimilated. Petra, my stylist, had been right: My sexy pajamas were bringing down the house.

On the internet, the first comments were raves: "I love her, she's so funny and has no filter." "She's so genuine, and stunningly gorgeous too." "Her success is totally deserved! She's so talented!" "No false pretenses with Cléo Louvent; she's natural and human, down-to-earth—why aren't all celebrities like her?" Of course, the praise was tempered by some cynical responses: "Anyone know who this is?" "Omg send help." "Meh." But no one criticized my nightie.

My cell phone vibrated. Stefani was endorsing my performance: "Exceptional. You nailed it. This interview is for sure going to be a turning point in your career." I had succeeded, I knew I had, because my manager said so—yet I was incapable of watching myself for more than three minutes, so I turned off the television. For some reason, when I saw myself on-screen, I wanted to hit myself in the face with a motorcycle U-lock.

Out the window: the sound of sirens, the frozen late-November streets, the bare trees in Central Park. At my feet, scattered on the hotel-room carpet: dozens of packages delivered to my dressing room that afternoon. A bottle of perfume, a candle, a box of tea, makeup, sunglasses. Stylish brands try to seek out celebrities where they are—namely, in the greenroom of the most influential TV show in the country. I gathered it all up as I left; it was enough to fill up my sleigh of Christmas presents for my family. Soon I would start abandoning them all behind me without even bothering to open them.

"There's what you actually think, and then there's what you say during an interview."

The advice I got from my team was clear: I should promote myself but be careful not to slip up. Alan, my image consultant, handed me a list of 207 subjects to avoid speaking about publicly. There were the obvious ones—abortion, gun-control laws, international politics—as well as the less obvious—blended families, the cattle industry, clowns.

During our media training sessions, Alan summarized the goal thusly: "Everyone needs to know you, and no one should know what you think." It meant talking all the time without saying anything, a skill that had to be learned; we spent entire days working on it.

My English was flawless, but my team told me to adopt an accent for certain expressions to add some French charm. They suggested I also pretend to forget certain words: "How do you say 'âpreté' in English, again?" I had French phrases at the ready to use when the time was right: lines from New Wave films, inspirational quotes by Napoléon and Simone Veil, and, most importantly, quirky proverbs that didn't exist in English. In one interview, I trotted out a makeshift literal translation of "remettre l'église au milieu du village," alluding to "putting the church back in the middle of the village"; in another, I bypassed the English "practice makes perfect" in favor of "you only become a blacksmith by working over a forge." I'd never been so funny and lovable.

They also helped me choose the right ways to describe my past, insisting I emphasize that *I did it all by myself*. This wasn't exactly true; it's not like I came from the middle of nowhere. My father had a degree from Yale, I grew up going back and forth between the States and France, I went to prestigious schools. But they preferred that I highlight the fact that I came from a family of reserved intellectuals. Unlike with most singers today, no one could claim that I succeeded only because of my parents, accuse me of being a nepo baby.

And last, they taught me to always compliment the journalist before the interview started *(I love your jacket/earrings/hat!)*, to never criticize a living artist (if people asked what kind of music I disliked, I answered Schubert), and to maintain that I preferred Coke to Pepsi (Coca-Cola was sponsoring my tour). I was ready.

Now all I had to do was charge into battle. That day I had fourteen straight hours of interviews, a ballet choreographed down to the last step, with my time divided into precise five-minute increments. It was the most intense period of post-album promotion.

They asked me if I had expected so much success. They asked me how I had come up with the idea to write a song about a woman who didn't have any feelings. They asked me what my morning beauty routine was. They asked me which lyrics I was the proudest of. They asked me how long it took me to write each song. They asked me how TikTok was upending the music industry. They asked me which artist I dreamed of collaborating with. They asked me where I grew up. They asked me to say something in French. They asked me how old I was when I started singing. They asked me what instrument I played. They asked me if I was in love. They asked me about my celebrity crush. They asked me what my favorite color was. They asked me what question I'd never been asked. They asked me if I ate stinky cheese.

The questions were always the same, and my answers were always the same. I repeated the same talking points, the same clichés, the same obvious facts, the same jokes pre-approved by my team. I would understand right away where the journalist wanted me to go; I'd let them finish their sentence, then start speaking on autopilot, hitting all the right notes.

I couldn't answer that I was exhausted, that my back hurt, that I was finding these interviews boring and superficial. I couldn't confide that all I wanted to do was sleep in my own bed, that I hadn't had a chance to go to the bathroom since the morning, that I wanted to call my mother and that there was an ever-widening rift between the two of us, that I missed my father desperately. Nor could I explain that I wasn't the one who chose the album cover and that in fact, I found it degrading (a half-naked woman in a starship . . . seriously?).

I was the guarantor of dreams. My label was using me to tell the world that fairy tales existed: I was the living proof, you could experience the magic vicariously through me, it could have been you! Everything I said was perfectly calibrated, watered down, inoffensive, inauthentically touching. I had to appeal to the public without being polarizing, consider my words carefully without losing my vivacity or sense of humor, pay attention to what I said without sounding scripted, please everyone without being too bland. I wasn't speaking as Cléo, I was speaking as Cléo Louvent—a name that was now a registered trademark.

I didn't have the right to complain: Media attention matches one's level of success. So I played along, pretending to be overjoyed, all the while reminding myself that the journalists across from me were meeting me for the first time. I owed them the same freshness, the same innocence, the same enthusiasm that I had in my very first interview that day.

So many professions are based on repetition. Politicians repeat the same slogans, sales reps repeat the same pitch, managers repeat the same instructions, professors repeat the same lessons.

And like everyone else, I put on a mask to go to work. Wearing a uniform helps: That day Petra had chosen a jacket with shoulder pads that I would never wear in real life. The diamonds borrowed from a jewelry designer did the same thing: They reminded me that I was in costume. It wasn't really me who was responding to the journalists. *Cléo, you're a star now, and everyone knows that stars don't exist.*

Everybody also knows that with fame comes excess. It's not that I would have any qualms about describing my new lifestyle of debauchery—the nights fueled by cocaine and champagne, the unsavory crowd I fell in with, the scenes of our crimes. I'd like to tell those stories, but I can't: I took the exact opposite path.

I stopped drinking, I no longer touched any substances, I had no sex life. No drunk driving, no hit-and-runs, no trashed hotel rooms, no stints in jail. I'm not claiming that celebrities don't ever transgress. I've seen Hollywood actresses shoot up heroin in luxury hotel bathrooms after walking the red carpet. Apparently, drugs can recreate the feeling of success: reproduce the giddiness, compensate for the drop in adrenaline. But I didn't feel the need. Completely the reverse, in fact. I was so thrilled by what was happening to me that I no longer felt like even smoking cigarettes.

Fame opened doors for me, and the expression wasn't just metaphorical. Luxury hotels, mansions, premieres, Michelin-starred restaurants, fashion shows for major designers, private parties. A week earlier, a high jewelry brand had invited me to a cocktail party at the British Museum in London; stunned, I tasted caviar a few steps from the Rosetta Stone.

Tonight I had been invited to the Academy Museum of Motion

Pictures's annual fundraising gala in Los Angeles. In reality, it was more about pageantry than patronage: Everyone in show business was there, dressed to the nines, to look at one another.

As a driver waited for me in front of the hotel, my team rushed around making crucial last-minute adjustments (for my messy chignon, should the loose strand of hair in front be tucked behind my ear or not?). Meanwhile, I gazed at my reflection in the mirror, mesmerized by my own appearance. I knew that I was beautiful, but I didn't think I had the potential to be *this* beautiful. The average person has the opportunity to experience this only once or twice in a lifetime—on their wedding day, for example. But I was the most beautiful version of myself several times a month. There was no black magic necessary: My dream physique required the work of four people for eight hours.

Wearing an haute couture gown is an unforgettable experience. Purple, backless, magnificent. I will always remember the moment when I first saw myself in Versace; it was like taking ecstasy for the first time at twenty and wondering how you ever could have thought you were having a good night before. I devoured my reflection, my dreamy dress, my ideal body, my perfect skin, my flawless face. I wanted to turn into a statue, preserve my beauty in amber, keep the precise waves of my hair intact, prevent my lipstick from fading even a little.

I say beauty, but I'm talking about a particular type of beauty: glamour. The open-backed dress, the diamonds, the exquisite and iconic hairstyle—this was an Old Hollywood ideal, not a New York one, and definitely not a Parisian one. From my mother I had learned elegance and the art of being well-dressed in a way that was seemingly effortless. Tonight Petra had added sequins straight from Tinseltown. Decked out in artifice, I had been deftly transformed into a goddess. An idol.

An hour later, the car was stopping, the door was opening, the flashes were dazzling. I struck a pose, displaying my best angle and wearing an expression of pride, my arms crossed like the *Mona Lisa*. Photographers shouted my name, and I counted to ten before turning around. A row of cameras waiting their turn on the other side. Behind me, a singer and an actress lingered in the vestibule. Every celebrity had their right to five minutes in the spotlight.

Once the photos and the interviews were over, two men removed my necklace and took it away in a gray briefcase. Bodyguards appointed by the high jewelry house, there to protect "the piece" around my neck, an octagon diamond surrounded by baguette and pear-shaped diamonds. When I had asked Petra how much it was worth, the only response I got from her was a burst of laughter: "Well, gorgeous, let's just say I'll never have you wear anything less than seven figures!"

Inside I found Hailey Bowen, the model who had appeared in my music video. We hugged as though we were the best of friends and chatted lightly. "What are you working on right now?" "Do you have any vacations planned?" I didn't bother trying to engage her on the downfall of capitalism or Cervantes's legacy in the history of the European novel.

After ten minutes, we found ourselves face-to-face with a world-famous actor. He was married to an actress who was equally famous, and they had four children together; the couple had been America's sweethearts for three decades. Being so close to him was a shock: I was getting used to my own growing fame, but that didn't mean that I was used to that of others. To our surprise, he approached us, and murmured:

"If I was single, I would lick both of your pussies."

Hailey was horrified. I wasn't against the idea.

Around me it seemed like everyone was having fun. However, being at this party didn't mean *partying*. I had to smile and be likeable, work my connections, chat intelligently, refrain from saying anything bad about anyone, confide in people while keeping some information strategically private, make sure not to tell secrets I shouldn't tell. I was encouraged to *make the most of it*. If fame was my destination, these events were a key part of the itinerary, and I had to navigate them just as skillfully as any other part. But in truth, I wanted only one thing: to be in a bathrobe in my hotel room, order a bowl of cereal from room service, masturbate under the sheets, fall asleep at 9:00 p.m.

I accepted a glass of champagne and brought it to my mouth to leave a faint stain of lipstick on the glass before abandoning it a bit farther away. The secret to pretending to drink without being discovered was to keep getting refills. Whenever a waiter passed right by me, I would take another flute and start all over again. These parties were agonizing enough as it was; there was no way I was taking my eyes off the road for even a fraction of a second.

Fame is contagious, so I forced myself to make contact. I talked to the people who were better known or more influential than I was, and fled from those who were less so. There were basic road traffic regulations that I had to follow: I respected those who were *in front of me* and ignored those who were *behind me*. The sole criterion for determining someone's value was their success. During my ascension, one of the feelings I experienced the most was contempt for the losers.

One peculiarity unique to celebrities is that they never introduce themselves. I'd been warned about that, and it was true. You'd better know who you were about to talk to before you struck up a conversation. And this party was filled with almost celebrities—

their face rings a bell, I think I've seen them somewhere, but where?
According to my initial estimates, the majority of people I crossed
paths with thought that they were between 20% and 30% more
famous than they actually were. On the other hand, no one had
prepared me for the fact that, in this environment, everyone imi-
tated this pretentious habit; even agents and producers didn't introduce themselves, as though we had any reason to know their
names. Luckily, on my phone, I had a list of the important guests
and their photos. I knew exactly whom I needed to get along with.

At the bar, I chatted with the CEO of the label I had applied to
work at when I had first arrived in New York. As he sang the praises
of my debut album, it all came back to me in a flash: the interview,
my phone on the side of the sink in my bathroom, my intuition
screaming at me not to pick up. Five years earlier, I had hesitated
to accept an assistant position paying $34,000 a year. Tonight I
was talking to the CEO about my future as an artist. A round of
applause for my meteoric rise.

While we were speaking, I spotted several people from my red
list. My Excel grid didn't lie: I still had the names of the idiots who
had ignored me when I'd sent them my songs. Would I find a way to
discreetly spit into their champagne glasses this evening? The vultures
circled around me, and I took pleasure in avoiding them. It was crazy.
I was the same person as I'd been a year and a half before. I had more
or less the same talent, the same skill, the same ambition. And yet now
I had access to a higher plane of reality. People looked at me, people
waited for me, people listened to me. Response rate: 100%.

The famous actor, the one who was married but famished with
lust, came back over. He smelled of sandalwood, a scent of up-
rooted tree trunks, Vietnamese temples, forests, climbing vines.
The message was still just as clear when he leaned toward me:
"Don't worry, my wife isn't here. You can suck me off. I know that

you want my cum in your mouth." I smiled before moving away. Very good-looking, but too old—and too married.

Ten minutes later, the singer Jane Cabello was telling me about her vacation in St. Barts. As a student, I'd considered her one of my most formidable rivals; concentrated and vicious, I'd analyzed her career during my public-law class. I still had the scar from the wound I'd inflicted upon myself on my inner thigh as punishment for having compared myself to her. Since then Jane Cabello had married Harry Miller before deciding to devote herself to acting, though with only moderate success (where was the Oscar?). My former nemesis smelled of crème pâtissière, almonds, blackberries, and sun. I smiled and nodded; I could just let her lead the conversation. She summarized for me the most recent film she'd been in, told me about her partnership with a prestigious leather brand, and announced her upcoming shoots. In fact, Jane was talking to me as though I were a journalist. I wondered if, given that she'd been famous since childhood, she had spent more cumulative hours over the course of her life giving interviews than having real conversations with other human beings.

Relatives often asked me what it was like to be around celebrities. Honestly, the conversations weren't any more interesting than with anyone else. I was rarely dazzled by famous people's sharpness or intelligence. However, I did immediately notice one big difference between them and the rest of the world: Stars smelled good. In their wake they left an extraordinary trail, a several-thousand-dollar concoction of perfume, moisturizer, soap, shampoo, detergent, oil, lotion, hair mist. I swear celebrity has its own scent.

I suppressed a yawn before pulling myself together. These parties were launchpads for my destiny; I needed these friendship and alliances. *Cléo Louvent, don't forget that you're here to be seen.*

Determined to make a good impression, I was weaving through the crowd to grab another glass of champagne I wouldn't drink when I spotted John Cutler. Superfamous, superrich, former child star, singer, actor, owner of a villa in Los Angeles; for years now, he'd been in a relationship with Lily Clayton, heiress to a hotel empire. The previous year, John Cutler had sold the rights to his musical repertoire for two hundred million dollars. With six albums and a dozen hits, he'd successfully reinvented himself to stay relevant, which hadn't been a foregone conclusion: The country had originally fallen in love with a twelve-year-old kid with round cheeks and a swoop of hair. John Cutler had navigated changing trends; he was shrewd in his collaborations with other artists, a musical king and marketing god. Honestly, the guy was a genius, and unlike most Americans I've met, I don't use that label lightly.

In short: He was a big fish. Catching his interest would mean catching the interest of the whole room. In fact, everyone was jockeying for his attention. I had to elbow my way through the crowd, pushing aside a passé English actress to get into his line of sight.

John Cutler came toward me. He congratulated me on my three Grammy nominations, told me that he loved my album, and wished me good luck on my tour. As surprising as it may seem, he appeared to be sincere. Truly sincere. My big fish was a nice guy. My heart pounded wildly; I was attracted to him.

"It was a pleasure to meet you, Cléo Louvent!" he said, then apologized before moving away. Five minutes later, he left the party.

Alone in my hotel room, I was restless and disappointed in myself. As punishment, I pinched myself with the zipper of my dress as I took it off. I should have stayed an hour longer. I should have worn a more daring outfit. I should have been more strategic.

I should have talked to that influential director—she must have considered asking me to write a song for the original soundtrack for her next film, why hadn't I gone over to introduce myself? I was too cold, or else too friendly. I said too much, or else I didn't say enough. I shouldn't have told Jane Cabello that I had started collaborating with a high jewelry house; I should have let her talk about herself without once interrupting her. Above all, I should have fought to keep the conversation going with John Cutler. His relationship status didn't bother me. It wasn't like he and Lily had committed to each other permanently. I should have charmed him with the kind of witty and relevant remarks that only I could make. Why hadn't I been capable of exchanging more than three sentences with him?

As I played back the tape of the last few hours, I saw only missed opportunities. Soon guilt gave way to paranoia. By the time I went to bed, a little after midnight, I had persuaded myself that everyone I'd spoken to at the party hated me.

My team gave me fifty-six hours off in Paris, from December 24th (10:00 a.m.) to December 26th (6:00 p.m.). The holiday break allowed me to join my family around the Christmas tree. I asked my relatives not to post anything on social media; I didn't want people to know where my mother lived.

In the living room, the presents were waiting to be unwrapped, my cousins were chatting as they waited for the food to be ready, the turkey was almost finished cooking, and my uncle was telling a story: He had nearly set their house on fire by throwing his underwear onto the lamp on the bedside table. My aunt's face turned red with embarrassment as my uncle acted out the scene, and the whole family burst into laughter. My heart sank. It was my second Christmas without my father—I missed him more in mirth than in melancholy; his absence felt more profound in times of festivity than it did in times of tranquility. My mother offered me a glass of champagne.

"I'd love one. It's been ages since I've had anything to drink."

"Really? You don't drink? But you're invited everywhere!"

"No, not a drop of alcohol."

"But why not?"

"Because I'm working, Mom."

". . ."

"You don't really understand what I do, do you?"

The cocktails, the parties, the red carpets: They were, quite simply, work. Tonight, surrounded by family, and for the first time in months, I was on vacation. I savored the first mouthful of bubbly before embracing my mother.

Foie gras, smoked salmon, turkey, potatoes, a cheese platter, a bûche de Noël with vanilla frosting. I ate in moderation; I'd put on weight during my ascension. I'd declined the glasses of champagne, but I hadn't refused the appetizers. The pounds of wealth. Before, in addition to my morning workouts, I walked or biked everywhere, I never took taxis, I went to restaurants only occasionally, I never snacked on the seven-dollar peanuts from the hotel minibar. But it's more difficult to stay thin when money is no longer an issue. The label paid for everything, even my cereal and orange juice in the morning. A little while ago, I'd learned to order a salad instead of lasagna and, above all, never to clean my plate.

In the late afternoon, Juliette stopped by for a piece of cake and some coffee. My family was happy to see her; my childhood friend hadn't changed since the days when she came on vacation with us to the Isle of Oléron. Next to her, sleeping in her stroller, was her daughter, whom I was meeting for the first time. My mother marveled over her, congratulated Juliette with tears in her eyes. She gave her a stuffed octopus toy that she'd knit herself, and it was obvious that she would have preferred for me to give birth to a baby rather than an album.

I hadn't seen Juliette for a year. She had a thousand things to tell me, but they were all about her daughter, Gabrielle. Everyone was fawning over her five-month-old baby. Unless I was mistaken, this infant wasn't a musical genius, so why was she the center of attention? Gabrielle was charming—that wasn't the issue—but she wasn't telling us much about her personality and talents. In my personal opinion, her communication was quite basic: crying, gurgling, smiling. I'd give her the benefit of the doubt, but all the same, she still needed to prove herself; there was nothing to get that excited about. And Juliette was ambitious—you had to be to become an ER doctor—so why was she dedicating so much time and money to someone other than herself? Children are noisy, they don't know how to modulate their voices, they speak slowly, they're dirty, you have to teach them everything, they need love.

"Do you want to hold her?"

As she handed Gabrielle to me, Juliette asked me to be her daughter's godmother. I accepted, reluctantly. Did I have a choice? It was the type of request that politeness dictated you had to accept. I couldn't tell her that I was planning to be much too busy to see the child, that I found the responsibility overwhelming, that I didn't think I'd be able to play fairy godmother, that I was a bad person, that I might corrupt her daughter, ruin her, irreparably damage her personality. Gabrielle fell asleep on my shoulder. I stroked her tiny fingers before carefully putting her back in her stroller. This infant was a piece of paper that I was afraid to crumple.

By 9:00 *p.m.*, the apartment was calm again. My cousins caught their trains back home, my uncles and aunts returned to their houses in the suburbs, I promised Juliette that I'd stop by to see her the next morning. And it was in this peaceful, festive atmosphere, amidst the blinking lights of the Christmas tree, that the terrible dishwasher incident occurred.

Soothed by the humming of the machine coming from the kitchen, I was responding to texts while my mother read quietly in the armchair across from me, her legs tucked under a blanket. Suddenly the dishwasher let out the high-pitched sound that signaled the end of its cycle. I got up from the couch.

My mother interrupted me. "Leave it, I'll do it."

"No, don't worry about it. I'll take care of it."

"You are not actually going to empty the dishwasher."

"And . . . why not?"

"You're tired. I'll do it later."

"But I've always emptied the dishwasher! Ever since I was six years old, I've emptied the dishwasher and set the table. That's how it's always been."

"Yes, but things have changed."

"How have they changed?"

". . ."

"What do you mean?"

". . ."

"Mom, just tell me what you mean!"

My mother wasn't letting me empty the dishwasher because I was famous. My face was on the cover of all the magazines, I was prepping for an international tour, and I had more money in my bank account right now than my mother had ever had in her whole life—but who was I if I couldn't put the silverware back in its drawer? What was my place in the world if I was forbidden to stack the bowls in the cupboard?

"Mom, this is my home. It's the only place where I'm not famous. You don't have the right to take that away from me."

"That has nothing to do with it!"

"Yes, it does! You're acting like I'm too good to empty the dishwasher, like I'm above all that."

"No, I'm not. I told you, that's not it at all. It's just that I'll do it myself later."

I wasn't the one who was changed by fame; it was the way others saw me. I was still acting exactly the same, but already people were treating me differently. I wasn't going to stand for it—I wasn't going to stand for any of it. I would be firm and merciless. I opened the dishwasher and looked at my mother determinedly.

"Mom, I'm going to put away these dishes, and you cannot do anything to stop me."

I didn't hear my phone vibrating between the couch cushions. Aria had tried to call me seven times. When I called her back, I could practically hear her pirouetting at the other end of the line.

"I got the part."

Aria's life was changing, a year and a half after mine had. Copycat.

Who was the most famous person in my phone contacts? Did I know what journalists were going to ask in advance? Were the shows actually broadcast live?

This wasn't a night out with friends, it was an interview. *Sweetie, you need a press pass to get me to answer your questions. I'm not working tonight.*

Aria had organized a surprise party for Celeste's birthday at a bar in SoHo. With its fairy lights and lanterns, the venue looked like a private garden, invisible from the street. I'd fought to clear my schedule so that I could go, convinced that this evening far away from the never-ending promotion was exactly what I needed. I was wrong.

"Have you met Jane Cabello?" "What is she *really* like?" "Did she actually cheat on Harry Miller with the director of *Snow White* while filming?" No one cared how I was doing; they wanted the juicy details.

Aria sulked in a corner. She must have hoped that everyone would be gushing over her and her new role, but she wasn't famous yet, and I was; I was taking up the whole spotlight even if I would have gladly stayed out of it. I answered reluctantly, lowering my voice so that neighboring tables didn't overhear our conversation. It wasn't anything confidential—it's not like I was revealing the secrets of the universe—but all the same, I whispered in public places to protect my privacy from prying ears.

I satisfied my friends' curiosity for five minutes, then tried to steer the line of questioning elsewhere. "Aria, when does your show start filming?" "Yasmin, how is your son?" "Margarita, have you visited Matt since he moved to Austin?" But the conversation always ended up circling back to me. I stopped making an effort, changed the subject, avoided eye contact. I was exhausted, and my coldness made me seem arrogant.

"Did you write your album all by yourself?" "Were you really naked in the shower in your music video?" "Can you keep the jewelry and dresses you wear on the red carpets?"

I had always dreamed of being famous, so I wondered why I wasn't happier when talking about myself. Truthfully, I wasn't satisfied either way: I hated being upstaged by Juliette's daughter, and I hated being the center of attention. Of course I thought I was superior, fascinating, brilliant. I craved admiration, but in silence and without effusiveness. What I actually wanted was to be looked at but not seen—or was it the opposite?

The waitress came over with a big smile to collect our empty glasses and lingered at the table. Had she recognized me? I couldn't exactly ask her to clarify: *You know who I am, right? You love me, don't you?* To create a distraction, I brought out Celeste's gift. Celeste opened the box and saw the bracelet; it was perfect for her. She thanked Lauren, Ellen, Margarita, Aaron, and the others, radiating joy. But I was dying of bitterness. I felt so sad, so distant from them. And that moment was the final nail in the coffin of my most fragile friendships.

A month earlier, Aria had started a group chat to brainstorm ideas for what we could give to our beloved Celeste for her thirtieth birthday. I scrolled through the messages on my phone; there were thirty or so of us, which meant we could dream big. Suggestions came in one after the other: a massage, Givenchy sunglasses, wireless headphones. I joined in, throwing out an idea: What about something from Cartier? This was received with a lot of enthusiasm—the Clou was an iconic bracelet, both delicate and classic, perfect for Celeste, what a great idea! I sent the chat the link to the product page. I wouldn't ever have suggested the gift if there hadn't been so many of us, but all the same, I wanted to make sure that everyone was okay with the price. The yellow-gold model without any diamonds cost $3,600; according to my calculations, this would mean individual contributions in line with what we'd all paid for previous group birthday gifts. Everyone agreed that it was the best option. A week later, I texted them to say that I'd picked up the bracelet.

"Thank you, Cléo!"

"Thanks for taking care of it!"

"Thanks, Cléo, it was such a good idea!"

They thanked me heartily, over and over. I was stunned. Holding my phone, I waited a few minutes, but nothing happened. Was I dreaming, or were none of my friends planning to contribute financially to this gift that we had decided to buy together? Why was no one offering to reimburse me? The underlying message was clear: *Now Cléo is rich, so she can pay. $3,600 means nothing to her.* Furious, I threw my phone on the tile floor of the hotel bathroom, and the screen shattered. Who did they think they were? My money was from *my* songs; I'd earned every cent. I wasn't living off Daddy. I hadn't inherited my fortune from my family; I was building it myself, without anyone's help. How could they act as though my money were a communal asset? I wasn't the World Bank.

Alerted by the noise, Stefani came into my room. I explained the reason for my indignation, but she looked at me uncomprehendingly. "Why would you care about four thousand dollars?" She didn't see the problem.

Two hours after my arrival at Celeste's birthday party, I was still the only subject of conversation. "So, Cléo, how do you go from being a bookseller to an international star?" "What's the secret?" "How do you explain your success?" "Your record label must have spent insane amounts of money to promote you, right?" "They're really good at marketing, don't you think?" I was a circus animal being thrown to the wolves, except the wolves were my own friends, and their questions weren't always well-intentioned.

"Did you ever think about doing a duet with Justin Bieber? That could be great for your career. And then you know what you should do after that? Acting. Lady Gaga's career really took off when she acted in that movie—what was it called again?"

Mike, a friend of Celeste's whom I'd met twice in my life, was standing in front of me, beer in hand. The look on his face was that of someone who thought they were smarter than everyone else, even though I heard the same comments forty-seven times a day. I could have stabbed his hand with my fork. As though I didn't have a team of thirty people already working on my five-year plan. What did he think I was going to say to him? *Wow, Mike, I hadn't thought of that at all! Thank you so much for giving me this brilliant idea! I'll ask my label to hire you immediately—you start on Monday!*

My lack of enthusiasm for this flood of unsolicited advice made me seem like a jerk, but I was too tired to pretend. As soon as Aria took a break to get some air, I slipped out with her. She didn't ask me anything about my album, my success, or my concerts; she acted as though nothing had changed, ignoring the elephant in the room that I was becoming a global celebrity. Drink in hand, she talked to me about herself—only about herself, always about herself. And this shift in focus was a relief. She updated me on her life, telling me emphatically about her audition, which she had been certain she had failed but which was now about to change her life. It was all still melodrama territory—the heroine saved just in time by a twist of fate. Filming would start in two months. Hers was a secondary role, but she hoped that the show would be a jumping-off point for her. The subject was niche, and yet she was sure it would reach a large audience.

"Do you want to sleep at our place tonight?" Aria asked me, finally. "Your old bed is waiting for you!"

"That's so nice of you, but all my things are at the hotel. I'm going to get a taxi."

All my friends went home via subway. I knew that they were already whispering to one another: "Cléo has changed." "She's so full of herself." "Success has gone to her head." But really, I asked them for only two things: that they treat me like a normal person and that they each pay back the $116.13 they owed me.

When I think about fame, the sound I hear in my head is one of obnoxious buzzing: the hum of requests. We should compile statistics on the nature and quantity of requests as a function of one's degree of success. The data would be easy to collect, and, above all, it would be a reliable barometer. It's true for an artist, it's true for a successful entrepreneur, it's true for politicians, it's true for influencers. Regardless of the field, the phenomenon is the same: With success comes requests.

At first, people asked me to *do them a favor*. Former acquaintances popped up out of the woodwork. Then the circle of requests started getting bigger. We used to live in the same neighborhood, we went to the same elementary school ten years apart, we shared the same sun sign, moon sign, rising sign. Then there were the friends of friends. My mother's colleagues and their children. Neighbors of my uncles and aunts. My cousin's boyfriend. My father's old dentist's childhood friend's cousin's brother-in-law.

My contact information got around. The messages always started the same way: "Louise gave me your phone number." "I'm a friend of Pierre's. He was kind enough to give me your info." "I'm writing you on behalf of Zoé, who used to live in the same building as your aunt in Brest."

"I've always dreamed of getting into the music industry; do you have any advice for me?" "I'd like to change careers and follow my passion instead. Would you be willing to meet me for coffee and tell me your inspiring story?" "My son would like to intern at a record label. Could you pass along his application?" "I'm about to launch my podcast about ambitious women. How about being my first guest and sharing the episode on your socials?" "One of my former coworkers is interested in becoming a publicist. Any chance you could put him in touch with someone you know in the field?" "My brother isn't feeling fulfilled by his career as an osteopath and he'd like to become your French agent. He knows everyone, he could set up your concerts in Lyon and Paris. . . . What do you think?" "My sister is an incredible writer, she'd love to write some songs for you. Could you chat with her and explain where she should start?" "And now that you're famous, would you happen to have Dua Lipa's number? My niece is a fan and she'd be so happy if she could meet her."

At first, I made myself available for these requests. Then I began to limit the time I would grant to each person; I still said yes, but they would have to be satisfied with a quick phone call while I was in a taxi or waiting between two flights. Eventually, I began to politely decline, responding that *it would be tough*, along with a few kind words and a heart. I already didn't have the time to wash my own ears; I wasn't going to go drink a coffee with you.

Requests also came in the form of *invitations*. I was invited to openings. I was invited to a screening of a short film about a family of circus performers. I was invited to test out a new organic cosmetics brand. I was invited to the launch party for a collection of Persian poetry. I was invited to wear designs from a brand that recycled fabric scraps. I was invited to listen to the first single of a promising Canadian singer who had fifty plays on SoundCloud. I was invited to test out a restaurant, a new car, a tree house, a hot-air balloon.

Overnight all the sick children in the country seemed to devise a plan to ask me to visit them in the hospital. I was begged to come sing at the wedding of a man with terminal leukemia, to sponsor a charity that was fighting cancer. I was also encouraged to speak up about the importance of nest boxes for helping to reestablish the population of Europe's largest bird of prey, the bearded vulture. My inbox was starting to look like the Cours des Miracles.

Finally, in addition to the requests, I began to receive an endless stream of *comments*. Everyone who listened to my music also took it upon themselves to give me specific feedback so I could improve: "I really like what you're doing, but I hate one of your songs, and I'll explain why." After every concert, I was subjected to a detailed evaluation of my performance: "I was in the audience last Saturday. I thought you seemed pretty tired. Honestly, I was disappointed."

Thanks to social media, everyone had the ability to send me a message, and apparently, they all felt free to do so. My phone felt like a nonstop open house: People would drop by, say hello, offer their opinions, lavish praise on me, criticize me, ask me questions. "What were the shoes you were wearing onstage yesterday evening?" "Out of curiosity, where did you get the idea to write a song about a person who doesn't feel any emotions? Were you a highly gifted child?" "There are fake tickets being sold for Friday's concert. I know some people who've been scammed. It's disgraceful."

I remember the day when I gave up. One morning I unlocked my phone to find 400 WhatsApp notifications and just as many texts, 1,852 unread emails, and tens of thousands of DMs on Instagram. I was already behind; it was impossible to sort through them and keep track.

I stopped responding. A year later, I deleted my old email address and delegated the management of my social media accounts to someone else. From then on, I had to change my phone number three or four times a year.

She lives in a different world." "She's completely out of touch with reality." "She has no idea what other people's lives are like." That's the type of criticism often leveled at celebrities, understandably so. Now it was my turn to leave solid ground behind.

I learned to say no, not to pick up my phone, to ignore my missed calls. We had to close the floodgates, and quickly. The intermediaries between myself and the outside world multiplied. Little by little, it became impossible to contact me directly: You had to go through ten middlemen first. By definition, a star is inaccessible.

Stefani took over from me in responding to the 209 proposals a day from other artists who wanted to remix one of my existing songs or feature in an upcoming one. The requests I answered personally were carefully selected. I'd noticed that important people often signed off with just a single initial—very chic—and I decided to do the same. I learned to keep my own messages brief (never more than twenty words) and to end with a period (no emoji): "Thanks for writing. Stefani's on it. Take care, C."

My entourage changed. Before, I had been alone, and now, I had a team: manager, tour manager, wealth manager, marketing manager, community manager; media coach, mental coach, vocal coach, driver, trainer, lawyer, producer, tax adviser, choreographer, assistant, accountant, artistic director, bodyguard, head of security, publicists in twenty-seven countries, stylist, psychologist, sophrologist, kinesiotherapist, shaman. Stardom is built layer by layer.

My friends and family said I was impossible to reach. My uncles and aunts wondered if they still had the right number and if

I would be attending my cousin's wedding. I was woken up in the middle of the night by a call from my mother; she didn't know I was in Tokyo to film a music video.

Celebrities have no choice but to set boundaries. During the first two years, the walls rose up around me before my eyes; over the next few years, the fortress only strengthened, becoming more and more impressive, more and more impregnable. But there was a paradox that was impossible to escape: Right from the start, the citadel isolated me as much as it protected me. The more I was surrounded, the more I was alone.

Breathe out through your mouth." "Do a set of push-ups." "Imagine that the audience is naked." I was given a lot of advice for quelling my stage fright before a show. I didn't dare admit that I didn't have any.

"The golden rule: Never apologize for being there," Stefani told me over and over.

There was no risk of that. In front of seven thousand people, I was exactly where I was supposed to be. As I warmed up my voice, I was offhand and cheerful, as calm as if I were going to play tennis with my girls. And tonight was a home game.

"It's all you now."

When I looked up, there was the crowd, standing before me. Upon my entrance, the massive, wriggling beast with seven thousand heads began to scream, its roar causing the ground to tremble beneath my feet. It was much louder than the stuffed animals on my bed, who had taken to listening to me in silence. Included somewhere in the audience at the Zénith arena in Paris: my mother, Juliette, my uncle and aunt, and three of my cousins.

I looked into the distance, avoiding the first few rows, where I could still distinguish the silhouettes, the faces, the phone screens.

I could sing in front of seven thousand people; all I had to do was not look any of them in the eyes.

Seven thousand people. Seven thousand people had bought their tickets, left work earlier than usual to catch the beginning of the show, taken line 5 of the metro, paid a babysitter to watch their kids. Some of them had put gas in their cars and assumed the risk of dying in an accident on the way.

Seven thousand people. And yet I pretended I was alone. I didn't draw on the energy in the room. The opposite, in fact—I went inward, retreating into myself. I'd followed the same winning formula since my very first concerts: ignore the public.

"Ten, nine, eight, seven, six . . ." The countdown was transmitted to my earpiece as though we were about to launch a rocket. "Five, four, three, two, one . . ." I began the opening verse of "I Feel Nothing," hitting the first notes without any effort; my deep voice sounded even more beautiful than it did in the studio. Right away, I was struck by the power of my mic. How antidemocratic those 120 decibels were: They promised that only I would be heard, that my voice would rise above the other seven thousand. Tonight my words would dominate. *Ticktock, ticktock . . .* The click track accompanied me in my in-ear monitor from the beginning to the end of the song, a metronome keeping time for me so that I stayed on tempo. *Ticktock, ticktock . . .* I finished my first song, masterful, joking around, relaxed. It was easier to sing in front of seven thousand people than it was to sing in front of seven. I didn't understand how that witchcraft worked, but it did.

Starting with the second song, I told the crowd when to sing the chorus with me and when to be quiet, forcing them to applaud at the right times. I was an authoritarian—perfect for being on-stage. When I was little, I had played with Polly Pocket toys, small figurines that lived in miniature worlds shaped like seashells or strawberries. Inside were scenes filled with charming details: a sled, a swing, a horse-drawn carriage, a bubble bath. My audience made me think of these tiny dolls; they were at my mercy. I wasn't the opening act for this show, and so much the better. I hated lending out my toys.

By the end of the fifth song, I still didn't feel any stress. Nor did I feel fatigue or joy. In fact, I felt nothing. I sang and I danced, but I was thinking of other things: John Cutler's smile, which had haunted my thoughts since we'd met; the dinner that was awaiting me; a movie I'd seen recently; my stomachache. In fact, without any shame, I relieved myself of my intestinal cramps in front of seven thousand people. Who was going to know? Nobody. The dissociation was wild. These songs had once been a piece of my soul; tonight I was reeling them off while farting, without meaning a word I was singing.

During the love songs, I pretended to be moved. During the upbeat songs, I pretended to be joyful. I paused to let the audience finish my lines, extending my microphone toward them: guaranteed shivers. I spun and twirled, shed a tear, joked around, improvised naturally. The magic formula: teach, delight, persuade.

"You've been wonderful! Thank you, Paris!"

The audience roared at the mention of their city. I blew them kisses, bowed in salute, did a pirouette.

"I love you! My heart will always be in Paris!"

The crowd screamed even louder. I exited the stage, throwing aside my microphone and ripping out my earpiece.

"I'm blown away every time," Stefani murmured. "It's like you've been doing this your whole life."

In a way, I had. So the next time I performed in Paris, we could multiply it all by ten. The Stade de France, seventy thousand people, all with total peace of mind.

"*Nothing can replace* the connection with fans. The stage is the only place where I truly feel like myself. I'm naturally shy, but in front of an audience, I become someone different. The real reward is the tour."

I've repeated these sentences hundreds of times in interviews. I have to say that being onstage is what I love most because it's what brings in the most money. I have concert venues to fill and a business to run. It's not that I don't love to sing—I do. But no one seems to realize how exhausting it is to play the same music over and over again.

My tour had barely begun, and already I was worn out from seeing the crowd demand the same three songs—the most popular ones, the ones that had made me successful in the first place. I had eighty-three shows scheduled for all over the world, plus private concerts, showcases, radio and TV broadcasts, and award-ceremony performances. I estimated that I had already sung some of my hits in public more than three hundred times.

In interviews they often want to talk about how I feel about being onstage. But they forget about the upheaval that takes place upon *leaving* the stage. At the Zénith in Paris, I exited through the wings, my heart beating furiously, and my team came up to congratulate me. To come back down, I had to replay the concert in my head ten times: I needed to hear that I was amazing and that the audience was captivated beginning to end, and I needed to be presented with rock-solid evidence in order to believe that this was true. For two or three hours, I was too intense and spoke too loudly.

But soon the euphoria began to mingle with regrets. I should have addressed the audience directly more often, taken advantage of being in Paris to build rapport with them. Why hadn't

I mentioned that my family was there tonight? My concert was *good*, but it could have been *better*. This simple idea was unbearable to me.

My mother came to join me in my dressing room. Her hands were trembling, and she looked bewildered. "When you came onstage, I didn't recognize you. I thought you were the opening act. . . ." She could barely articulate her thoughts; it was as though she had just witnessed a battle scene, not her daughter's concert.

In the suite of a luxury Parisian hotel I'd never even set foot in before (it came with my own personal majordomo named Théodore, who was available 24/7—excellent), I paced back and forth between my bed and the bathroom. To calm down, I opened a meditation app on my phone, but I couldn't focus. I needed a lover; I always slept like a rock after an orgasm. I thought about masturbating before abandoning the idea. I couldn't tell if I was being cautious or paranoid, but I was scared of being hacked, so I'd stopped visiting my favorite porn sites. For a while now, I'd had to touch myself while watching movie clips or reading novels. Actually, I could have really used a joint. It seemed like cannabis was invented for this exact situation, when artists were struggling to wind down after a performance. I nearly asked Théodore to get me some but reconsidered. It wasn't the time to develop an addiction. I had a world tour to get through.

Already I'd played shows in New York; Detroit; Cincinnati; Nashville; Atlanta; Washington, DC; Philadelphia; Boston; Montreal; and Paris. Ten out of eighty-three. Using a razor blade, I traced a thin line on the inside of my thigh. Ten shows, ten cuts. I always had something to punish myself for.

My lifestyle while on tour resembled that of a top athlete. I warmed up. I trained. I hydrated. I took power naps. I ate balanced meals. Ventolin, vitamins, probiotics, protein, corticosteroids, stimulants, painkillers. I wouldn't have passed most athletic anti-doping tests.

One image kept coming back to me: a clementine being squeezed. Soon I wouldn't have anything left to give. They were paying me well, but they were also taking everything.

I was scared of doing one concert too many—the one where I collapsed onstage. I was scared of doing one interview too many—the one where I rolled my eyes and sighed. I was scared of fainting in public, of vomiting on a journalist, of bursting into tears, of screaming to be left alone, of slapping my assistant, of strangling a fan, of hanging myself in my hotel room.

I was very busy. And yet I no longer handled anything myself. I was told when to get up in the morning, what I was eating for lunch, if I had interviews for local TV, how long the sound checks would last, the time at which I needed to start getting my hair and makeup done. I essentially had two full-time babysitters chaperoning me, as though I'd regressed to childhood, a pampered and coddled little girl. They never informed me of technical problems or issues with the costumes or ticketing malfunctions; I was also spared from the shaman's predictions of bad weather for outdoor concerts (I didn't care about being rained on, anyway). Other than singing, I wasn't supposed to think about anything. I had an army behind me, but every night I was alone on the front line.

I was very busy. And yet I had never spent so much time waiting. I spent my life in transport, getting into cars, planes, buses. Performances with holograms seemed like an appealing option. Or perhaps teleportation? I knew I was richer than I'd ever been because I began to desire things that couldn't be bought.

We deployed a whole regiment for a concert, covering staggering distances for twelve songs. I alternated between emptiness and fullness. There would be no one in the venue; an hour later, there'd be five thousand of us. We'd vibrate to the rhythm of my melodies and the audience's screams; two hours later, the tech team would be silently packing up the cables. The excess would change into absolute calm; I'd be too much in demand and then suddenly have nothing to do, and I was incapable of appreciating either extreme.

There is a number of adjectives that could be used to describe my behavior the evening of my show in London. You can choose the one you like best: despicable, moody, foul, abysmal, appalling, unbearable, irascible, obnoxious.

I'd slept four hours the night before, hadn't eaten anything since 7:00 a.m., had a sore throat, and had spent the afternoon filming a video for *Vogue* in which I had described the contents of my purse. Each object had been chosen by my image consultant and negotiated with the brand. Smiling, I pulled out of my Dior tote bag some makeup (that I'd never used in my life), perfume (who carried around a seven-ounce bottle?), and an enormous tube of sunscreen (these product placements were really lacking in subtlety)—but also both volumes of *The Second Sex* by Simone de Beauvoir (one would have sufficed) and a coffee-table book about eighteenth-century female painters (who was going to believe that I lugged around a ten-pound tome every day? While we were at it, why not a Van Gogh painting, a circular saw, or a catamaran?).

Next I had to go do a meet and greet with the fans who had shelled out for VIP tickets. They lined up obediently, single file, and I had to take seventy-three photos in record time: "Hello, thank you, goodbye." After that, my record label's local team presented me with a gold record (or maybe it was a diamond record?) for the English market, and I shook their hands, pretending to know whom I was talking to. And then it was time for me to get ready to go onstage, to put on my costume. But first I wanted to take a shower.

"Unfortunately, that won't be possible. There's no shower for us to use here, and we're already behind schedule."

I remember saying to my father at the age of six or seven: "Dad, I hate putting clothes *on dry skin*." I've always been disgusted by the feel of fabric on skin that isn't damp. Everyone has their little quirks. Except that by this point, forty-seven people knew about mine. If my stage manager had a sudden craving for a banana before a concert, he was free to indulge himself in private—meanwhile, I couldn't steal away to rinse myself off in the hopes that no one would notice my disappearance, not even for five minutes. If I had the slightest desire for something that wasn't already accounted for, I had to let my team know and get their approval, impacting the schedule of nearly fifty people.

Calmly, Stefani intervened. "Cléo, the shower is going to be tough. We're really behind."

"We're in London, not on Mars. You can find a way for me to shower. Get some water, boil it, put it in a basin, I don't care. I need to rinse off. It's nonnegotiable."

"Right after the concert, I promise."

"No. Now."

"It's not possible, there's no time. . . ."

"I never ask for anything. You all live off me, and you can't even give me a shower? A fucking shower? What's next? I won't be allowed to go to the bathroom and I'll have to wear diapers?"

". . ."

"You've got to be kidding me."

". . ."

"This is absolutely ridiculous."

I'll remember that shower my whole life: It was my first *star tantrum*. Under the scalding water, I didn't feel the satisfaction of having gotten my way; instead, I thought about the rumors that circulated about certain celebrities. The musician whose contract stipulated that there be five KitKats and Japanese tea in his dressing room before every concert. The actress who would cancel ten interviews on a whim. The musician was criticized for being *difficult*, the actress accused of being *a diva*. When you become famous, you no longer have *needs* or *wants*. Only *tantrums*.

I pulled on my costume—my skin was still damp, with water dripping down my back—but I couldn't even savor the pleasure of not *putting clothes on dry skin*. This shower had made me into a horrible person. And the worst part was that I had every reason to be one. You try being shuttled from one town to another for months on end to give concerts. You're an object, passed from hand to hand. Each of these evenings is monetized, and the product for sale is you. You have to smile when you're sleep-deprived, when your stomach hurts, when you're hungry, when all eyes are on you. You're supposed to kindly welcome all requests: "My daughter loves you, could you record a message for her birthday?" "My aunt saw you in concert in Boston, she was in the front row wearing a gray hat, does that ring a bell?" "I wanted to tell you that your album changed my life—it helped me get through my divorce. Without you, I wouldn't be here." You need to listen attentively, stay focused, give everyone a dose of love. You're expected to answer the same questions, take the same photos, sing the same song, dance the same choreography, and then do it all over again the next day. So ask yourself: Are star tantrums really tantrums?

Since 5:00 a.m., I'd been forcing myself to remain sweet, attentive, and cheerful. But what they'd remember was the shower incident, not all the other hours of professionalism, patience, and smiles.

After I left the stage, I was told that I had a last-minute interview that I absolutely had to accept. Despite my fatigue, I plastered on a radiant smile: No problem! It was time to make everyone forget about my shower of shame. When I arrived at my dressing room, I was pleasantly surprised to find that the journalist was exactly my type. His name was Vikram, though everyone called him Vik; he had a charming English accent, big hands, a friendship bracelet. We couldn't take our eyes off each other; I'd eat that guy for lunch. I got his number as I left.

Finally, I closed the door of my hotel room behind me, exhausted from all the commotion. I was alone for the first time since the morning. Most celebrities grow up in big families, and it's true that the lifestyle of a star isn't compatible with the solitude you're used to when you're an only child. As I brushed my teeth, I thought of Céline Dion, who had thirteen siblings.

I should have just given in and *put clothes on dry skin*, dealt with it, kept my fatigue hidden; punishment awaited me, and I was the only one who could inflict it upon myself. I took a belt out of my suitcase.

I had to prove to my team that I was up to the task, show them that I was capable of withstanding such a high level of pressure. The kind of career I aspired to was about more than just music and talent. It required endurance. I looked at my reflection in the mirror. *Okay, baby, it's time to prove yourself. Everyone's watching.*

On my nightstand, my phone didn't display any new messages. I picked it up and dialed.

"Hi, Mom?"

"Hello, sweetheart."

"Why don't you call me more often? For once we're almost in the same time zone."

"I'm afraid of bothering you. I know you're very busy."

The paradox was so devastating, I could feel it in my throat. I had just sung in front of five thousand people, but I didn't have anyone to talk to before going to sleep. And during my tour, my packed concert halls overflowing with love would never keep me from crying myself to sleep alone at night.

The next evening, I invited the cute little journalist to join me at the bar of my hotel. Before he arrived, I informed the bartender that I didn't want any alcohol in my cocktails, but that I needed his discretion on this point. I planned to ply my new friend with drinks while staying sober myself.

Two hours later, Vik's eyes were glassy, and I asked him to come to my suite. When the elevator doors opened for us to enter, I announced the schedule: "We'll go up, and I'll undress you."

I wanted him, very badly. He couldn't walk straight. I took off his clothes, and he let me do it, deliciously drunk. As a bonus, he was impressed by my alcohol tolerance: "How many drinks did you have? You hold your liquor better than I do. . . ."

Everything about him enticed and seduced me. His eyebrows, his pecs, even his feet—all looked like they belonged to a Greek god. His defined muscles, sculpted arms, powerful abs. Vik was a journalist, but his body was that of a personal trainer. Or maybe a windsurfing instructor (who else wore friendship bracelets after the age of thirty?). His English accent and anonymity only added to the allure. I felt like I was acting out *Notting Hill*. Too bad he wasn't a bookseller.

I pulled his boxers down to the ground before getting on top of him. It was so good to release the pressure. The effect was immediate; it relaxed my muscles, released endorphins in my brain, regulated my blood pressure, reduced the lactic acid in my legs. According to my smartwatch, fifteen minutes of sex with Vik was equivalent to fifty minutes of yoga. Miraculous and efficient.

Underneath me, Vik couldn't get over the fact that he was inside Cléo Louvent. It wasn't the beauty mark on my shoulder blade that was turning him on, it was my fame. I put a pillow over his face and pretended he was John Cutler instead—because I was surprised to find myself thinking about him often, looking him up online, fantasizing about his freckles, and because it would be strategically smarter to sleep with John Cutler than with a stranger. The superposition was so pleasurable, it was dizzying. It's morally questionable to think about someone else during penetration, but who can claim they've never done it? I came and then climbed off him. All there was left for me to do was pay for his taxi home.

In two days, I would play a show in Glasgow. My assistant would reserve a plane ticket for Vik. I really needed to relax.

When he was sober, Vik was an extraordinary lover. His palm slid over my body like a bar of wet soap, gliding easily over my breasts, stomach, and pussy. Rolling across the bed, he opened a box of condoms and busied his hands between his legs with focused precision. My mouth was watering, as though I were watching a waiter arrive with our plates. Sometimes people say that putting on a condom ruins the moment, but personally, I took pleasure in the interruption: It gave me a minute to savor the imminence of the act, sixty seconds to grasp the exact moment when our kisses would lead to penetration. Vik looked up. He was ready. It was time.

I fell asleep around 2:00 a.m., but he woke me up with kisses an hour later. "I'm not going to let you sleep all night . . ." he warned, then spread my legs and disappeared beneath the sheets.

We made love. We really *made* it. Seven hours of physical labor, working on each other's bodies. We both assumed an active role, applied ourselves to the task, took it seriously—no rushing. With my fingers in his mouth and his fingers in mine, Vik looked me right in the eyes, and I wished it would never end.

I got up several times during the night to eat; we had to take breaks to keep our energy up. At our feet were six or seven empty bottles of water, our fuel while Vik introduced me to new earthly pleasures.

"You're tireless."

"I can adapt," he replied, flipping me over on the mattress.

The next morning, I was rattled by the soreness in my thighs, glutes, and abs—deep muscles that my Pilates sessions had never required. I struggled to walk, limping slightly; my cheeks were rubbed raw from the friction of his beard, my lips chapped. My tangled hair was tied up in a ponytail, forming one big, messy knot. My hairdresser was going to pass out.

Vik adapted to my schedule, took time off from his own job, organized his life around mine; it was impossible to imagine it working any other way. He was like a sailor's wife, patiently waiting in my hotel room while I attended to all my duties. Fortunately, my next destinations were nearby: Dublin, Brussels, Amsterdam, Cologne, Berlin, Copenhagen.

As soon as I felt like seeing him, all I had to do was tell my assistant to bring him over. While I was at it, I asked Vik to take naked selfies for me. Obviously, I didn't reciprocate; it was unthinkable for me to assume such a risk. Vik submitted to my desires, sending me everything I requested, accompanied by explicit messages outlining the plan for the night. A thrill ran through my body hours before he would even touch it with his tongue.

Vik, meanwhile, trembled whenever there was too long of a silence between us. He was afraid of saying or doing something that would cause me to leave him forever. He walked on eggshells, terrified at the thought of my telling him that it was over. But he had no reason to fear. I was feeling good. With him, the balance was easy to find: 99% for me, 1% for him.

All day everyone touched me. They touched me when they were applying my makeup. They touched me when they were doing my hair. They touched me when they were painting my nails. They touched me when they were massaging my sore wrist. They touched me when they were stretching my back. They touched me when they were helping me put on my costume.

Onstage I wore a custom catsuit created by a renowned designer, a tight-fitting, opaque nylon one-piece with geometric cut-outs that remodeled my figure. Basically, my ass had never looked so good. The only problem was that I could neither put it on nor take it off alone. Three people were required to dress and undress the queen.

Backstage the team repeatedly told me the name of the city where we were that night, a new ritual I valued. "Dallas, Texas." "We're in Dallas." "Welcome to Dallas." I drank one last sip of water, ignoring the applause that I could already hear. I had to commit to memory the one piece of information I needed to be certain of before going onstage: I was in Dallas. *Okay, Cléo, don't shout "Hello, Houston" or "Bonsoir, Perpignan."*

I made a triumphant entrance, followed by five dancers, three backup singers, and a ray of blinding light. As I started the second song, I pretended to forget the lyrics. Bursting out laughing, I started over from the beginning. The audience was entranced—they went crazy for these moments of realness. "Cléo Louvent made a mistake, she's human, this performance is totally unique." I finished the track with a knowing wink at the crowd.

And then, inexplicably, the rest of the concert slipped from my grasp. The strap of my leotard snapped; this time I hadn't done it on purpose to elicit a sense of complicity from the audience. During the next song, I couldn't hear myself well enough in my in-ear monitor, and, even worse, I was distracted by one of my backup singers, who was too loud. Did I have to remind her that she was only there to enhance the sound of my voice? For this ballad, what I needed was to be surrounded by soft vibrations, not the piercing sound of a bugle. I turned around and she smiled stupidly, carefree and joyful. Between songs I ordered her to shut up. She wasn't the one the fans had come to see; my concert was not the time or place for her to launch her solo career.

I stormed offstage. Sometimes saying nothing is more brutal than shouting, so I stalked through the hallway in glacial silence, poison emanating from me in waves. No one dared utter a word.

In my dressing room I was simmering with rage, holding my hand over my mouth to stifle a scream. Unfortunately, Stefani had the wrong impulse, which was to try to comfort me.

"You're tired. Performing four nights in a row is intense . . . but I promise, you were great," my manager said soothingly.

"Obviously I was great. It's the others who weren't doing their jobs."

"That's not true—it went very well."

"You didn't see what happened onstage. I had to compensate for everyone else's mistakes."

"No one could tell."

"That's not the point. You're asking a lot of me without giving me the right support. I can't work in conditions like that."

"Okay, I'm going to let you rest. I'll come find you in fifteen minutes."

Stefani was treating me like she treated her three-year-old daughter, giving me a time-out in my room for as long as it took for me to calm down. But her punishment had the opposite effect. Anger clouded my vision until I could see only red, and I couldn't contain myself any longer. I was livid. Stefani didn't live my life; what made her think she could lecture me? She wasn't the one going onstage. She had an easy job, sheltered and comfortable in the wings. Should I remind her who was the one paying her salary every month? Why were people so disappointing? My manager, my costume designer, my sound engineer, my backup singer: Was I the only competent one in the whole country? Music may not attract top-tier talent, but couldn't we find some professionals who met the standards of what I wanted to offer the public? I was surrounded by mediocre *employees*: For them, it was a job; for me, it was my life. Not everyone in my orchestra was a first violin, and the fact that they were bringing us all down was unbearable. If I were trained for just half an hour in each of their duties, I'd be better and more effective than them, would achieve better results. If only I could multiply myself, create an army of Cléos to fill every position.

Vik was waiting for me in my hotel room. He'd taken a week off to join me in Dallas.

"You were incredible tonight . . ." he began.

"Shut up."

I took a shower to calm down, taking the opportunity to self-mutilate. This time I chose my kneecap to punish myself for having failed so miserably. *I hate myself.*

A half hour later, I came out of the bathroom, my knee disinfected and bandaged. Vik knew, my whole team knew, but no one said anything. As long as I stayed functional and performed well at each concert, they turned a blind eye.

Vik was sitting on the bed, looking sheepish. He had to excuse my bad mood—I was under insane pressure, and it was nothing to take personally; I just had to decompress when I left the stage. My lover understood and forgave me. He told me about his day, then his week, describing emphatically his latest argument with his boss, the unfair workload distribution at his office, the scandal of unpaid overtime, his desire to quit.

"What do you think?" he asked me.

"I don't think anything, Vik."

" . . ."

"You should do whatever you want."

If he wanted to quit his job because he was fed up with it, then fine. What did it matter for anyone else? I was considering canceling three concerts at the end of the month because my vocal cords were raw and my doctor had prescribed rest. Just imagine the millions of dollars in insurance claims, thirteen thousand would-be concertgoers asking to be reimbursed—and that's not to mention the headache of rescheduling for later dates. How could I not feel that, in comparison, Vik's problems were less important? How could I not find his concerns trivial? Did the famous Anna Scott think the same thing whenever Will complained about his bookstore's financial troubles? Had Julia Roberts and Hugh Grant lied to us?

Vik continued to hold forth on topics that interested only him. I watched him, my chin lowered and eyebrow raised, exasperated. *You haven't done anything. You're a nobody.*

The next day, I was in Houston. Then in Austin, Denver, Salt Lake City, Phoenix, San Diego, Los Angeles, San Francisco, Portland, Seattle, Vancouver. Later in the year, I fell asleep in ritzy hotel rooms in Osaka, Chiba, Tel Aviv, Hanoi, Brisbane, and Auckland.

One day I woke up without having any idea if I'd slept two hours or twelve. I squinted my eyes halfway open, disoriented. Underneath my head, the pillowcase was embroidered with my initials.

Fame is soft to the touch. The memory of my ascension will always be associated for me with the padded comfort of plushy fabrics: cozy goose-down duvets, Egyptian combed cotton sheets, thick towels in hotel bathrooms, fluffy bathrobes, velvet slippers at the foot of the bed, silk negligees—and, of course, my cashmere pajama set, the most pleasant wearable invention since the sleep sack.

I walked around my room. A walnut fireplace, decorative wood paneling on the ceiling, a leather couch with tufted cushions. There were three chocolates on my bedside table and a glass bottle of water. The bath mat was laid out in front of the freestanding tub. In the entryway was a handwritten welcome note from the manager that I ignored, though surely it was charming and personalized. By this point, I didn't even know which country I was in.

Opening the thick velvet curtains, I discovered a terrace overlooking the garden below. In the distance, the mountains were bathed in a feeble, hazy golden light. I stayed still for a moment, trembling. Was the sun rising or setting? Was I looking at the first rays of daylight or the last? Looking at a landscape and not knowing whether it was dawn or dusk was an astounding experience, the most intense disorientation imaginable.

I found a charger in one of my bags. As I waited for my phone to turn back on, I kept looking out at the view from the terrace. The unplaceable light was heart-wrenching. A few minutes later, the blue GPS dot on my phone indicated I was in Bogotá. It was 5:50 a.m. Daybreak.

I have no memories from Colombia. Nor do I have any memories from Chile, Brazil, or Argentina. I can't even tell you if I went to Paraguay. Did I sing at outdoor festivals or in intimate concert venues? Did I give three concerts or eighteen? Was the audience shy or excited? Did I participate in interviews with local media? Did I go on television? Did Vik visit me? I have no idea. I passed through those countries without registering even the slightest feeling; the only traces that remained were the gashes I inflicted upon myself after every mistake. And then I continued my world tour—vacant, withered, not really there at all.

When I left the stage in Saint Petersburg, I had a sudden desire to talk to Vik. Luckily, he picked up on the first ring.

"Vik, I'd prefer if we stopped seeing each other."

"Well, hello, Cléo."

"Yes, I'm sorry, hello."

"You want to stop seeing each other, and you're telling me this over the phone?"

"What, did you think I was going to teleport to London to tell you?"

"When did you decide on this?"

"Five minutes ago."

"Oh, thank you for not waiting to give me the good news."

"Are you being sarcastic?"

"You think?"

"So you'd rather I take six months to tell you? I've made my decision, and now we can move on to other things. You can always come to see me from time to time."

"..."

"Anyway, are things any better at work now?"

I like to declutter my relationships the same way I do my closet: without waffling. I throw things away, I donate them, I empty it all out. No regrets.

Vik was an excellent lover, but it was impossible to bridge the gap between us. I couldn't fall for someone who wasn't famous;

we would never live on the same planet. My kind journalist was sexy, but he bored me to tears and, more importantly, I didn't admire him enough to ever hope to love him one day. Also, I didn't like how cheap he was. When he stayed over at night, he always brought his toothbrush, but never his toothpaste. It was a stingy move. I was infinitely richer than he was: I was fine with paying for his plane tickets, the taxi from the airport, the room service. But I felt like he could have brought his own toothpaste.

"Okay, Vik, I have to go. I've got errands to run."

A private plane was waiting to take me to New York. I was taking advantage of a break before the end of my tour to spend three days in Manhattan. I had an apartment to buy.

Stefani had put me in touch with a real estate agent who specialized in working with "clients of my type." I realized what the expression meant during my first tour: a three-million-dollar penthouse with a brick ceiling, roof terrace, and Jacuzzi. Not my style. Or, for the same price, I could buy myself a family home in Brooklyn with three bedrooms, four bathrooms, a fireplace, and a yard. Equally wrong; I dragged my feet as I walked around the property.

The agent put her last card on the table with a more reasonable proposition: a two-million-dollar apartment in Chelsea with a view of the High Line. Better, and yet still not right.

"It seems like you can't see yourself here, Ms. Louvent," the agent said.

No kidding. I'd been living in hotel rooms for months, and I needed a place of my own where I could drop anchor. But I could not imagine myself munching on cereal in that kitchen, throwing a crêpes party in that dining room, sobbing all the tears out of my body in that marble shower. That wasn't to say that I didn't still want to live in the top .00001% of luxury, but now that I was well on my way there, I needed some time to adapt. When you'd earned as much money in two years as I had, how much was reasonable to spend on an apartment? Half? A third? A quarter? It was explained to me that properties upward of two million dollars were the best investments, that I should be careful not to buy *too low*. But in truth, I wasn't familiar with these new orders of grandeur, and I still feared that my precious millions would disappear. I was learning to be famous, but I was also learning to be rich and discovering that wealth did not always come with a feeling of abundance.

Besides, I wasn't rich: *I had made a fortune.* The money I'd earned from my music was nothing like the salary that I'd received as a bookseller or from giving piano lessons. We weren't talking about building a nest egg by sensibly setting aside a small sum each month: These were astronomical amounts sent to a bank account every so often on random Tuesday evenings. I felt like I had stumbled upon a gold mine—enchanted, but anxious to know how long I would be able to draw a profit.

I was offered life insurance, investments, and financing packages; I surrounded myself with lawyers, fund managers, wealth optimization experts. I thought about the soccer players swindled by shady advisors and the pop stars regularly pursued by the IRS. So I fumbled my way along, even considering calling Celeste's parents to ask them for tips. At first, my instinct was to live *below* my means. Relatively speaking, my lifestyle wasn't particularly imperial. Now was the time to earn money, not to spend it. And I was making my first paid appearances, at parties and for brands: The fees were staggering, and I let myself be bought, ready to play the marketing game. At the end of May, I made a killing when one of my songs was used as an ad for a next-generation dishwasher in Japan—elegant, silent, connected, with a heat-exchanger drying system and an illuminated floor display. I left a little bit of my dignity behind, but I cashed a fat check.

Finally, at the end of my long weekend in New York, I decided to rent an insane apartment on Airbnb for the next six months. Two floors, a sculptural staircase, concrete columns, skylights, designer furniture. I fell for the oversized sofa and bronze coffee table. The rent was unreasonable; it would have been much better for me to invest the money instead. The fear of misplacing it led me to simply throw it out the window. And that right there was real luxury.

Barefoot, wearing only underwear, my hair tangled, my eyes half-closed, I dragged myself to the kitchen. It was 4:00 p.m. I didn't feel like I was waking up after a good night's sleep; instead, it was as if someone had knocked me out—a sharp blow to the back of my head, then complete darkness. The stench of my armpits followed me, putrid and foul. I hadn't showered in five days.

My first world tour was over. Despite my earlier idea to call off three shows for vocal rest, I hadn't canceled a single show. Incredulous, I repeated this to myself in a low voice several times, illuminated by the light of my fridge: "I didn't cancel a single show, I didn't cancel a single show, I didn't cancel a single show. . . ." Fuck, I was as proud as if I had survived a plane crash, a bear attack, a game of Russian roulette.

In the microwave was a plate ready for me to reheat—a white truffle risotto prepared by my private chef. My assistant was the one who found Matteo, a Venetian man with green eyes. They both had a list of the 75 foods that caused me to bloat and the 42 ingredients that were inadvisable for my vocal cords, and they created the menus accordingly. I'd made sure that I didn't have to make any more decisions about how to feed myself, even though tonight I might have preferred macaroni with ham.

I left the remains of my food on the kitchen table and headed back to bed. In the hallway, I crossed paths with my cleaning lady.

Surprised, I froze for a second before deciding to continue on as though nothing had happened. Contractually, she didn't have the right to address me if I didn't speak to her first. I walked by her, ignoring her completely, without bothering to cover my bare chest. At least I didn't have to worry about my pathetic appearance; her phone had been taken away at the entrance to the apartment.

The early days of my fame were inextricably linked to a profound transformation in my domestic life. My time was precious, and I could no longer spend it cleaning my own shower, choosing my own clothes, or cooking my own rice.

My greatest revolution was named Rachel. As my personal assistant, she was an extension of myself. Every day she busied herself in my shadow, her little hands carrying everything out on my behalf. When I'd returned to New York a week earlier, she had unpacked my suitcases. The night before my arrival, *someone other than me* had emptied my toiletry bag, lined up my shoes, dropped my clothes off at the dry cleaning, stowed away my luggage, and hung my clean blouses up in the closet.

Unlike most celebrities I've encountered, I refused to ask a childhood friend or a cousin to be my assistant. The system I put in place was unequivocal: I hired a professional; she signed a contract for one or two years; at the end of it, I found a new one. The position was a learning opportunity—and an excessively well-paid one—but it was for a limited period of time. I didn't want for us to become friends, for her to get too comfortable hanging out in my apartment, or for her to nurture ambitions she couldn't fulfill by working for me. I was looking for a personal assistant, not a future songwriter or artistic director. There was *no* room for growth. My assistant could not be drinking mojitos with me at 3:00 p.m. and then sorting my socks by color at 4:00 p.m. Everyone needed to stay in their place.

With my domestic staff came new obsessive fears: that my dirty underwear would end up on the cover of a tabloid, that details of my private life would come out via an anonymous Twitter account. Or, worse, that a journalist would disguise themselves as an assistant so that they could write a juicy book about me. I needed custom-made armor, so I suited up with NDAs. Everyone swore by them. I enlisted Leonardo DiCaprio's lawyer, the very best, to draft the contracts for everyone I hired. They weren't allowed to talk about anything they saw at my place, not today, not two thousand years from now. Their silence was golden, and I knew its exact price.

If I'd been aware then that five years later, I'd shell out for the most expensive vacation of my life so that I could be alone on a desert island . . . How could I have predicted that my greatest desire would be to cook an omelet myself in a kitchen without running water? And yet hadn't I already vaguely sensed that I might end up missing those daily tasks when I'd argued with my mother about unloading the dishwasher? Without those trivial little chores, reality could seem so far away.

I gave myself ten days to recover. So I slept for five more hours. I drank two glasses of water. I slept for six more hours. I ate some pasta salad. I slept for seven more hours. I heated up some soup. I had never slept so much.

I sniffed my underarm; the smell of sweat was repulsive. It was time to take a shower and scrub myself with soap. Tonight I had a date with the love of my life.

had a date with the love of my life, and there was just one detail left to figure out: He didn't know that he had a date with me.

There's a concept in ancient Greek that I'm very fond of. καιρός. Kairos. You can translate it as "the right moment to act." When the stars align and it's time to forge ahead. It's the only thing success is made of: kairos galore.

Tonight my kairos was named John Cutler. He was single for the first time in years and in New York for a week. I spotted him sitting at a table in the back of the room, underneath one of the ten Baccarat crystal chandeliers. My sources were well-informed; John was indeed attending this dinner, which was a fundraiser for ocean protection. Thank you, coral reefs; thank you, whales. My big fish was right in front of me.

In Greek mythology, kairos is represented by a little winged god of opportunity. I pictured that figure flying over the room now, circling us—mischievous, chubby, impish. When that figure came near me, I reached out and grabbed him by the hair. It was time to take action.

"John! What are you doing here? It's so crazy to run into you. . . ."

John was just as I'd remembered him: kind, sweet, attentive. As though he were a fuzzy little chick, newly hatched. I touched my bangs nervously and did everything I could to make him like me. After the dinner, he invited me back to his place. Bingo.

Vaulted-ceilinged living room with a view of Central Park, two glasses of wine, my stilettos on the polished concrete. The apartment wasn't his; a filmmaker he knew was letting him stay there. The posters for his friend's films lined the hallway, and four Oscars served as the legs of a low glass table—you had to see it to believe it. On the wall, the masterpieces weren't reproductions. *What's up, Picasso. Hey, Frida Kahlo.*

John suggested I join him on the couch. We talked for a long time, passionately, carried away by a thousand different conversation topics. I asked him about his latest song, which was brilliant and effective; I had a hard time hiding how much I liked it. John opened up easily, without ulterior motive or equivocation. His sweetness was mind-blowing to me. His innocent blue eyes, his strawberry blond hair. He was humble, honest, gentle, simple, balanced. How had he survived more than fifteen seconds in showbiz without being devoured by wolves?

As we talked, a phrase kept coming to mind, one that would later serve as the chorus for the first song I wrote about him: He was *untouched.* John had been famous since he was a kid, and yet it seemed fame had left him unscathed. He made me think of an antique vase—you always have to wonder how a thousand-year-old artifact could have lasted so long without being damaged, how it preserved its color, resisted the elements, survived lootings. I stared at his arms, his freckles, his transparent skin. *John, sweetheart, surely you're not going to tell me that you have no cracks?*

John asked me questions in return about my own journey; he was impressed when I told him that I'd been a bookseller, attended prestigious schools, come from a family of academics. "You must be so smart," he marveled. "I wish I read more. Don't tell anyone, but I have a tutor who gives me gen ed lessons once a week." Had John recognized the Magritte we were sitting under?

John could flirt with anyone on earth and seduce the most beautiful women in the world, but I sensed that he was attracted to my frankness, my ego, my culture. To him I was coming across as blunt, funny, wild, talented, cerebral. And I was no longer the infinitely-lesser-known neophyte he'd met a year ago. Now I was the rising star who had brought part of the music industry to its knees.

Did I actually like John, or was I attracted to how famous he was? The pairing of our names would give me an incredible media narrative, an unparalleled strike force. Next to him, I would climb to a whole new level of celebrity. Was I in love, or was I cynical? I could debate the question for hours and end up at the same aporia: John and his fame were inseparable.

Try falling in love with Madonna, with Kylian Mbappé—or even with me. Imagine, for a moment, that you're at a candlelit dinner with one of us. It would be impossible—and stupid—to ignore the fact that we're well-known, but that wouldn't prevent you from falling under the charms of our personalities. You can't dissociate a star from their fame. The subtraction will always be an impossible operation.

I was surprised to find that on the coffee table were several packs of neon-yellow chick-shaped marshmallows covered in thin layers of sugar. John explained to me that these treats—Peeps— were his favorite. Such innocence.

"John, you are a pure heart."

"What do you mean?"

"You are a pure heart."

"And what are you?"

"A brat."

Suddenly John grew quiet. I wanted to do it right; I wanted to do it with him. I leaned over to kiss him. Kairos, again and again. His lips still tasted like sugar.

We spent the rest of the evening making out on the couch like high schoolers, John caressing me through my clothes. Obviously, I was a hundred times more turned on than if he had put me on all fours. He wasn't inventing anything new; dallying is more erotic than doing.

To move things along, I began to unbutton my dress, but John stopped me. "Let's take it slowly. . . ."

What had gotten into him? He hadn't invited me over for a game of Basque pelota or to start a book club.

"I'd prefer if we took our time," John murmured.

"Yes, of course, I understand."

No, I didn't understand. I was there to go down on him, not to solve differential equations. Why was he refusing to go any further? Maybe John had a genital deformity. Erectile dysfunction. Perhaps he'd gotten back with his ex, Lily Clayton. Or else he had unusual sexual preferences: BDSM, scatology, exhibitionism, fetishism . . . some kink that was too revealing to bring up the first night (and without signing a 450-page NDA). I stroked him through his pants; his cock was hard and seemingly normal-sized, with all parts of the Holy Trinity present and accounted for. I kissed his neck, and he lifted his eyes to the heavens. To heaven. Was he too afraid of God to sleep with me outside of marriage? I always forgot that puritanical America never had sex on the first date.

"Cléo, don't push it, please," John said firmly.

Shit. Shit. Shit. What had I done?

I got up off the couch. "Well, I'm going to head out. . . ."

John didn't try to prevent me from leaving. He walked me to the door, kissed me on the cheek, and helped me into my coat, promising to call me before he returned to Los Angeles in two days.

I was a fucking idiot. In wanting to move too fast, I'd forgotten my manners. In the elevator, I slipped my hand into my underwear. I was bitter and hurt, but I hated not finishing what I'd started.

My shoulders were covered with a shawl, and I wore an ebony-black dress—mourning attire, fit for a widow. I'd debated wearing a hat and a black veil.

The name of the Best New Artist was in the envelope. Olivia Grace. *Oh no, not her.* I announced it into the microphone as though I couldn't be happier. Applause; Olivia took the stage. I paused for a second before handing her the award and stepping back into the shadows. She was now holding in her hands the same prize I'd received the previous year.

It was outrageous to expect me to attend the crowning of my replacement. Do they ask you to congratulate your ex's new girlfriend? But I didn't have a choice; tradition dictated that the previous winner be the one to present the trophy. *Look: Here's the new model! Soon you will be obsolete.*

Olivia Grace seemed to be searching for the microphone, disoriented, as though she had no idea what was happening. I didn't believe it for a second. Behind her lost-doe-in-the-forest look, I could sense her satisfied smile. She was so pleased with herself. *Keep singing, Olivia Grace, because you're a terrible actress.*

Everything about her annoyed me. Her unbearable conceitedness. Her grotesque apple-green dress. Her large torso. Her rodent-like face. Her purity ring proclaiming that she wouldn't lose her virtue before marriage. Her faux-ingenue way of looking at you. Her feigned clumsiness. Her exaggerated naivete. *Sweetie, the child-woman thing won't work forever.*

The music industry was a slave to youth; they loved female singers, and they especially loved to rob the cradle for them. In interviews Olivia Grace always specified her age, even when nobody asked her. Insolent child. She'd throw out the number as though she were spitting an insult in your face: I knew this because she'd always pause briefly afterward to give the other person time to react. "You're only eighteen—how impressive!" *Shut up, Olivia. With two actors for parents, of course you became famous quickly.* A well-known last name slapped onto songs you didn't write, a voice corrected by auto-tune, zero original artistic vision. *I have no respect for you.*

The audience listened to her in silence—I wondered if any of them were fooled. Holding the trophy to her heart, Olivia reeled off a string of bombastic absurdities: "Thank you to my fans, for allowing me to be the best version of myself." *Well, now we'd heard it all.*

My management had been encouraging me for weeks to collaborate with her; we were at the same label, had signed the same contract, had made a pact with the same sea witch. But I would have rather put a bullet through my head. Anyway, then what? Did she want me to write her second album for her too?

During the party that followed the ceremony, I made sure to pull Olivia to one side to inform her about the Best New Artist curse. The prize recognizes the music industry's *brightest hope*, the most promising artist of the year, but legend has it that the trophy brings bad luck. Musicians whose careers were in full swing had failed to do anything else after receiving the coveted miniature gramophone. As a friend, I wanted to warn her.

"*You know, another* person's success doesn't take away from your own," preached Stefani when we were in the car heading back to the hotel.

I found this hard to believe. My manager knew better than anyone that this industry was a zero-sum game. When one player wins, the other loses. But obviously, I denied it flat out.

"Are you kidding me? I'm so happy for Olivia Grace. I love her."

"You do?"

"Of course. Her latest song is great. What's it called again?"

Stefani smiled. I was saying the right things but making no effort to hide that they were completely insincere; the melody had been stuck in my head for weeks. Anyway, why wasn't I the one who had written it? Really—why hadn't I come up with the idea first?

Once I was alone, I listened to the entirety of Olivia's album. Once, twice, three times, thirty times. It really wasn't bad. Honestly, it was excellent. Effective, innovative, catchy. I made thirteen gashes on my thighs: one for each of my replacement's songs.

A week later, I started a rumor that Olivia had made advances toward me; on the night of the awards ceremony, she'd suggested a threesome. It spread like wildfire. *A seductress, a libertine, a vixen*, people whispered. *She sleeps with everyone, even women.* Everyone loves a young virgin, preferably a demure one, so I'd gone for her most precious asset: her purity.

Every year female singers who looked like me turned eighteen. Every month new musicians were discovered and signed. Every week the media heralded the arrival of new talent. Every day new songs hit the top of the charts.

I hadn't written anything of substance since the release of my first album. Meanwhile, the music industry wasn't standing still. And no one was waiting for me.

No accomplishment was irrevocable, and no defeat was definitive. The it singer of the moment could fall into oblivion with their next album; the artist who had just failed could make a glorious comeback three years later. I had no choice but to get back into the ring and defend my title.

I hadn't envisioned beyond my first album, convinced that that was the hardest part. But now I was thinking about all the one-hit wonders through the decades, all the singers forgotten as time marched on. Keeping my spot was going to be even more difficult than getting it in the first place.

I was promised free time after my tour. And yet with all the fittings, the photo shoots, the dinners, the society events, the red carpets, the trips abroad, the brand collaborations as time-consuming as they were lucrative—the pace wasn't slowing. In truth, the requests were endless, in accordance with one major principle: *Strike while the iron is hot.*

How was I supposed to create when I was so busy? I hadn't released a new song in almost two years; why was I the only one to see that this was an eternity?

My alarm went off at 5:00 a.m. I woke up in a hotel room in Dubai, a six-star skyscraper on an artificial island off the coast. Tonight I would be paid $50,000 in cash to make an appearance at a dinner alongside the royal family. At 7:00 p.m. I was supposed to be on the roof of the Burj Al Arab, 689 feet aboveground, where a helicopter would be waiting for me.

I took advantage of the early morning to search for inspiration, work on a tune on the guitar, compose a first verse. But it had been the same story for months: I was never happy with the result, starting dozens of songs without ever finishing one. And the free time was over in an instant. It was already 7:00 a.m., and my phone was vibrating—my assistant calling from the room next door to go over my schedule for the day.

"Carmen, could we cancel a few things today?"

"No, unfortunately, I checked with Nikki and we've already cut it back to the essentials."

For weeks the head of my label had been dismissing my worries with a simple shrug: "You can't write any songs? No worries, we'll find someone! I know some great songwriters." But I still refused to play by those rules: There was no way I was going to be replaced in the studio while I played ditz for the photographers.

I put my phone on speaker and let my assistant continue talking while I paced around looking for a way out. No one seemed to understand that I couldn't keep enjoying the banquet, basking in my good fortune, making appearances, pleasing everyone. I wouldn't make the mistake of coasting off the success of my first album for three years without preparing for what was to come. One morning I would wake up and people would have moved on; my empire would have fallen, and I'd find myself without anything left. *Cléo Louvent, no one is going to get you out of here. Remember, no one came to find you and hold your hand for the first album. You're a big girl, sweetheart. What do we do when we have a problem? We figure it out all by ourselves.*

I needed to use my brain. I needed everything to stop. I looked out the window. The height. The drop. I found it. The solution could be found somewhere between my knee and my heel.

I stood on a chair and jumped off, but the garish carpet cushioned my fall. I tried again a second time, then a third, in vain. I kept catching myself—impossible to bypass the reflex.

"Is everything okay, Cléo? I hear something in the background."

"Hold on a minute, Carmen, I'll call you back."

Sitting cross-legged on the bed, I scrolled through YouTube. Perfect—a compilation of the worst injuries in the history of soccer. Four minutes of twisted ankles and feet facing the wrong ways. Each of the accidents shared one point of similarity: the angle. Sketching a quick diagram in my notebook helped me understand the torsion: According to my research, what I wanted was to injure the lateral collateral ligament. Even better if the ligament were to tear off a small piece of bone along with it. That would guarantee a cast. I could do it.

Standing on a chair, I jumped with my foot turned inward, but once again the damn reflex saved me at the last moment, and my attempt fell flat. I needed to make sure not to catch myself with my arms—I had to be able to play the guitar and piano—so I somehow managed to tie my wrists behind my back with a scarf before climbing back onto the chair. I was eighteen inches off the ground, high enough; the important thing was to get the angle right. Why wasn't it working? I climbed up and jumped once more, twice more, five times more. On the sixth, I heard the snap. The pain took me by surprise—sharp, red, stabbing. A little giggle of shock bubbled up from somewhere inside me. Holy shit, I'd done it.

A minute later, the pain was gone. Adrenaline, I guessed. I sat for a while watching my ankle swell up.

Finally, I called Carmen back. "Hi, Carmen, I think we have a bit of a problem."

"What happened?"

"I fell."

My sprained ankle cleared my calendar efficiently. The cherry on top: People felt sorry for me and hoped I'd get better soon. I could lock myself up and write my second album. Problem solved.

I artificially recreated the conditions under which I'd written my first songs: alone in only my underwear in an apartment in New York with a piano and a guitar. I wasn't sensitive to cold, and it seemed like inspiration struck when my breasts could get some fresh air. I settled in to tweeze my uninjured leg; nothing helped me concentrate like focusing on a single hair. But as I approached my calf, I realized that ever since my laser appointments, I had no more hair to pluck. People often talk about regretting tattoos afterward, but no one ever talks about regretting permanent hair removal.

The doorbell rang. A delivery person handed me a bouquet of flowers and a card from John; he'd learned of my accident and hoped I was doing better. It was the first I'd heard from him since that New York night I would have rather forgotten. I stayed silent for a long time, holding the peonies in my arms. I wasn't sure I owned a vase.

My second album was born in the contingency of rainy March afternoons, my mood, my ankle injury—and an intense craving for gnocchi and grated carrots. I hopped around on one foot from the kitchen to the bathroom, from the bed to the couch. I hadn't been so happy in months.

For me there was no freedom to be found in the trips, the dinners, the outings, the appointments. It was in the stillness. I finally stopped leaving bits and pieces of myself everywhere. It was an incomparable joy.

My only companion was a two-thousand-piece puzzle of the northern lights over the Lofoten Islands. I'd found a new way to occupy my hands and empty my brain—a substitute for the tweezers. I sorted the pieces while thinking about ideas for songs. What did I have to say? I kept a notebook close by and frequently abandoned the Norwegian landscape to add to a list of my current fears, remembering that my anxieties were often an effective starting place:

disappointing people, missing the boat, shooting myself in the foot, self-sabotaging, wallowing, being incapable of producing another success. I'd had my fifteen minutes of fame; what if it didn't last? I thought about all the shooting stars who'd been forgotten: "Hey, you never see that actor anywhere. He totally went under the radar." "Hey, that singer isn't doing anything anymore." I finished my inventory, knowing that my bogeymen would bring my future songs to life: *beginner's luck, dashed hopes, a flash in the pan.*

I circled my subject for hours before seizing it: hope. I had the title and the theme of my first song. Hope, which I no longer considered a cheerful idea. How could I have confused hope with success for so long? Hope was a possibility, not a certainty. Soccer clubs in France had *pôles espoirs*, hope hubs—training academies for the most promising young players—but by definition, not all of the hopefuls would become champions. Hope always comes with a cemetery of broken dreams.

I followed the same formula as I did with the first album: I talked about myself but blurred the details to make it universally relatable. In my song about hope, I referenced my music career, but you could also hear it as a tale of thwarted love. The beginnings were glorious, but what if we didn't make it?

Every night before going to bed, I listened carefully to my first album, fighting with all my strength against the demon of idealization. I focused on each song: The twelve tracks that had brought me international success weren't insurmountable. I wouldn't have any problem doing better; I was at only 10% of my capacity.

But beyond capacity was guts. My rival was a version of myself who had disappeared, anonymous and aggressive; who better to succeed? Yet from now on, I had to write from the comfort of success—and the height of a pedestal wasn't an easy one from which to write songs. I'd set the bar so high; tripping over it now would be extremely painful. Each past success meant potential future pain if I couldn't replicate it. I had everything to lose; what was there still to gain?

The puzzle pieces scattered at my feet, I listened to my first album while noting down all of its flaws, telling myself over and over that it was overrated until I came to believe it. It wasn't particularly good. And I was like a fine wine; I could only get better with age—right?

Since childhood I'd thought that my greatest joys were in the future, not the past. I was the opposite of nostalgic, a futurist of happiness. It was impossible for me to believe that my biggest success was behind me. The best was yet to come. Always.

When you've sold this many records, people consider you part of the *system*. They imagine complex games of influence, money, and power, that there's some kind of secret committee working behind the scenes to determine the music of the future. Everything, they assume, is rigged, calculated, planned: Global superstars are just puppets in the hands of the powerful. In fact, that's my critics' favorite insult. On the internet they say I'm an industry plant, created by my label and foisted on the public via millions of marketing dollars.

I was the first to think it, and the first to be surprised. Even at the highest level, even on an industrial scale, creation is artisanal. Even with twenty-five people paid to write bland tracks for starlets, even in the biggest record label in the world, songwriting is an uncertain endeavor. It's impossible to know whether the result will be a hit or a flop.

When writing my second album, I pushed the artistry as far as I could by refusing the aid I was offered. My ankle remembered: The only person I could count on was myself. And all the money in the world couldn't help me. If I wanted to keep my spot, I had to write good songs. I had the wealth and the power, but I was in an extremely precarious position: make good music and *you can stay*; make bad music and *you should go away*. Nothing personal. You couldn't be paranoid, nor could you be naïve. There was no one plotting either my success or my failure. If my music was great, I would have another resounding success. If my music sucked, my label would graciously show me the door. The secret was that there was no secret.

I didn't use social media to understand what my fans expected of me, I didn't ask AI to write lyrics that would resonate with my audience's current preoccupations, I didn't use Google to find trendy subjects and turn them into songs, I didn't delegate my artistic direction to an algorithm.

I belonged to the star system, but it wasn't the system that decided: It was me. Trying to imitate whatever was working elsewhere was the best way to spend your whole life two years behind. By the time the album came out, everyone would have moved on. The music industry was made of trends, but I wasn't there to follow them. I was there to create them.

My second album was written in two phases: first craftsmanship and then heavy artillery. I wrote pared-down ballads, demos that I sang alone at the piano or with my guitar. Once I finished my song, my label would arrange it so that it would go viral on social media and streaming platforms. In concrete terms, this meant a producer would add notes of funk or disco, whatever was selling at the moment. In this superficial way I couldn't avoid trends.

Once the product was created, the machine would kick into gear—a whole ecosystem working to make my music into a world-wide success. Industrialization, promotion, commercialization . . . My label was a success accelerator. But they couldn't do anything without a launching pad. The money machine started up only when it was given high-quality, original material. And that living material was me. Even for a pop song calibrated for Ibiza nightclubs, there had to be extra soul. Mastering the market required a masterstroke.

I could pretend as much as I wanted, but unfortunately, I couldn't pretend to create. It would be a lot simpler if it was all fake, if I didn't put any of myself into it. If only I could be a cynical bitch right up to the end. But the nuclear reactor core was made up of my own guts; it always would be.

My second album was even more successful than the first. No surprise there. I always succeeded at everything I tried. Afterward I forgot the mountain of doubts I'd had to climb to record those sixteen songs. When the story ends well, you tend to expunge anything that happened along the way. My second album was a triumph; how could it have been anything else? In my memories I retained only the happy epilogue.

My song "Hope" was everywhere, number one on the charts, quickly followed by two other singles, "Untouched" and "Girls." I was Cléo the talented, a magician, a meteor, a little rocket, a powerhouse. It was the natural order of things for the lion to devour the gazelle. The artists who collapse after one success are the ones who didn't deserve it in the first place. Those imposters know that you can fool the world once, not twice.

History was repeating itself, better and stronger now: the top spots on the charts, the media frenzy, the awards. I scaled up, filling stadiums with fifteen thousand spectators, then thirty thousand, then sixty thousand. And time kept accelerating.

On the jet taking me to California for the start of my second world tour, my team presented me with the schedule for the next ten months. Ninety-one concerts that would span the whole globe. Phoenix, Zurich, Perth, Kuala Lumpur, Mexico City. October 31, November 20, January 27, March 31, April 16, July 6. The places seemed imaginary, the dates made-up. As Stefani scrolled through the calendar, a tear started to roll down my cheek. This was never going to stop.

I'd arranged my own return to hell, sacrificing everything to put myself back at the center of a machine I found unbearable. Of course, I wasn't the first person to be trapped by a contradictory dream. There were parents who wished for a child with all their hearts, then ended up shaking the baby violently, causing irreversible brain damage, because they were exhausted from being so alienated from themselves for so long. I understood them. Imagine: It wasn't one small being but millions who were holding their arms out to me, begging for my love and every speck of my attention.

I was looking out the window watching the city lights grow distant, Manhattan disappearing into the night as the plane dove into the clouds, when my father's warning came back to me, tangible and cruel. "Sweetheart, be careful what you wish for," he'd whispered to me on the evening of my twenty-fifth birthday. I had thought that I wanted more than anything to be famous. For the first time, I was now wondering if I'd been wrong. The real problem with wishes is when they come true.

Being a victim of your own success. Years later I still think about that expression. I've never been a victim, of anything or anyone. I'm not looking for sympathy; my destiny is as grandiose as I'd ever wanted it to be. However, it is true that success like mine comes with a heavy price.

At that time, I didn't realize just how much I was giving up permanently: my privacy, my social life, my place of residence, my bodily integrity, my discretion, my right to be forgotten, my autonomy, my freedom.

I was about to internalize the universal rule of celebrity: The more famous you are, the more you belong to them.

On the island there's no corporal punishment, no lessons to engrave, no failures to absorb through blood. Instead of cutting my thighs, I cut the wooden wall with the blade of my knife to count the days, like a prisoner in her cell tracing her sentence in white chalk. Strangely, nobody else had the idea to do this before me. There aren't any carvings, graffiti, or drawings inspired by the extended hiatus far from civilization. Has anyone actually stayed here? As the sun sets, I mark that it's the end of my second week on the island.

I'm less scared now. I no longer jump at every little noise; I'm used to the birds shrieking, the wind blowing against the cabin, the flapping of my towel drying outside. I'm less scared, but I do feel alone. It's not surprising: I'm on a desert island. No one knows where I am, not even me, not even the inner circle of my team; my new assistant was surprised that she didn't have to book my plane tickets or hotel reservations. But I don't feel more alone here than I do in my daily life—at least not *much* more. The loneliness of the powerful isn't just a cliché.

In the mornings, I guess the time by watching the sun's journey through the sky, keeping an eye on the shadow of the hut moving across the sand. I talk to myself while drinking sweet coconut juice, or else I ramble to the birds drying their feathers. "My friends," I say to them, "have you ever met any celebrities around here? Who have you seen on this island other than me? Did Selena Gomez end up coming? Was she as terrified as I was the first few nights? Be honest. And while you're at it, could you tell me exactly where we are?" But the ugly little chaps just squawk and ignore my questions, indifferent to my curiosity. They're either white with long beaks or black with a light spot on the top of their heads. One day while I'm gathering wood, I observe that they don't build nests, but rather lay their eggs directly on tree branches. I eat the best omelet of my life.

In the afternoons, I write masterpieces, the best songs I've ever composed. Then I allow myself a break to swim, plunging into the water with my fins, mask, and snorkel. I swim among schools of multicolored fish; I can see their tiny gills opening and closing. I encounter giant gorgonians, jellyfish, seahorses, and turtles, as though I'm right up against the glass in a mind-blowing aquarium. A stingray undulates in the water; it looks like a black-spotted ghost with two horns protruding upward from its head.

The silence of the ocean chases away my worries. I observe my surroundings calmly, propelling myself with leg kicks. Concentrating on the site of my injury, I test my right ankle's range of motion, flexing my foot, then pivoting it inward and outward.

Suddenly I sense a presence. I turn my head: a dark mass, fifty or sixty feet away. I freeze, hold my breath. My brain orders me to flee, but I'm afraid of attracting the shark's attention. Luckily, I haven't cut myself since my arrival. The most important thing is not to act like prey. I need to avoid sudden movements, and I don't want to turn my back to it, so I stay right where I am, petrified. My vision blurs; salt water seeps into my mask, stinging my eyes. This is the second time in less than a year that my survival is a toss-up.

I prepare my defense strategy in case the shark attacks. "Wait a second, do you know who I am?" I'll ask. "I'm not just anybody— I'm Cléo Louvent. This is ridiculous. I can't die here. When I go home, I'll wire you ten million dollars to keep you and your family safe. Your shark wife and baby shark can live happily under the ocean. Besides, I'm in the middle of writing songs that will make history. Soon I'll be an even bigger star. So let me live." But nature is indifferent to my fame, my money, my power, my talent. On a desert island, I'm a nobody. You're only famous in the eyes of others. And wild animals don't count.

The shadow stretches out; it's now ten or fifteen feet long, a slender silhouette with a distinguishable dorsal fin. Is this even possible? Is my vision playing tricks on me? The predator moves away and then disappears. For a few seconds, I fear it will suddenly reappear, lunging at me from behind.

Trembling, I come out of the water. What did I see? Was it really a shark? I can't believe it—it's not possible. Or maybe there were three scuba divers ready to intervene in case of an attack. Or else it was a species that doesn't prey on humans. There has to be some explanation. No one would send a celebrity to an island to be eaten. I'm not in danger. I'm Cléo Louvent.

Suddenly I understand. I'm part of a reality show, or a movie. Where are the hidden cameras? These three weeks are a setup; I'm being filmed for a future show that sends celebrities to a desert island for an extraordinary experience. I should have guessed. It was the image they'd been waiting for: the diva facing a predator, completely staged from start to finish for entertainment value. This wouldn't be the first show to send people back to nature; Robinsonades are eternally popular. In the hut there are two chairs, not one—didn't that prove that someone else was about to arrive? But who? The host? I wonder who's in on it. Who from my team is behind all this? Who had the idea? And to think that they all feigned surprise, as though they didn't have any clue where I was going. Frantically I search for the cameras in the coconut palms, the rocks, next to my bed. I turn everything upside down, scattering my things everywhere. I don't find anything.

I'm so anxious that I can barely breathe, as though something is sitting on my chest. I'm going crazy, I'm losing my mind; what must I look like, hunting cameras that don't exist? I'm having an episode of paranoia. Fuck, why did they have to confiscate my cigarettes?

I have to calm down. Nothing will happen to me. I might not have actually encountered a shark, and even if I did, there's no reason for me to get worked up. Shark attacks are rare; why did I panic like that? I can't stand losing control—I've fought against it my whole life, with all my strength, so that I never appear vulnerable. And yet I've ended up there anyway. The shock made the images resurface: the stairs, the sounds, the tears.

I pace back and forth along the beach. I'm rattled, frustrated, confused, but I refuse to pick up the emergency phone to ask to go home early. I have to see this experience through to the end, trace the story until its conclusion. There's only one week left. I have to hold on.

I let the sand slip through my fingers. In front of me is the turquoise lagoon, the coconut palms, the beach. The island is incredible, but make no mistake: This atoll is also a prison. And I'm not here by accident.

PART THREE

Glory

Losers are in vogue, both in literature and in the movies. Characters fail all the time. We go crazy for obstacles, setbacks, defeats, redemptions, and comebacks. Success is the reward at the end of the journey, as though only failure makes for a story worth telling. It's never the starting point, it's the end point. Once the sun smiles down on us, the narrative stops.

And yet triumph has just as many twists and turns as defeat. In its own way, success is also an ordeal; victory is neither ataraxia nor nirvana. As my fame grew, this was a new discovery for me, one I feel in my bones. Success is more difficult to live with than failure.

After the explosion of my second album, the overabundance continued: more fans, more money, more opportunities, more fame. But when it works, it's never too much.

The evening of December 31st, I gave a concert in Times Square, broadcast live on the country's biggest television channel; like magic, millions of Americans celebrated the New Year with my face and voice. A month later, I sang Édith Piaf's "La vie en rose" at the White House in front of the president of the United States. And then, one morning, Stefani announced that I had been chosen to write and sing the song for the next James Bond movie. The British royal family invited me for tea when the film premiered; magnanimously, I didn't hold it against them for not having invited me to the wedding—instead, I just spread jam on my scone, blushing with pleasure.

In March I performed at the Oscars in front of A-list movie stars; it was a privilege granted to the five nominees for Best Original Song. I said hello to Meryl Streep. Scarlett Johansson whispered a joke in my ear. Brad Pitt extolled the merits of his vineyard in the south of France—I'd be welcome there this summer, he said warmly. I was mingling with the most famous people in the world and, more importantly, they considered me their equal.

I walked through the audience to the sound of applause, commanding and brave in a see-through sequined mermaid gown. I wasn't apprehensive or trembling; I was floating above the crowd, self-assured and untouchable. Nothing could get to me once I stepped up onto my pedestal. My pointed-toe stilettos heightened my confidence exponentially as I sat down at the grand piano, my red nails flashing over the black-and-white keys. Atop my head was a tiara set with precious gemstones. I'd gotten the idea from the Duchess of Cambridge when I'd spoken with her at Buckingham Palace; why should the royal family be the only ones who got to wear crowns?

An hour later, they were about to open the red envelope. I'd won. Thanks, James Bond. It was the ultimate achievement; I'd touched the Holy Grail. I jumped into Stefani's arms, ecstatic. Behind me, Nikki, my favorite sea witch, gave me a triumphant wink. If only my father could have seen me. I was beside myself with joy. I'd dreamed of this. I'd fought for it. I'd succeeded.

The happiness, the pride, the career milestone of this achievement: There were a thousand reasons to truly rejoice. Yet it took me a minute to adapt to this new reality. And once I did, it no longer meant anything to me. The disproportion was a smack in the face: I'd worked on this for months; I was happy for sixty seconds. In the end, all it boiled down to was one minute of pleasure.

In the limo, Stefani showed me pictures from my performance. My dress had been unflatteringly wrinkled around my torso when I'd been sitting at the piano. "Give me my phone right now," I yelled. I dialed Petra's number and hurled a stream of insults at her; there went our collaboration. Then I slammed the car door behind me, forgetting the gold statuette on the seat.

My greatest victories no longer brought anything more than a fleeting joy. In fact, they quickly became insufficient. I always needed more to get the same effect.

And since I was entitled to everything, I became obsessed with what I still couldn't get. Another singer was invited to perform in Paris at the Champions League final at the Stade de France. I thought this opportunity was rightfully mine, given that I spoke French and my songs were objectively better than hers; incredulous and hurt, I protested: "Why her?" The same week, I made myself sick when I learned that I wasn't one of *Time* magazine's 100 Most Influential People. It was a powerful optical illusion: I could see only what eluded me.

Tonight I had dinner plans with Aria. Kristen, my current assistant, had reserved a table for us. I'd given her just two criteria for the restaurant choice: a panoramic view (of the Empire State Building, if possible) and a menu with spiny lobster (flambéed with Cognac, if possible).

I skimmed the menu while waiting for Aria. No spiny lobster, just Maine lobster. I kept calm. Kristen had never tasted either one; how could she have known that the flesh of the spiny lobster was firmer than that of the Maine lobster? I sent her an informational text: Spiny lobster had antennae, Maine lobster had claws; thanks in advance for learning the difference. I ordered a salad.

Aria burst in like fireworks, explosive and magnificent, conspicuously noisy in the subdued atmosphere of the restaurant, looking incredible with her hair in a messy bun. She was late, she couldn't warn me, her phone had died; to top it off, her purse had been stolen the day before. She updated me on her life, alternating between radiant outbursts and loud sighs. As I listened, I stole peeks at her cleavage. Her career had taken off since the success of her show— her name was out there, she was desirable and desired, her phone was ringing. And yet she too was waiting for the next step. She was waiting for a part in New York's biggest play. She was waiting for an auteur filmmaker to choose her for a demanding film so that she'd become a respected actress. She was waiting for an even bigger director, one who would give her a rich and complex leading role that would earn her a best actress award in Venice or Cannes.

The mirror she was holding up to me was cruel: I could see reflected in it the trap of permanent dissatisfaction. In this regard, Aria and I were the same: We would never be happy about just having gotten our slice of the pie. We also wanted the next one, and everyone else's too.

Sitting on the sixtieth floor of a skyscraper in the Financial District in Manhattan, I contemplated the Empire State Building twinkling in the distance and realized that I would never wake up one morning thinking, *I've made it, this is it, the race is over, I'm growing wings, I'm an archangel, I walk on a cloud, I'm on a first-name basis with the divine, that's eternal bliss for me.* Even at the top, you never say to yourself, *It's all good now.* You look out at the view and wonder, *What's next?*

They pressed their faces against mine once, twice, fifteen times to take selfies with me. They kissed me on the cheek once, twice, fifteen times without asking my permission. A woman with purple hair clutched my wrist. I recognized her—she'd turned up at every location I'd been in since I'd landed in Milan two days ago. She stared into my eyes wildly, looking possessed. I got the feeling she could have lunged at my neck, strangled me, or bitten me; the pressure of her fingers on my skin hurt. She succeeded in yanking my sunglasses off my face before being pushed to the side by one of my bodyguards.

A hundred fans had been waiting for hours outside the entrance to my hotel. Security ordered them to stand back—some of them were pressing against the barriers, others were circumventing them to try to get closer to me, their arms extended in front of them in desperation. The scene encapsulated everything that's abnormal about fame. No human being is programmed to hear a crowd scream their name.

Have I explained how disappointed I was by my fans? Even in a city as rich and sophisticated as Milan, they were badly dressed, with yellow teeth. Any Hollywood star would tell you the same thing: Fans are rarely the pick of the litter. Besides, *why the hell are you in front of my hotel at 3:00 p.m. on a Wednesday? Don't you have anything else to do? Don't you work?* I was sure that they'd traveled here via subway and that they hadn't washed their hands.

Because my public persona is warm, the way people talk to me is disconcertingly familiar. They feel like they know me, so they address me as though I were an old friend. While an obese teenager pressed his body against mine to take a photo, I fantasized about saying to him, with all the hatred I harbored inside me, *Take your hand off my hip. We don't know each other.*

A little farther away, a man passed out. Next to him, his friend burst into tears. They were literally starstruck: There I was, in the flesh, and they completely lost it. I'd observed this phenomenon transform thousands of faces, seen every possible resulting expression: shock, astonishment, paralysis, crying fits, muteness, stammering, aggressiveness, violence, lust, ecstasy, spasms, dizziness. It was as though they'd all seen the Virgin Mary.

The man who fainted was carted away by hotel security. I approached his friend; she was convulsing with disgusting hiccups, in borderline respiratory distress.

In an attempt to calm her, I looked at her warmly and asked, "What's your name?" She eventually caught her breath enough to tell me that I'd changed her life, before handing me a chrome frame. Unsurprisingly, it was a charcoal portrait of me. You could sense the dedication and the hours of work that had gone into it, but it portrayed me with bulging eyes and a lopsided jaw; it looked like I'd just stuck my fingers in an electrical socket. Why were my fans so eager to draw me? Did they seriously think that I dreamed of hanging my own face above my bed? Even my narcissism had its limits. If only my fans had a soupçon of irony—I could ask a national museum to organize an exhibit displaying all the hideous portraits of me that I'd been gifted over the years.

I thanked this fan several times before hugging her. "It was so nice to meet you, Veronica! Thank you for your support, and thank you so much, from the bottom of my heart, for the drawing. You're an absolute angel." I had to go out of my way to pretend that I actually gave a shit. Fame is a radically asymmetrical experience: She'd been waiting for hours, she'd been preparing for this for weeks, she'd remember it for years; meanwhile, for me this was a blip in my calendar. A minute later, I would not only have forgotten this girl's name and face but I would also have forgotten her entire existence.

I'm not a monster. The situation made me a monster. Of course, the first hundred times I was touched by the attention, the declarations of love, the gifts. I was flattered by the shrieks, the tears, the trembling. But I'd challenge anyone to experience an emotion to the point of overdose and then try to feel it again afterward, even the tiniest bit. If ten fans were to tell me they loved me, I might be moved by it; if a hundred thousand fans were to tell me they loved me, I couldn't any longer. The human heart isn't that elastic.

So I grinned and bore it. I waved, I agreed to take photos, I hugged. Around me, the team collected the letters, the presents, the flowers. A man with a shaved head asked me to autograph his wrist, promising that he would get it tattooed immediately afterward. I was amused by this insane idea and tried to dissuade him, then signed my initials with a heart. Our exchange ended with a burst of laughter.

Like any good schmoozer, I used the techniques of a politician: placing a hand on the other person's arm or shoulder to respectfully establish physical contact, looking them right in the eyes to prove I had nothing to hide. My authenticity was completely fabricated, but it worked—I came across as charming and approachable, *so connected* to my fans. It was what they all said: "Cléo Louvent is actually *so sweet* in person."

We calculated the time I'd stay based on the size of the crowd: a minute for every six people, or ten seconds each—at the higher end of average for such a famous star. After seventeen minutes of this veneer of affection, my bodyguard coughed. I recognized the signal and disappeared into the hotel lobby amidst the shrieks.

In the elevator, I gritted my teeth. Being famous had become a profession in addition to my own profession. I now held two full-time positions: that of an artist who wrote and played music, and that of a public figure who inspired and enthralled millions of people. I had to juggle between the two, exhausted.

The most beautiful hotel room in Milan was located on the top floor of a fifteenth-century convent that had been transformed into luxury accommodations. I walked through my suite to get to one of the three bathrooms and turned on the gold tap. I scrubbed between my fingers with soap, lathered it up to my wrists, cleaned my nails with a brush. Frantically, I washed my hands for a long time—until they were covered with red patches, until my skin cracked, until it burned.

CLÉO LOUVENT

CLÉO LOUVENT + RELATIONSHIP

CLÉO LOUVENT + JOHN CUTLER

CLÉO LOUVENT + HUSBAND

CLÉO LOUVENT + PREGNANT

CLÉO LOUVENT + HEIGHT

CLÉO LOUVENT + WEIGHT

CLÉO LOUVENT + MEASUREMENTS

CLÉO LOUVENT + AGE

CLÉO LOUVENT + SPEAKING FRENCH

CLÉO LOUVENT + DOES SHE WRITE HER OWN SONGS

CLÉO LOUVENT: 230,000,000 results in .49 seconds. Unless I changed my identity, I would never be able to change my life. I belonged to the public domain.

Locked in the bathroom, I typed my name into Google for the third time since that morning. At the bottom of my screen, the most frequent search terms appeared automatically. Moral of the story: I could toil my life away writing a Major Work, and still people would wonder if I was shorter or taller than five foot seven. I noted that, in particular, my fans seemed genuinely concerned about my love and sex lives; while they were at it, why didn't they ask about the date of my most recent sexual encounter, or when my most recent menstrual period had begun? I rolled my eyes, dismayed by the amount of stupidity, even though I knew perfectly well that I couldn't ignore the people's court. The public always had the last word: They were the ones who could make or break a celebrity's fate; they were the ones who had crowned me a queen.

The internet allowed me to take their pulse. For several weeks now, John Cutler had been at the center of their concerns—Google alerts kept me informed in real time of every mention of our relationship in the media. He'd attended one of my concerts during my second tour; his presence in the VIP tent in Miami hadn't gone unnoticed. And last Monday, we'd been photographed with his friends at a lunch in New York. The rumor mill was going strong, even though we were not actually together. We saw each other intermittently: He sent me chocolates, I played hard to get. This time I was following the rules of chaste and courtly love. I'd learned my lesson.

CLÉO LOUVENT. I'd gone down a rabbit hole, skimming articles, photos, videos, comments, declarations of love, declarations of war, threats, various oddities. Oh, look, last week I apparently infiltrated the subconscious of a stranger somewhere in Japan—"In my dream, Cléo Louvent was wearing red cowboy boots, and she stole my couch."

I was part of the collective unconscious, which was also capable of unleashing violence. I was heartily admired and heartily insulted; you couldn't have one without the other. It would be unrealistic to think I could receive so much adulation without being equally lambasted. You could never separate love from hate. "That girl is unbearable." "We all agree she's useless, right?" "It's too bad she always does the same thing." "She's overrated. . . . I've never understood the hype." "I liked her music at the very beginning, when she wasn't famous yet, but now she's changed. She's too commercial." "My ears are bleeding and she's singing out of tune." "I'm tired of these preprogrammed clones; they're such a cliché." "She's so blah." "Ms. Louvent, maybe it's time you thought about having a baby."

People often ask me how I deal with criticism. Believe it or not: I couldn't give less of a shit. It rolls off me like water off a duck's back. Those buffoons don't have the power to rob me of a single cent or a single second. Obviously, I take comments into account because they contain information that's essential for my positioning as an artist—I have to actively monitor my brand—but the criticism doesn't wound me. I've seen celebrities in their Beverly Hills villas get so upset over insults on the internet that they cry; to me, that's insane. It would take more than that to shake me. My foundations are basically rock-solid, and I've learned to protect myself. That summer I'd sung in front of two hundred thousand people at a festival, no stress. Just imagine the level of detachment you need to have in order not to feel any surge of adrenaline; suffice it to say that an unkind comment written by some jackass on his couch would never get to me. I made the decision early in my career not to give a fuck, and I've always stuck to it. Peace can sometimes be as simple as a silent but firm agreement with yourself: *Cléo, we've decided not to care, okay?* And if worse came to worst, if one day I found myself sad and affected by it, I would take my cue from Scrooge McDuck diving into his pool of gold pieces: I would console myself by thinking very hard about the millions of dollars slumbering in my bank account.

"What are you doing in there? Is everything okay?" Celeste asked me through the door.

"Yes, I'm done."

"Are you doing drugs or something?"

"Yes, that's exactly it. I'm doing drugs."

"Are you making fun of me?"

"Yes."

There was no way I was admitting to Celeste that I had locked myself in the bathroom to read articles about myself. I'd rather have her thinking I was fueled by cocaine or constipated. I unlocked the door. Sunscreen in hand, I headed out to the patio.

"Girls, you haven't seen my hat, have you?"

Apparently, friendship is a plant that has to be watered, requiring a lot of attention and care. So to maintain my connections with Celeste and Aria, I suggested to them that we go on vacation in Ibiza together this summer. My two former roommates the first week of August, Juliette and her kids the second week. My inner circle hadn't changed much; I'd shut the door on most of the relationships fame had granted me access to. There was nothing new under the sun: Once you were successful, how could you tell whether sudden friendliness was genuine? I was afraid of being used, so instead I chose from the friendships that had begun before I was famous. I'd established the cutoff as the day I'd signed with my label, four years earlier. On September 20th, prospective friends were full of good intentions; on September 21st, they had something else in mind.

"Shall we have breakfast by the pool?" Celeste asked.

"Sure, anything's good with me," I replied, indifferent.

"It'll be nicer that way," she decided.

Since we'd arrived, I'd observed my friend move naturally around the villa on the northern side of the island that I'd paid a fortune to rent. She called the concierge to ask them to adjust the air-conditioning, made a spa reservation, requested housekeeping services. Even with my brand-new millions, Celeste was still richer than me.

The three of us sat down facing the ocean. Celeste took a photo of her eggs Benedict and French toast, which she posted half-heartedly on Instagram. Her baking account had become obsolete, long deposed by the merciless competition for pâte à choux sovereignty. Celeste didn't mention my presence at the table in her post to try to cannibalize my social media followers. It would seem that she still didn't need to be followed by millions of strangers to feel alive.

Between two graceful mouthfuls, Celeste told us about the challenges and joys of her new job. Recently, she'd been running her own art gallery, a project financed by Daddy, though she held the reins skillfully. She also outlined the preparations for her wedding; Tom had proposed back in April, dropping to his knees in their kitchen one Sunday morning, ten years after they'd first met. Celeste wanted the ceremony to be in New York next summer, but her family insisted they have it in her grandparents' vineyard in Napa Valley.

"I gave in on the guest list. There will be seven hundred people, and I can't do anything about it. But I would have liked to be able to choose the location of the reception."

"Do whatever you want," I told her. "It's your wedding, Celeste."

"It's my wedding, but they're the ones paying."

As for Tom, he'd accepted the situation with gentle fatalism. Celeste's fiancé hated conflict; as such, he was willing to get married in California. His happiness revolved around two things: Celeste and the restoration of old books. Right now he was fussing over an atlas from 1661, enthralled by its hand-painted engravings of our solar system by the German astronomer Andreas Cellarius. The couple still lived in Celeste's parents' apartment in Brooklyn; Aria's and my old bedrooms had been transformed into an office and a home gym.

Celeste asked me about the success of my second album, my tour, and what was next. Without a doubt, she deserved the Palme d'Or of friendship, with a special mention for her unfailing enthusiasm. She was a tireless mascot on the sidelines: "Oh, that's amazing, good for you, you really deserve it!" Across from me, Aria was silent, her huge owl eyes fixed on her plate. I could read in each of her reactions the pangs of jealousy—*You weren't number one in England, were you?* To keep from hurting her, I found myself exaggerating the bad parts—the constraints, the doubts, the disappointments. And I downplayed my victories, as though a euphemism could protect her when my face had been plastered everywhere ever since I'd become the new face of a luxury perfume. My smile was in every airport terminal, every bus stop in the major cities around the world, on the outside of the Palais Garnier, on the glowing billboards of Times Square.

Then the discussion drifted to the plagiarism lawsuit I had just won. It wasn't hard for me to talk about it; it hadn't exactly kept me up at night. I'd never listened to the song whose chorus Kyle Havens had accused me of stealing. My former studio neighbor, whom I'd met when I was recording my first album, would have been better off if he'd just shelled out for writers to rework his lyrics instead of wasting his money on legal fees. Aria said that he was doing it for the attention and the cash. I wasn't so sure. I thought he really believed that I'd been inspired by his music. Sometimes it's easier to fight against an imaginary enemy, to go after those who are more talented, than it is to confront your own mediocrity—and your own inability to create anything worth creating.

After breakfast Aria dove into our private pool. She'd cut her hair above her shoulders, and she wore a white one-piece swimsuit; her beauty was irritating. I had to force myself not to drool or dwell at length on her curves. So I settled into a lounge chair in the shade, phone in hand, and reimmersed myself in my favorite subject: myself.

I Googled my name again before looking at a social media account that documented, with photos, every single one of my appearances. "Cléo Louvent Tracker" on Instagram was startlingly accurate.

July 24, 2:30 p.m.: Cléo Louvent coming out of Greenwich Village Italian restaurant L'Artusi with a group of friends that includes John Cutler

July 25, 9:30 p.m.: Cléo Louvent spotted in the Hamptons

July 26, 10:00 a.m.: Cléo Louvent ordering a maple latte at Ludlow Coffee Supply in New York

July 27, 5:10 p.m.: Cléo Louvent takes the time to chat with a fan in St. John's Wood in London

July 28, 10:00 p.m.: Cléo Louvent leaving her hotel in Oslo

I had missed one post. Seeing it now for the first time, I was flabbergasted. A fan wrote in about being in possession of a bandage that belonged to me. Last week, as punishment for having slept in two days in a row, I'd plugged in an iron—and then clapped my bare left hand over the metal. The pain had woken me up. Fair, motivating, redeeming. I bandaged my hand and left my hotel in the center of Oslo to get coffee. When I got back, I realized that the bandage that had covered my palm had fallen off. And there, in my Ibiza deck chair, I learned that a man was bragging about having found it. He'd posted several photos of me entering the café with the bandage clearly visible on my left hand, and others a few minutes later without the bandage. The pièce de résistance: three close-ups of the bloodstained gauze after he'd picked it up from the ground.

According to my research, the bandage thief was named Ivar. He was thirty-seven years old, he was a pediatric nurse in a hospital on the outskirts of the city, and he lived alone with his dog, whose nickname was Zola (turns out Ivar was a Gorgonzola cheese enthusiast, not a nineteenth-century-literature buff). Despite my extensive investigation, I couldn't figure out whether Ivar had kept his precious finding or whether he'd auctioned it off to the highest bidder.

I called Stefani, beside myself with anger. My manager didn't pick up. She called me back twenty-seven seconds later. Twenty-seven seconds of agony. I unleashed the full extent of my fury: What was the point of my security detail if they weren't picking up whatever I dropped? How could my team have let a thing like this happen? Why was I only learning about it by lurking on social media? If I understood correctly, no one was keeping an eye on what was being posted about me online. Did I really have to do everyone else's work all the time? My bodyguard had to be fired immediately—the bandage situation wasn't a *mistake*; it was a *misdemeanor*. Had anyone even thought about the consequences? What could this lunatic do now that he had my DNA? Clone me? Voodoo rituals? Track down my mother? What information could he collect using a tiny drop of my blood? My cholesterol levels, my vitamin deficiencies, my sexually transmitted diseases?

"Fuck! I'll just send them a sample of my shit if they want it so badly."

Those were the last words I barked at Stefani before hanging up. Aria and Celeste were staring at me, stunned.

"Is everything okay, Cléo?" Celeste asked me.

"No, everything is not okay."

"Who were you talking to on the phone?"

"Stefani."

"But what time is it in New York?"

I shrugged. "I don't know."

"We're six hours ahead here. . . ."

"Okay. So it's three a.m."

"That's a little early, isn't it?"

"Given the mountain of money I pay her, I'm not too worried about it."

I circled the pool like a wounded animal, disturbed and dangerous, unable to be soothed. To lighten the mood, Aria joked to Celeste, "You better get your bulletproof vest—you might be hit by a stray shot."

I hated Aria's mockery. I hated Celeste's gentleness. I hated Stefani's carelessness. I hated my bodyguard's incompetence. I hated everyone. No one could understand me. I'd already given *everything* to my fans. I'd done thousands of interviews, I'd written songs about my most intimate thoughts, I'd just finished a second worldwide tour and sacrificed another year of my life. What more did they want from me?

Celeste tried to hug me, but I was shaking with anger. I staggered away from her toward the table with the remains of our breakfast and hit the glass tray with all my strength. It shattered upon contact with my fist. I watched the blood drain from my hand. This time I would make sure that none of my bandages went missing.

An hour later, my wounds had been disinfected and I had eight stitches and a bandaged hand—and was wondering how I'd gotten here. My anger had vanished. I'd poured out all my hatred, a torrent of bile, and now I felt empty, ashamed, and weary.

Fame hadn't changed me; I'd always been impatient and hot-headed. But what it had done was remove all the guardrails. No one spoke to me normally anymore. Other than Celeste and Aria, who dared contradict me?

So I raged. I sulked. I screamed. I hit. I grumbled. I punched. I complained. I scowled. I stamped my feet. I lay down on the ground. Basically, I was a four-year-old child without any boundaries. At this point, my tantrum about not *getting dressed with dry skin* seemed far away. During my second tour, every detail of my daily life was negotiated in the contract: my shower before each concert, its length, the brand of donkey milk soap that would be made available to me there. And also my arrival time, the bouquet of white roses in my dressing room, the composition of the fruit basket, the obligation to call me "ma'am" and not "miss," the ban on the smell of cigarette smoke in a 1,500-foot radius, the ambient temperature in my hotel room, the thickness of the carpet, the presence of three humidifiers to protect my voice, the name of my massage therapist, my nail technician's wages, down to the cent.

I kept telling my teams: "Let's keep things as simple and efficient as possible." But it was an impossible request. As soon as I crossed the threshold, everyone was warned, prepared, on the alert. Silence. Concentration. Fear. *Look out, she's coming.*

My career hit a new strategic milestone: Finally, the tabloids were interested in my cellulite. It's a privilege for your ass to be an object of such concern. Most people feel scrutinized on the beach, but you have to be rich and famous in order for your skin dimples to be truly worthy of interest. Not all fat deposits are matters of substance.

The shift took place on the beach in Ibiza. It was impossible to ignore the paparazzi scuttling like crabs over the sand and toward the sea. In front of me, kids were playing in the waves, shouting, throwing themselves on floats, sliding onto boogie boards; to my right, Aria and Celeste were diving into the water headfirst. I flexed my abs, hating myself for having chosen a badly cut bikini.

I do want to make one thing clear: I've never had cellulite. I have firm breasts, a flat stomach, and a well-rounded posterior. However, at certain angles and in certain lights, some people have thought they saw faint traces of fat on my upper thighs. The photos taken by the paparazzi in Ibiza bear witness to this. After that unfortunate incident, I sought out the necessary correctives: a vigorous anti-cellulite massage and a touch of cosmetic surgery. Even though I've *never* had cellulite, strictly speaking.

In January I went to visit my mother at Harvard, where she'd been invited to teach for the semester. I wanted to celebrate my thirtieth birthday with my mom.

We hadn't seen each other for six months when she hugged me awkwardly. She looked older, which I hadn't expected. I buried my face in her neck; she smelled of mimosa flowers. My mother walked around my hotel room, commenting on the weather in a feeble voice as she opened the blinds. She didn't know what to say. She was afraid of asking stupid questions, afraid of bothering me. After five minutes of hesitation, she tried a new approach:

"Sweetheart, I saw on your Instagram that you went to Sydney. In the photos you took in front of the opera, you had the same smile as when you were little. You looked so happy!"

"I was in Australia for barely seven hours, Mom. I had a fever on the plane, and they loaded me up with meds right before the photo shoot. . . . I was shivering under three blankets."

"Oh, I didn't know that, honey. Are you feeling better now?"

"That was six months ago. Photos are never posted right away. It was for a shitty partnership that wasted too much of my time and didn't pay enough."

". . ."

"What did you think? That I went to Sydney for fun and visited the kangaroos?"

". . ."

"It's called product placement. I earned $300,000 for the post." I slipped into my coat to put an end to the conversation. "Mom, you have to stop following me on Instagram. It's not real life. If you want to hear what I'm up to, call me instead."

After yet another heavy silence, I suggested to my mother that we go to the pool. Why didn't we take advantage of the faculty-only athletic facilities? It had been snowing for several days, and most of the students had gone home for the holidays.

Only a handful of professors was still on campus. I was safe: My boobs and cellulite couldn't possibly be of interest to political philosophy researchers, molecular biology PhD students, or algebraic geometry specialists.

There were seven of us in the water, and then there were three. My mother swam breaststroke without putting her head underwater; it looked like she was mid-coitus. I was ashamed of her. Why hadn't she opted for an elegant backstroke? In the next lane over, I did lap after lap, berating myself for having told her that I'd earned $300,000 for posting one photo on social media. Why hadn't I kept my mouth shut? That sum represented four or five years of her salary. I couldn't just drop bombs like that. Moreover, I hadn't yet officially decided: Now that I was ultrarich, how many hundreds of thousands of euros should I offer, reasonably, to each member of my family? Was it better for me to send them a check or buy them a car? Did I give the same amount to my relatives in Boston, who already had a lot of money, as to my uncles and aunts in France, who had been struggling financially in the past couple of years? And what about my distant cousins? For that matter, what about their spouses and children? Where on my family tree was I supposed to draw the boundaries of my generosity? I had no idea. In any case, nothing good could result from exposing my bank statements to my mother. *Next time we will think before we speak.* As soon as I was alone, I would find a way of punishing myself for my mistake.

Suddenly I saw a woman get out of the pool, go into the locker room, take her phone out of her bag, and return a few moments later to take photos of me—and also of my mother (what the fuck?). I could almost admire her dedication: She had to brave the cold, dry her hands, and open her locker. It might have even been touching if she didn't make me want to plunge a knife into her stomach.

The woman was photographing us while pretending to use her phone to send a message. She was so convinced that she was being discreet that I didn't know whether to laugh or cry.

"Did you just take a photo of us?"

The sound of my voice startled her. I pulled myself up out of the water, and she took a step back.

"No, um—excuse me—" she stammered.

"You know that's punishable by a fine?"

"I'm sorry. . . ."

I seized her phone and threw it into the pool. "You stupid bitch," I said to her before turning away.

For once, there were no witnesses; she would pay for the sins of all the others. Behind me, my mother was silent. She too was afraid of me.

Marilyn Monroe was harassed by the paparazzi: We had that in common. But for years now, in addition to the threat of their camera flashes, there had been a new, ever-present danger: cell phones. I could shake off the paparazzi; I couldn't escape the entire population of Massachusetts. During those three days at Harvard, I was filmed walking down the street, coming out of a restaurant, throwing my gum away in a trash can.

I don't know what horrifies me the most: people photographing me without my consent, or people asking me a hundred thousand times a day for permission to do it. There's no hoping for a normal conversation. Everyone has only one sentence on their lips: *Can I take a picture with you?* Autographs are barely a thing anymore. A signature is nearly worthless—you need proof in the form of an image. People take photos with celebrities as though they're posing in front of the Leaning Tower of Pisa or the Taj Mahal because they then have to share the miracle immediately with everyone they know: *I was there. I saw Cléo Louvent in real life.*

In a café right by the university, a man requested a selfie with me. His girlfriend was one step behind, then five other people, then ten, then twenty. A throng formed around me. Meanwhile, the rest of the group was offering their opinions as though I couldn't hear them. "She has incredible skin." "She's taller than I thought she'd be." "I love her, her latest album is so good." "My brother hates her music. He can't stand the sight of her." It was wild that no one was bothering to whisper. I was a painting on display at a museum: People approached with curiosity, judged me, admired me, denigrated me, and eventually went on their way. My coffee was cold by the time I was able to pick it up at the counter.

On the private jet that took me back to New York, I had a strange dream in which I was invisible. I was walking through a crowd, glimpsing faces that were preoccupied, distracted, absent; I got closer, and then even closer, and their gazes slid off me, went through me. I was transparent. Then I was in an amusement park, a big-box store, an airport terminal; the lines got longer, bodies were brushing up against one another, jostling, but no one was shouting, no one was trying to get my attention, no one was encircling me. I was the invisible star: Cléo Louvent had become a ghost. I took an escalator so that I could look down at everyone—there they were, all at my feet—then I retrieved a gun from my bag and began shooting.

I woke with a start. The plane had just landed.

I returned home resigned and sad. My daily life was like a city under siege: I retreated and ceded, neighborhood by neighborhood. The beach. The pool. The café. The drugstore. Running in Central Park. The movie theater. My world was shrinking rapidly.

I learned to climb in and out of a car without risking my crotch being photographed. At restaurants I left excessive tips; all I needed was for one person to steal a photo of the check for the entire country to accuse me of being stingy. I wasn't even allowed to scold a child who was behaving badly in the hallway of my hotel anymore. I couldn't let my guard down anywhere.

So I limited my activities. My friends came to visit me and not the reverse. I placed orders, got deliveries, hired a driver for my excursions. I now understood the appeal of the insane apartments that the real estate agent had showed me in New York—when you're under house arrest, it's better to have outdoor space, a Jacuzzi, and a gym. It was time for me to move.

In theory, I was free to live wherever I wanted. I could afford any house in any city in the world. But reality was more complex: My schedule was carefully planned and my geographical location strategic; any move I made required precise logistics, with my security a constant concern. Before becoming famous, I had no idea that such a level of constraint could exist. Nothing was ever left up to chance. With my career, the expectation was that I settle in Los Angeles. I chose to live west of the city, in Malibu.

I bought a house right on the ocean and soon adopted the local custom of beginning every morning with an hour of yoga on the terrace before breakfast. The Pacific was my backdrop during downward dog; my new assistant would go over the day's schedule with me as I stretched my back in cobra.

I missed New York and Paris, but it wasn't for nothing that Los Angeles was the city of celebrities. I was finally in an environment adapted to fame: gated communities with guards, houses accessible only via private roads, hilltop villas shielded from neighbors' prying eyes. I didn't buy a $15 million house because it had six bedrooms and nine bathrooms; I bought a $15 million house because it promised peace. It wasn't the infinity pool that raised the price, it was the discretion.

After living in apartments for my whole life, I felt like Tom Thumb living in a giant's home. My house came equipped with three elevators and sprawled into a maze of hallways. Moving from room to room took a ridiculous amount of time: three minutes between the kitchen and my office, seven minutes between my bedroom and the pool (better not forget the flip-flops).

For the first few weeks, I spent all day looking for my things. Where had I put my phone? Where were my sunglasses? Where had my sandals gone? I wasn't used to being in spaces where I couldn't see everything at once. A whole room was dedicated to my handbags, another to my shoes, a third to my books. The architect had installed a custom library next to the dining room; the little book-lined lounge was a delight. As for the decorator, he'd gone crazy with antiques (I chose to turn a blind eye to the prices of objects from another era); as a nod to my paternal heritage, there were several Greek and Roman vases, a Tyrrhenian amphora, a mummy mask, a bas-relief from the New Kingdom. And then there was the recording studio of my dreams: I could compose while facing the ocean, with the window open and Zuma Beach, the most beautiful in California, at my feet. The waves gave me the rhythms for my songs—they made me want to write ballads, slow the tempo down a bit.

Was it because my house was too big that I started losing sleep? Ever since my move to the West Coast, insomnia kept me up all night, exhausted and powerless. So tonight I had a light dinner, meditated, took a lukewarm bath, drank a glass of milk, pulled on wool socks, and tried a weighted blanket and an ergonomic memory-foam pillow. Unfortunately, all these preparations were in vain: I tossed and turned in bed for hours, unable to sleep. I was this close to asking my new assistant to come to my room and chant nursery rhymes. Linda had an extremely monotonous voice.

I tried changing beds. I lay down in one guest room, then another, then a third. The bedding was from Hästens—each Swedish mattress cost $80,00 and was handmade from cotton and horse-tail hair—yet I finished my night outside, lying on a yoga mat on the ground. I dozed off on my terrace around 4:00 a.m., wrapped up in a duvet, thanks to the sounds of the waves below and a horror movie. Watching a group of friends get chopped into pieces by a masked psychopath finally enabled me to relax—apparently, gore cinema was more effective than Sleepytime tea.

When I opened my eyes, it took me several seconds to figure out where I was. It was 7:00 a.m., and my face was moist with a light dew; I'd slept under the stars.

I put some water on to boil for my tea; it was one of the few tasks I still performed for myself, and I clung to it. I no longer opened the shutters of my house, chose my clothes, closed the car door, ran the water for my baths, or toasted the bread for my breakfast. Recently I'd even stopped washing my own hair.

On a wooden tray I placed a mug, the hot teapot, a jar of honey, and the glass straw I used for drinks that might stain my teeth. I savored my tea alone, facing the ocean. No one was allowed to come down to the ground floor between 7:25 a.m. and 8:05 a.m.—not my assistant, not my cleaning lady, not my manager, not my private chef, not my gardener, not my yoga instructor. No one. This bubble of solitude was written in black and white in the latest amendments to their contracts.

I listened to the voice notes that Juliette had sent me three days earlier on WhatsApp. In them, she recounted her recent adventures—just like when we were eight, just like when we were eighteen. She still called me Cléou. And she'd always been indifferent to my fame. She saved lives and had created lives; it would take a lot more to impress an ER doctor and mother of two. So much the better. In return, she'd never asked me for anything: no internship for her niece, no three-thousand-euro loan, no gifted plane tickets when I invited her on vacation. On Saturday Juliette had spent the evening with our old high school friends, and she gave me the detailed rundown. "Everyone wanted to know if I was still friends with you!" "Clémentine is a French professor in Athens, and her boyfriend is a ceramicist." "Henri sold his IT company to Darty for seven million euros and bought a house in Tours with his wife, Amandine. She's a clockmaker." "Oh, and Nathan was there too, did I tell you that? He left everything to become a pyrotechnist like his grandfather, and he moved to Toulouse two years ago. He was crazy about you when we were in high school."

I took a sip of tea before starting my response. "Hi, Juliette! Okay, first of all, I must remind you that Nathan was never in love with me. . . ." Several seconds later, my phone vibrated in my hand. It was a message from John. My new neighbor was quite a morning person.

He was welcoming me to Los Angeles and asking if I'd received the gift he'd had delivered to me the day I had moved in—a rare orchid from Japan. He ended the text by asking me out to dinner that night. The man was eating out of my hand. I would respond to him in a week or two.

I sent Linda across the city to buy a slice of Mexican lime pie. When I gave my new assistant orders, she carried them out, but I didn't feel a sense of sincere submission to my authority. Having to drive through LA traffic for this errand would teach her respect. *Linda, don't forget that you are a vassal.*

5:59 p.m. Linda set the dessert in front of me. Meringue, whipped cream, raspberry sauce. I'd given her an hour to accomplish this impossible mission—had she teleported? My negative sanction landed with a grimace of disgust. "No, thank you, I'm not hungry anymore."

My assistant kept staring at me, her arms dangling at her sides. Why weren't her eyes oozing with love and fear, like those of her predecessors? Kristen couldn't tell the difference between a spiny lobster and a Maine lobster, but she was fascinated by me. Besides, everyone knows that a dog chooses its master—bringing them its favorite toys, warning them of danger, rejoicing every time they're reunited. I observed the same phenomenon with all my assistants: affection, protection, devotion. But unlike the others, Linda never *chose* me.

The girl was quite efficient, but without much enthusiasm, as though she had better things to do elsewhere. I wanted to see her tremble, struggle, run herself ragged, go one better, transcend herself. I needed to get the sense that she was prepared to throw herself under a truck just to satisfy me. Which was the way it *should* have been. I'd seen *The Devil Wears Prada*, and I never understood why people saw Miranda as the villain. She didn't ask for masochistic submission from her assistants, and nor did I—just loyalty. At the end of their contracts, I'd open my address book and fulfill my end of the bargains. My first assistant, Rachel, was recruited by the most prestigious fashion magazine in New York. Carmen was hired by my label. As for Kristen, she went back to school to become a lawyer; my network and influence (as well as a generous donation) got her into Stanford.

"Can I do anything else?" Linda asked me.

Young, athletic figure, brown hair styled in precise waves, a metric ton of foundation. Linda was fairly pretty, and yet something was off with her. But what was it? Was it just her way of occupying space? I wanted her to be both everywhere and invisible at the same time—but for now, it was like she didn't know what to do with her arms and legs.

It had only been a month since Linda had started working for me. I opted for a gentle and kindhearted lesson. "Linda, I need you to be comfortable here and to feel like you're welcome on my team. So I'm going to start by clearing up any misunderstandings. If you don't feel like you're capable of this job, no problem—I'll find someone else who is. Thousands of girls would kill for your position. So, no pressure, everything is fine, don't stress. If it's not you, it'll be someone else." Then I talked to her about my ambitions (high) and my expectations (even higher).

"Linda, I imagine that a friend has invited you over for dinner before. Right?"

"Yes."

"Good. Know that there are two types of people on this earth. There's the friend who sends you a message with the time, the address, the codes for both doors, the floor number, which door it is, instructions for parking. Can you visualize that?"

"Yes."

"And then there's the friend who you have to ask for the address. When you get there, you have to call them for the codes. Of course, they don't pick up, so you wait outside like an idiot. Once you're in the stairwell, you realize that they didn't tell you which floor. So you have to send them another message: 'What's the floor again?' You see where I'm going with this?"

"Yes, I do."

"Linda, you have to understand one thing: I surround myself with only the first category of people. If I arrive at a dinner and I have to wait ten seconds because my host didn't bother to send me the code beforehand, I turn around. Their loss."

"..."

"I have a second example for you. If I ask you to set the table, you have two choices: You could take out a plate, a knife, a fork, and a glass. But that's not what I expect. It's not *sufficient*. On the table, in addition to that bare minimum, I want to see a pitcher of still water. A bottle of sparkling water. The saltshaker. The pepper grinder. The trivet. The serving spoons. The cloth napkins. If you're in France, I'd even add a basket of bread."

"..."

"Listen to what I'm about to say. There's one last subtle thing: I want you to set the table and be happy while you're doing it. Show me that you're motivated."

"Yes, but . . ."

"If you want to work together peacefully and happily, please don't interrupt me."

"..."

"And don't stammer when you're stressed."

Linda's shoulders were slumped and her head tucked in like a turtle. I allowed her to be dismissed. *That's all.*

As soon as she closed the door to my office, I threw myself at the pie, both hands in the meringue, devouring it in three bites, wolfing it down like an animal, mouth full of whipped cream. I had raspberry sauce everywhere—my fingers, my cheeks, my neck.

The next morning, Stefani and Linda went with me to a meeting at the Beverly Hills Hotel. A famous Spanish singer wanted to meet me to propose a collaboration. We headed toward the hotel bar at 10:00 a.m.: shaded terrace, palm trees, $48 omelet. I was eagerly looking forward to it. But unfortunately, Linda still did not know how to *move* correctly.

"Linda, stop walking duckfooted. It looks like you have to have a bowel movement."

"Yes, sorry."

"And stop following me like a little dog."

"But we're going to the same place . . ."

I wasn't getting any help. You had to explain *everything* to her, even how to put one foot in front of the other. But I didn't have time. I wasn't running a day care. I was trying to maintain my career stardom.

At the top of the hill, the winding streets all had avian names. John lived in the Bird Streets, an exclusive, upscale residential neighborhood in West Hollywood. It was the beginning of February, and it was the first time I'd set foot in this private enclave where celebrities could nest in peace. The sky was bright and cloudless; I was wearing a navy-blue dress with a ruffled collar. I was delighted, though determined to hide it.

I'd imagined that John's house would look like mine, with an infinity pool and full-length windows. But when the gate opened, what I saw wasn't an ultramodern residence built like a cube of glass—it was a Mediterranean villa with red roof tiles and wrought-iron fencing. In the yard: olive, orange, lemon trees. Inside: a fireplace, white-washed walls, hexagonal terra-cotta floor tiles. I felt like I was at my grandparents' house in Aix-en-Provence.

When John opened the door, he was dressed simply—bare feet, sunglasses, a multicolored T-shirt. He launched into a tour of the property; I followed him, suddenly shy, charming, fluttering around. His sports cars weren't particularly interesting to me, but I had a weakness for his impressive open kitchen: a central island with a six-burner stove, a sous vide cooker, an ice-cream maker, a meat slicer, Japanese knives, pink marble mortar and pestle, a walk-in fridge. Unfortunately, after two cocktails on his couch,

John decided to invite me to dinner at a private club on Sunset Boulevard instead of slaving over the hot stove.

"I'm so happy that you moved to LA!" "The server must be bringing our food soon!" "My pool has been leaking for four months, but I'm sure they'll find a solution!" John marveled at everything and saw the best in everyone—he was optimistic and untroubled. *Good news, that's good timing, we're lucky, everything will end up in the right place.* While he savored his fries with delight ("The burgers at the Bird Streets Club are delicious!"), I thought back to the depressive fatalism of Justin, my first producer. I wondered what would happen if you put the two of them in the same room—if, as it did in math, the negative would outweigh the positive.

We talked about our careers, projects, lawyers, asset management, vacations, friendships. John was part of my world, and the conversation unfolded naturally—I didn't need to explain any of the trappings of fame to him. When my friends and family from home spoke to me, I could always read in their eyes the same astonished observation: *You're famous now.* They didn't know what to say. Except that fame wasn't me, it was an exceptional thing that had happened to me, and this nuance was a chasm—it made all the difference. With John, on the other hand, fame was a given: It didn't change our relationship at all. All his friends were celebrities—why make it into a big thing? When going to the restaurant, he suggested, unprompted, that we take two separate cars and make our entrances a half hour apart. Plain and simple.

"Are you enjoying your salad?" "Are you cold?" "Do you like this place?" I liked his version of the world. I liked his big heart. I liked his moral code. I liked his freckles. I liked his delicate features, the way his face looked like it was drawn with a pencil. I liked his long light eyelashes that touched the tops of his eyelids. I liked his stability. I liked the way he admired other artists and was capable of saying good things about them. I even liked his somewhat-uptight nice-boy manners and his puritanism. I hadn't thought that I could like someone so much.

During dessert John took me by the hand and squeezed my fingers over my fruit salad, trembling, vulnerable, emotional. He confided that his breakup with Lily had been painful, they had spent five years together, he still had an enormous amount of respect for her, his ex was a wonderful woman, and now he'd turned over a new leaf, a year and a half after their separation, he was ready to love again, but his personal life was endlessly scrutinized and he didn't want to make a mistake, I had come into his life early, too early, but now he wanted me by his side, he was certain of it, I was an absolute gem, he wouldn't let me get away, not for anything, not ever. During this entire declaration, John didn't blink once.

That night John finally decided to make love to me for the first time. He lifted me up by the hips to set me on his bed before unwrapping me like a present: "I feel like I'm in a dream, you're so beautiful. . . ."

The love bombing could begin. We were in fusion; John agreed with me on everything; I noted the thousand things we had in common, told him over and over that he was different from other people, and he was, because I was in love for the first time in my life. He undressed me morning, noon, and night—we couldn't spend a minute together without devouring each other. He took French classes, I talked to him for hours about my father, I organized surprises for him just for the pleasure of seeing his face light up. I cut myself off from everyone but him, I was inspired by him to write my most beautiful love songs, I called him seventeen times a day, I sent him a list of movies to watch, I gifted him my favorite books.

I'd never been so happy, as though being at the top finally

allowed me to feel something. I was in the right place, with the right person. I could love—intensely, even; I was capable of it.

I loved him so much that I nibbled at him like a puppy. I wasn't a cannibal, but I could understand the temptation. My mouth watered when I thought about his skin. I loved him so much, I wanted to eat him all up.

I felt sure of myself, John kept me focused, I was able to sleep again. Whenever I lost patience, when I started acting over the top or got carried away, he would lean toward me.

"You're looking for a fight, huh?" he'd murmur between kisses.

I'd hang on to his neck, pulling him closer to me. I'd inhale him.

With time, I've developed a lot of respect for the paparazzi. They have a difficult job, and it's one that's destined to disappear thanks to cell phones. Their golden age is behind them; they can no longer sell a photo of a celebrity pumping gas for $15,000. The only way they can make a living now is with shattering revelations. Accordingly, they were risking shattering their own necks to snap the first photo of John and me.

One evening we were eating dinner on Natalie Holmes's terrace. She was John's closest friend, an actress who had just finished filming a postapocalyptic psychological thriller for Netflix. To celebrate her new ten-million-dollar role, she'd invited twenty honored guests to sit by her pool to sip cocktails and eat Kobe beef sliders. Suddenly a helicopter appeared in the hills, and a man in combat uniform leaned perilously far out of it, a camera hanging around his neck. The scene made me smile; I poured myself another drink. If I wasn't holding John's hand, if we weren't kissing, the shot was worthless.

Every day I watched the paparazzi battle to get an exclusive photo. I appreciated their competitive spirit; I'd rarely encountered such inventive, tenacious people. That said, there was no way I was giving them this victory. John and I were going to go public and announce the good news ourselves.

After several weeks of deliberations with our teams and pillow talk, we made our relationship official: As a public announcement, John posted a photo of me on his socials. I was sitting on a white couch, my head tilted to the side; my cheeks were rosy and my hair tousled, the sun glinting in my laughing eyes. I looked like I'd recently woken up from a summer nap, or like we'd just made love. I was heavily made-up to give the illusion of wearing no makeup, and I'd spent two hours getting my hair done to achieve the perfect no-effort look. I wore no jewelry and a tiered dress with a peach pattern that added just the right bucolic touch. In forty-eight hours, there wouldn't be a single item left for sale on the Brazilian brand's website, and their stores across the country would be mobbed.

My nail polish sparked the same frenzy. I'd swapped my signature fire-engine red for a pearly white, almost transparent, which shimmered on my nails like confectioner's sugar. In a few hours, my "glazed donut nails" were the subject of hundreds of thousands of internet searches, and just as many hashtags on social media— everyone wanted to know how to reproduce the effect. The next morning, the biggest cosmetics brand in the US asked me to create a nail polish for them. My well-negotiated partnership (one meeting to choose a color, two photo shoots, three posts on my social media accounts) was more lucrative than a week of concerts in front of thirty thousand people. These days singers no longer get rich from their music; they become multimillionaires by creating their own makeup lines. I've searched in vain for any artists who don't sell foundation between their albums.

In this now-iconic photo, the whole world saw a flouncy dress and a new nail polish. When I looked at it, what stood out was the sincere part: my smile. I was delighted, and for once my happiness was lasting a little while. The blessed parentheses of a romantic idyll. I was becoming a better version of myself—less rigid, less severe, more patient, more tolerant. I stopped harming myself: no more cutting, no more burning, no more hitting my head against the wall. Around me everyone was benefiting from the lull. I was even pleasant to Linda. During those magical first few months, John filled me up and calmed me down—until, despite myself, the venom of my irritation began to disturb the raptures of our nascent love.

John was kissing me in the elevator of our hotel in Madrid. He had one hand under my blouse, the other snaking its way up my skirt. When the doors opened, he pulled me by the arm toward our suite.

Four days later, the footage was making its way around the world. My team had warned me to keep an eye out for security cameras.

The world's fascination with us hit an all-time high with this illicit peek at our tantalizing lust for each other. The reactions to the video made me realize that millions of people would pay a lot of money to watch us have sex.

Upon my return to Malibu, I borrowed Linda's computer and spent a night entering my name into the search bars of adult websites. There were hundreds of fake sex tapes of John and me in the look-alike category featuring porn stars who resembled us: a blond woman with bangs, a redheaded man with freckles, done. I also found hentai, erotic Japanese manga starring animated avatars of us in various positions. Thanks to the astonishing capabilities of artificial intelligence, there were thousands of pornographic photos of me created from montages of existing images—I had to admit they were disturbingly realistic. And then, on certain sites off-limits to anyone under eighteen, there were the compilations of the parts of my music videos in which I was partially naked—where my tits were visible through my tank top or where you could glimpse part of my ass when I bent over. Basically, if someone could just film me giving John a blow job, it would be a gift to humanity, and they would all be extremely grateful.

What actually happened in that Madrilenian hotel room? No acrobatics. No complicated experimentation. And, unfortunately for me, no spanking or anal sex. John made love to me as though we were in a romantic comedy, gently and conscientiously, asking for consent and complimenting my body.

I have clear images from that night. A flick of black eyeliner on my eyelids. My blond bangs falling in a curtain over my forehead. John on his knees at the foot of the bed, spreading my legs; it was like he was eating a papaya. The outline of my silhouette was visible in the mirror next to the bed, and I observed my reflection, pressing my hand against the wall. My braid slid down my back as I arched, conscious of the effect. I was taking full advantage of the erotic potential of my hairstyle—I'd grown up with Lara Croft's films. While he licked my pussy, I kept looking in the mirror, making love to myself. I came, turned on by my own beauty.

"I feel like you're dancing," John whispered in my ear as he climbed on top of me.

To please him, I whispered to him in French, murmuring on and on about anything I could think of. He didn't understand any of it, and that turned him on.

"Continue John, continue encore. Prends-moi plus fort. Allez, tu n'es pas très dégourdi, je pensais que tu aurais plus d'animosité en toi. Mon petit chou, il va falloir être un peu plus viril." Keep going, John, keep going. Take me harder. Come on, you're a bit slow; I would have thought you had more vigor in you. Darling, you're going to have to be a little more of a man.

During my last orgasm, I suddenly had an idea for a new song. I quickly got dressed again and ran to take out my guitar so that I wouldn't forget the melody. I strummed a few chords, improvised the lyrics to a chorus, I had something, the inspiration was there, I was almost finished—and then I heard John's footsteps behind me.

"What are you doing?" he asked.

Such a stupid question. What did he think I was doing? Did I look like I was going ice-skating with my friends? *Figure it out— you can see very well for yourself that I'm in the middle of composing something.*

"I'm writing a song. I'll come join you in five minutes."

I continued singing, my phone within reach so I could record myself.

"Do you want a glass of water, my love?"

Irritated, I shook my head. John finally walked away, then turned around and retraced his steps.

"Cléo, I wanted to tell you something."

"What now?"

"You put your shirt on backward."

I turned my head brusquely to look at him, my expression stony. I let the silence linger.

"I was just saying that your T-shirt was on backward. . . ."

"That's not a very interesting thing to say, is it?"

"Excuse me, I didn't want to bother you."

"Not only are you interrupting me, you're also bringing down the level of conversation."

The next morning, I felt bad about having been so curt. John had the right to offer me a glass of water and tell me my T-shirt was on backward. His observations weren't exactly relevant, but they came from the heart. To apologize, I wrote him a fawning text that ended with some French endearments. But autocorrect changed my message: Instead of sending "Je t'aime," "I love you," I accidentally sent "Je t'abîme"—"I'm damaging you."

Have you read them all?"

John was standing in front of my sculpted-wood library, incredulous. I handed him a glass of white wine to go with the oysters.

"Of course I have."

"There are so many of them."

"I was a bookseller, remember?"

". . ."

"You can open them, they're real."

We were eating dinner together facing the ocean, just the two of us. Shrimp, clams, mussels, calamari, sea bass: My chef had prepared a bouillabaisse with local ingredients. My grandparents probably wouldn't have appreciated this Californian rendition of Provençal cuisine.

During the meal, I questioned John about his definition of success. He'd been in the industry for so many years. Unfortunately, he interrupted me once to ask if I preferred the window open or closed, and a second time to determine whether I thought he should light some candles. What a waste. Here I was trying to get him to develop his reasoning, to gain maturity, nuance, and depth so that he could improve himself, but he persisted in staying exactly as he was.

The rest of the evening was a car crash; I was on the scene but unable to react. I'd spent a crazy amount of time preparing myself for this dinner. Full of noble intentions and determined that we would have a nice time together, I'd chosen the menu, the music, my shoes, my lingerie. But reality didn't live up to my beautiful vision. I hated the way he answered my questions; even worse, I despised how he'd interrupt the conversation with such mundane commentary; I didn't like his red jacket or his unstylish haircut; I was irritated by his appetite—one portion of tiramisu would have sufficed. And why was he so determined to stare at me like that? Wouldn't his corneas get dry? How many times was a human being supposed to blink each minute? Ten times? Twenty? Discreetly, I started a timer on my phone and began to count. Once, twice, three times . . . my intuition was right. John had blinked only eight times in the last sixty seconds. In all seriousness, I made a note to get him some gel eye drops for his birthday.

Now that the shrimp and the calamari had offered their bodies for the sake of John's pleasure, it was my turn to do the same. He laid me down on the couch, full of enthusiasm, and undressed me, full of desire. Unfortunately, after that, he showed less initiative. I liked a lively, rousing session, while his tempo was endlessly slow. We'd been together for six months—it was time to transition from rom-com to porno.

On the other side of the floor-to-ceiling window, the moon, massive and bright, was reflecting off the waves. I studied John's white skin over his shoulder; it was almost transparent, dotted with constellations of freckles. He was active in bed, demonstrating plenty of goodwill, but I had to face the truth: As a lover, he kind of sucked. He lacked imagination. He had no vision. He couldn't carry out his ideas. He didn't know his body. And, worst of all, he felt vaguely guilty whenever I sat on his face.

After fifteen minutes of labor, I took our lovemaking into my own hands. I climbed on top of him and started to work, undulating my hips while varying the intensity and rhythm. After ten seconds, John moaned in ecstasy, his eyes contorted in pleasure. I really had to do everything myself: I was both the brains and the driving force in my career, in our relationship, in bed. And I was tired of it.

The Amalfi Coast was quite pretty, but I was bored on the yacht. Amalfi, Positano, Capri. We swam, we drank, we fucked. There was nothing else to do. Rating: 1/5.

"So, what do you think of the yacht?" John asked me the first day.

"Honestly?"

"Yes."

"I think yachts are tacky."

Luckily, the boat wasn't his. When you're a real celebrity, you don't own a yacht—someone lends one to you. Thanks to the generosity of a rich businessman with whom John had become friends, we were spending fifteen days in the Tyrrhenian Sea without paying a cent. It killed me inside to take out my credit card to buy a sarong. The richer I got, the more I wanted to stay that way. You quickly get used to not spending any money.

John joined me on the deck. He had just come out of the shower; I recognized the smell of his Eau d'orange verte soap. As he approached, a smile on his lips and his chest puffed out, I lowered my sunglasses to stare at his stomach, rounded like that of a little boy. John had gained weight since we'd met, and I could no longer stand seeing him devour his favorite Peeps; I felt like his whole body was turning into a marshmallow. He sat down next to me and I pinched his love handles, laughing. Maybe my tickling would make him consider going on a diet. I had a perfect body—I deserved a partner of whom I could say the same.

However, it didn't seem like my pointed displays of affection bothered John, because he kissed my neck and pulled me toward him. I was expecting him to whisper sweet nothings into my ear, but when he opened his mouth, it was to talk hardware.

"The light in the bathroom is broken," he announced solemnly.

"Yes, I saw. But it's not broken, it's just that the bulb blew out."

"It's the same thing."

"No, it's not the same thing."

I responded more sharply than I'd intended. I stared at his privileged face, his all-American head, and remembered that John had been famous since he was twelve. This meant that he'd never changed a lightbulb and definitely had never looked for the right kind in a store (Edison screw or bayonet cap? LED or halogen? E14 base or E27?). For that matter, John had never crossed the street carrying a secondhand coffee table. He'd never taken a commuter train to the airport with two suitcases and a backpack. He'd never stayed up all night studying for an important exam. He'd never recaulked his bathroom. He'd never washed the walls of an apartment. He'd never helped his friends move in exchange for half a pizza and two beers. He'd never bled a radiator. He'd never carpooled. He'd never slept on the overnight bus from New York to Montreal. He'd never kept a ridiculous blog in high school. He'd never peed between two cars on the way home from a nightclub. He'd never shit in a public toilet. He'd never tried out sofas at IKEA on a Saturday afternoon. He'd never borrowed a drill from his parents to put up shelves. He'd never waited seven hours in the ER for a wrist X-ray. He'd never cried after his favorite sweater shrunk in the wash. He'd never made apricot jam. He'd never filled out his own tax forms. He'd never dropped off his car at the mechanic, worried about the next inspection. He'd never repotted a plant. He'd never sprouted an avocado pit. He'd never walked out of the supermarket with rolls of toilet paper under his arms.

Lounging on a thirty-two-million-dollar yacht somewhere off the Italian coast, I realized that there was one experience John and I would never have in common: normality.

On a yacht, all the days are alike, and I dreamed of bike rides in the countryside, cappuccinos on a terrace, endless flea markets, jaunts to antique stores, pistachio ice cream by the port. After intense negotiations, I got what I wanted: a trip to the National Archaeological Museum of Naples. My security team warned me that our visit would elicit curiosity, that we should expect to be photographed. All the better. For once we could inspire the world to seek out culture instead of buying nail polish.

At 10:00 a.m. we were wandering down the museum halls with a guide who was explaining the building's history to us; it had been constructed during the Renaissance in the historic center. On the second floor, I went into raptures in front of the bronze statues from Herculaneum. John heard about Vesuvius for the first time ("Oh, really, a volcano erupted?"), while I asked for details about fishing techniques during the first century AD ("By the way, was Herculaneum also a vacation destination?"). I got a lump in my throat in the basement as I looked at the Egyptian collection, the treasures of which my father had described to me when I was a kid.

By 11:00 a.m. visitors were running from room to room to catch a glimpse of us. Several families were shoved, a pair of twins lost their parents, a group of Germans was out of control, the guards were overwhelmed. The mob was dangerous: for us, for them, for the art. Museum security was forced to escort us to the exit.

Obviously, seeing me holding John's hand was more exciting than looking at a marble Hellenistic statue from the third century. Obviously, a pop star was more fascinating than a mosaic unearthed in the Pompeii excavations. Obviously, I was an endless source of admiration and inspiration (+400% more visitors in two months at the museum). Yet I felt stupid. I knew that we wouldn't slip by unnoticed, but I hadn't anticipated that the crowd would behave like that. I was angry with myself, with John, with the whole world.

"It's not a big deal, babe."

"Nothing is ever a big deal with you."

"We were able to visit part of the museum. It's better than nothing."

On the ride back to the yacht, I kept rehashing the same complaints, frustrated and disappointed.

"I should have guessed."

"..."

"You should have told me it was a bad idea."

"..."

"Why didn't you tell me it was a shitty plan?"

"..."

"What a stupid fucking thing to do."

"..."

"We should never have gone."

"..."

"They should have opened the museum early for us."

"..."

"Why didn't they organize a private tour?"

"..."

"I don't understand why you didn't warn me."

"..."

"I'm always the one who has to think of everything."

"..."

"Obviously, you're not saying anything."

"..."

"I can't deal with this."

"..."

"I can't deal with you."

In September a series of paparazzi photos from us on the yacht was published. The photographers were already interested in my ass, but now that the whole planet knew that John was up close and personal with it, its value was priceless. In the shots, I was wearing a sky-blue thong that made my posterior look amazing, and, more importantly, I wasn't wearing a bikini top. This time the angle was flattering. My chest looked round and sensual, like that of an Italian singer from the eighties. And it was a great idea to have kept my earrings on while swimming; my gold hoops gave me a diva vibe. But I was ashamed of what John looked like next to me. He was too fat, too soft, too gentle. In the photos where he was coming out of the water, he looked like a wet dog.

It was time, once again, to sell myself. Luckily, I was good at hustling. My new single had been released two days earlier, and I was promoting it through a Los Angeles radio show. The recording took place in the early evening at their studio in Hollywood, just a few blocks from Santa Monica Boulevard.

One hour of ab exercises directed by my personal trainer. Two hours of putting together my outfit with my stylist. Three hours of hair and makeup. I was ready for my twenty-five-minute interview.

There were some weeks when I worked more on my appearance than I did on my songs. My success was measured by the success of my music, but I was its vehicle. People liked my music because they liked my being in the world. To put it simply: I wouldn't be so famous if I weren't so pretty. They admired my appearance—my signature bangs, my California blond, my thin and toned body, my fashion sense, the way I'd shaped my eyebrows. Granted, I starved myself a little and spent $2,000 each week on my hair, but these minor sacrifices were part of the deal.

I was crabby on the way to the station and an angel as soon as I stepped out of the car. Linda had a hard time reconciling these two versions of me—but it was very simple: I got into the character of my public persona, who was thoughtful and funny, grateful and humble. An ice queen in private, a little ray of sunshine in public.

I'd earned the right to be difficult with my team, but certainly not with my fans or the media.

Five minutes before the show started, I rehearsed my talking points. My song was called "Malibu," and it was "an ode to hearth and home." In this rhythmic folk ballad, I sang about "my new life by the seaside" in which I enjoyed "simple pleasures." With this song, I was "going back to my roots"; I'd written it one Sunday evening on my patio, "inspired by the ocean." Malibu was "an incredible place"; I'd found "my little perch," somewhere where I felt "happy and safe." I was repositioning myself as "a radiant, calm young woman" who was "in love and at peace for the first time," offering the public a version of myself who was "less melancholy and tortured" than the Cléo Louvent of my first two albums. In the very pastoral music video—which had garnered more than five million views in the past twenty-four hours—I danced on the beach with pigtails and a checkered dress, surrounded by colorful balloons and the setting sun; I sang next to a waterfall; I rolled around in the grass; I petted a border collie, my bangs blowing in the wind. No lascivious poses, no tits visible through my shirt, no suggestively parted lips. I channeled the mindset of a bucolic shepherdess. I was ready.

Every sentence I uttered on air would be interpreted, commented on, taken out of context in articles with questionable journalistic ethics. Everything I said could and would be used against me in media court. The slightest awkward remark might haunt me for five or ten years; the slightest controversial statement could, in a worst-case scenario, annihilate my career on the spot. So beneath my relaxed smile, I was extremely focused when I entered the studio. The live broadcast was starting in ten seconds. I assumed my interview voice—it was easy to recognize, higher and more cheerful. *And we're off.*

"What would you say to those who insist that you're talking about your boyfriend in this song?" "Is it hard for you when everyone speculates about the hidden meaning of your lyrics?" "Aren't you annoyed when interviewers constantly ask you about your personal life?"

The journalist wasn't inquiring about the release date of my third album: He wanted details about my relationship. It was fair enough; the lyrics didn't leave much ambiguity about the person involved. "You visit me in Malibu / I'm in love for the first time / With you I'm not famous, I'm just me."

Since our relationship had become official, my love songs had ceased to be disembodied. They now had a known subject: John Cutler. John had pulled my songs from artistic limbo and tethered them to reality, so now the public could dissect every verse in search of nuggets of truth. Every day the power of this shared frame of reference became clearer to me—and I even played with it. I concealed fewer personal details than in the songs of my first two albums; my publicized love life was a new string to my bow when I wrote songs—why deprive myself of it? Now you had to read the tabloids to understand my lyrics.

The problem was that, between the time I'd written the song and the time it had come out, eight months had passed. This interval was a punch in the stomach. I'd had the idea one evening in February, the day after we'd first spent the night together, when I was content and happy. Today this song reminded me of an old wedding announcement for a couple who'd been divorced for three years. Last night John had burst into tears after I'd reprimanded him for not asking me enough questions about myself, then came scratching at my door like an abandoned puppy. Exasperated, I'd locked him out and turned on some music so that I didn't have to hear him whine.

"Are you inspired by your personal experiences?"

"'Malibu' is about the feeling of having found the one. It's universal."

To avoid talking about *my* love life, I talked about love lives *in general*. The secret: extrapolation.

"This song isn't just about me. It's about anyone who's fallen in love."

"But the lyrics refer to one person in particular, don't they?"

"My hope is that my fans will see themselves in my lyrics. That's the most important thing. This song transcends the circumstances in which I wrote it."

Pirouette, somersault, dodge, leap, arabesque, sidestep: I didn't answer the question, but I got away with it. Most importantly, I kept smiling so that I wouldn't let the slightest sign of irritation slip through.

"I talk to my fans through my music. All that counts is the music. My personal life isn't really that interesting to my listeners."

My personal life isn't really that interesting to my listeners. A magnificent example of a bad-faith argument. It was irrefutable—I often used it in interviews to imply that my fans cared more about my music than my sex life. Completely untrue, but no one dared contradict me.

After the chapter on my love life, I was asked about my new role as the face of a luxury brand, my upcoming collaborations with other artists, my relationship with France. The host also asked me to give a speech on the little woes of fame: the paparazzi, the pressure, the fear of disappointing my fans after the success of my first two albums.

I wasn't offended by the vacuousness of his questions. I reacted as though I were finding our conversation fascinating: I elaborated, I was surprised, I was touched. It wasn't for nothing that I was a media darling. In the industry they said I was a *good inter-view*. "Cléo Louvent is *very generous*." I knew what the journalist expected from me: spontaneity, anecdotes, something new, something unexpected. He wanted me to confide in him, to expand on my answers, to burst out laughing, to have my phone ring in the middle of the broadcast and for me to pick up and ask my mother to call back later. He dreamed of getting a piece of me that I hadn't given to anyone else.

There were only three minutes remaining in the interview; it was time to give the journalist the happy accident he'd been hoping for. I pretended to accidentally reveal the title of my next song. Then I clapped my hand over my mouth, eyes wide, feigning confusion.

"Shoot, did I say that out loud? My label is going to kill me! It's so bad, I'm incapable of keeping a secret!"

I granted him a perfectly calculated slip of the tongue; he ended his show with a scoop. Win-win.

For this interview, my army of publicists had laid the groundwork firmly: "Please note that Cléo Louvent has only twenty-five minutes, she has a hard stop at 6:55 p.m., she will be pressed for time. Be quick, and no photos." That was their job: play the bad cop, tighten the screws, crack the whip. The exaggerated severity allowed me to always be the good guy.

After the broadcast, I continued chatting with the radio presenters and technicians and took selfies with everyone on the team, as generous off the air as on. But thanks to my guard dogs' warnings, my presence was seen as a *gift* rather than an *obligation*. *Her assistants said she didn't have a lot of time, but she ended up staying forty minutes—Cléo Louvent is so nice!* The calculated goal was for everyone to think: *Her team isn't exactly accommodating, but Cléo Louvent herself is the best.*

The car that was to bring me back to Malibu was waiting in the underground parking lot. Stefani and Linda congratulated me on my performance—"You were perfect, as always. A boxer and an acrobat." On the way home, I leaned my head against the window and thought about all the stars who didn't want to talk about their personal lives in interviews. There were the celebrities who chose not to share the names of their kids. Or the actress who refused to reveal the names of her pets on live TV. A ploy for attention. *We know what your face looks like from every angle, we've seen you half naked in three different movies, so what are you on about? You can't say the names of your hamster and canary?*

We passed through the mountains of Santa Monica to follow the ocean along the Pacific Coast Highway. I rolled down the window—something I never did, but I was nauseated. The fog obscured my view; it was like the car was moving through a smoke machine. I imagined, without being able to see them, the houses on stilts, the restaurants, the beach, the sun setting on the waves. And then I understood. It wasn't a silly whim, refusing to talk about your personal life in interviews. It was a question of survival.

When I replayed my conversation with the journalist in my head, realizing how much I'd given away of myself, my chest seized up, and I gagged. I'd shared how happy I was to live in Malibu and see the ocean when I woke up every morning. I'd mentioned that it was sad for me to be so far away from New York and that I was nostalgic for Paris. I'd chosen what to divulge, but still, it was too much. At the end of the interview, I'd confessed my recent passion for horror movies. Why had I talked about that? Of course, I didn't specify that it was because they lulled me to sleep, but I felt dirty anyway. I was overcome by the same self-disgust whenever I told a new story, whenever I revealed the name of a friend or family member, whenever I confessed a previously unknown detail of my daily life. As soon as I relinquished any part of my inner self, my world shrank, and I would leave the interview with a bitter taste in my mouth. Often after returning home, disheartened, I would drink a glass of salt water and then jam two fingers down my throat. Vomit it all up, and quickly.

The electronic gate opened, and my driver parked in the driveway. There was so much fog that I could barely see the contours of my house. Unsteady, I struggled to get up—I vomited in Linda's purse before I was able to get out of the car. If I gave everything away in interviews, what would be left for me once I closed the door of my own home at night?

I crouched down and rapped three times on the parquet. Nothing happened. I stood up, knocked on the wall. Still nothing. So I clapped, grumbling that I needed a bell or a portable ringer. After eight long seconds, Linda finally appeared.

"I'm sorry, I was on the phone."

"You thought that this was a good time to call your mom? You want a cup of tea too?"

"No, not at all, I was talking to the label about . . ."

"Don't tell me your life story."

". . ."

"That's not why I asked you to come."

". . ."

"We are actually going to talk about geometry."

". . ."

"Linda, do you know how to calculate the area of a rectangle?"

". . ."

"You understood my question perfectly well. Do you know how to calculate an area?"

". . ."

"Wonderful. So go get something to measure with."

". . ."

"Figure it out."

". . ."

"Very good."

" . . . "

"Now, measure my nightstand."

" . . . "

"How long are the sides?"

" . . . "

"Okay."

" . . . "

"Do you know the formula?"

" . . . "

"If I'm understanding correctly, you are three hundred thousand dollars in debt for your college education and you don't know how to calculate the area of a rectangle."

" . . . "

"Not a very wise investment."

" . . . "

"You have to multiply the sides."

" . . . "

"There you go."

" . . . "

"Now, can you tell me the surface area of this nightstand?"

" . . . "

"Mental math isn't your forte."

" . . . "

"You're as bad at algebra as you are at geometry."

" . . . "

"Yes, you may use your own four-function calculator."

" . . . "

"What answer did you get?"

" . . . "

"Yes, that's correct."

"..."

"And what can you deduce from that?"

"..."

"Nothing?"

"..."

"I'll answer for you: My nightstand is narrow."

"..."

"So please do not put so many things on it."

"..."

"If you don't mind, let's count them together."

"..."

"One, a pair of sunglasses. Two, a bottle of water. Three, my throat lozenges. Four, my bedside lamp. Five, the novel I'm reading. Six, my earplugs. Seven, a bottle of vitamins."

"..."

"Earlier I tried to grab just one of these items, and, of course, half of them fell."

"..."

"The problem is that when you carry out my orders, even ones as basic as placing items on a flat surface, you don't put yourself in my shoes."

"..."

"You don't think."

"..."

"You act like an idiot."

"..."

"Use your brain."

"..."

"When you are *setting up for my bedtime*, I need to have all these items available to me. I'm not telling you anything new; you know the list by heart. But these items do not count as being accessible if you place them all right next to each other on such a narrow surface."

"..."

"Are you understanding what I'm saying?"

"..."

"While I'm at it, I would have appreciated it if you'd noticed that my nightstand does not consist only of its top shelf."

"..."

"It also has two drawers and a lower shelf."

"..."

"But you continue to not use them."

"..."

"You put everything on the top without thinking."

"..."

"In fact, you are an idiot."

"..."

"I don't see any other explanation."

"..."

"Or maybe, Linda, you need to take responsibility for your prejudice."

"..."

"I'm serious—follow your logic to its obvious conclusion! Contact my interior designer to get me a wider nightstand."

"..."

"Do you want me to give you his phone number?"

"..."

My assistant remained silent; I could no longer stop myself. My clever barbs flowed out of me effortlessly, with a boundlessness that was as intoxicating as it was dizzying.

"Okay, we're done with this conversation."

"..."

"Is my bath ready?"

"..."

"Did you jam all my beauty products onto the rim of the bathtub, or did you arrange them intelligently?"

"..."

"Fabulous. I hope that it's the right temperature."

"..."

"I hadn't planned on boiling myself or doing a cold plunge."

"..."

"In the meantime, I want you to think over what we've just talked about."

"..."

"You are punished, Linda."

"..."

"Go to your room."

We've been looking for faults in our all-powerful gods ever since antiquity. The deities live on Mount Olympus, inaccessible, immortal, haloed with glory—and yet they resemble us. Athena is pretentious. Hera is mean. Aphrodite is egocentric. Ares is cowardly. Hermes is a playboy. Zeus is a rapist. What could be more human?

In the same way, celebrities are a species unto themselves. Ordinary mortals have nothing in common with the mythical creatures who buy villas in the hills of LA. But everyone dreams of finally being able to say: *Stars, they're just like us.*

That actor slept with his kids' babysitter. That brilliant billionaire left his wife for a younger woman. That singer cheated on his pregnant wife when he was out at a nightclub. You can be rich, beautiful, famous—and also unlucky in love. For the regular people, it's extremely reassuring news.

John and I formed a two-headed mythological beast known by the public as CléJo. We were the most prominent couple in Hollywood—magazines referred to us as the quintessential power couple. Our tumultuous love affair encompassed humanity's most intense and ancient emotions; like classic Greek plays, it was an outlet for general public catharsis. Our audience couldn't tear their eyes away.

We began arguing more and more often; I left John once, regretted my decision, went back to him. I left him a second time before sending him a text late at night, struck with sudden lucidity: "Why did we break up again?" Our reunions were exquisite.

"Why did you come back?" John asked me, his eyes wet with happiness.

"Because I wanted to." What a question—there could be no love without want. "Because I wanted to": It would make a good title for a song.

In a villa in Hamburg that I'd been dreaming of visiting for weeks, John and I celebrated our first anniversary. Three hundred and sixty-five days, if you didn't count the breaks and reconciliations. Villa Jako, a jewel from the 1920s, was located in the hillside Blankenese neighborhood on the west side of the city. Neoclassical architecture, Roman columns, rococo porcelain figurines, genre paintings. After breakfast I sat down at the grand piano in the small salon next to the living room. It felt like I was in an opera set; my notes resounded with unprecedented brightness.

At the end of the tree-lined, sloping park, I spent the evening hypnotized by the gigantic container ships that entered and exited Germany's largest port. I reproached John for having his eyes glued to his phone instead of enjoying the view; why wasn't he interested in the Elbe or the history of the house?

And that was the moment he chose to give me a diamond-studded pendant of the first letters of our names intertwined. His present was ugly, tacky, unsophisticated, garish. John definitely did not have any taste. I should have known that as soon as he showed me his collection of gleaming sports cars—spending so much money on Lamborghinis was very nouveau riche. How could I have thought that his automobile fixation and my snobbery would be a good combination?

I sulked openly (because I was disappointed with the necklace), I was turned off (and I let him know when he brushed his hand along my neck), I went to bed at 10:00 p.m. (without wishing him good night).

The downfall was equal to my expectations: enormous. I could no longer be the easygoing, sweet woman he'd fallen in love with. I was angry, irritable, cruel. John was passive, naïve, lazy. Our story was unbalanced, disappointing, mundane. The whole world could rest easy: *Stars, we're just like you.*

On this particular morning, you were better off having a poster of me above your bed than actually having me in your life. In other words, I was in a bad mood.

Stefani had been waiting for me for an hour when I deigned to join her in the car. Along the way, I called my stylist, Margot, a French woman who lived in Beverly Hills. She sometimes had good ideas, but Margot spoke slowly. How many words did she say in a minute compared to a normal person? Was there a connection between her extreme slowness and the fact that "Margot" rhymed with "escargot"? According to my initial estimates, she was somewhere around 180 words per minute, while my threshold of tolerance began at 210. I was allergic to sluggishness—it might have been at that moment that my life started to spiral.

Margot was mentioning different clauses in the contract for my new brand deal; I was to be paid for appearing in the front row of a runway show for twenty minutes (did anyone still go to Fashion Week if they weren't being paid?), and she was in charge of choosing my outfit alongside the clothing label. I only half listened, wishing desperately I could program her to play at double speed. It was a bad habit I'd picked up while listening to my WhatsApp voice notes. Irritated, I abruptly hung up. Margot would think that my phone had died or that I'd lost signal.

"Did you just hang up on her?" Stefani snapped at me.

"No, of course not. The call dropped."

My manager wasn't fooled. And I remembered I'd done the same thing to her the previous week.

We had a meeting in Santa Monica at my label's California offices. I had to finish my third album (something I was taking care of), but I needed help strategizing. At this point, my career essentially consisted of making choices: what to *say yes to*, what to *say no to*.

Should I be collaborating with the Nigerian singer everyone was talking about? Or would a duet with a French singer be preferable? Was it a good idea to keep releasing singles like "Malibu" to take up as much space as I could, or was it better to finish my third album as soon as possible? What were their thoughts on a detour through the movie world—always risky and unpredictable? Was it time to assume a political bent and pick a trending issue to get behind (eating disorders, cyberbullying, fourth-wave feminism, the migrant crisis)? Should I agree to license my voice for AI software or give a virtual concert in Fortnite? Other promising possibilities: become a judge for a well-known music-competition TV show, host a podcast, set up a social-media book club (darn, Dua Lipa had just beat me to it), start my own cooking show (whoops, this time Selena Gomez was faster), write a children's book, launch a brand of moisturizer or nonalcoholic cocktails.

Like any good captain, I needed to set a course, and my teams were supposed to help me navigate. If I wanted to stay at the top and continue to be relevant, did it behoove me to stick to what I was known for or to diversify myself? Then there was the fact that an artistic career was made up of both stunning feats and disappearances—you had to know how to fade away from the public eye for a bit, to make your fans miss you so that you could come back in full force. At what rhythm was I supposed to be shifting between present and absent? More than anything, I was terrified of the thought of going backward by accepting proposals that were beneath me. I was scared of tarnishing my image, of lowering my ratings, of making myself a less desirable commodity. When I agreed to a new project, I wanted to be sure that it was profitable for me and not the opposite. Were they exploiting my fame? Were they using my name? And what was I getting out of it? Short-term? Medium-term? Long-term?

I arrived at the label and got out of the car, still irritated and in a bad mood. It took the receptionist six seconds to open the security gate. One, two, three . . . I counted out loud, sighing. No one ever talks about it, but the truth is that when you become an international celebrity, it takes exceptional moral strength to stay pleasant with an underling who makes fifteen dollars an hour.

In the hallways, I didn't greet anyone so that I could save my voice. My sunglasses were perched on my nose so that I could roll my eyes in peace. When I entered the meeting room, Linda was already sitting there. I finally realized what was off about her: She had the face of a dolphin. Little round eyes that were very far apart; tiny, gritted teeth; long nose. Another sizeable issue: She always looked like she'd just come from the hairdresser—and that wasn't a compliment. She needed to spend less time with her curling iron and more time developing her personality. I asked her to leave the room because she was drinking her coffee too loudly.

Everyone had been waiting for me for two hours, but they forgave me with revolting ease. And yet I had a chef, a driver, and an assistant; honestly, I'd never had so few reasons not to be on time. To think that at the beginning of my ascension, if I was running two minutes late, I would send a note to the whole team alerting them and apologizing.

Nikki and Stefani greeted each other with hugs and big smiles, though their relationship had been strained over the last few months. The reason: a strong-armed new negotiation of my contract (and therefore my compensation). Around the table, next to the two powerful women, were a handful of men: the marketing director, the artistic director, the creative director, the director of promotions.

Ryan, the marketing director, was sitting directly across from me. I immediately despised his perfect-son-in-law smile, his well-combed hair, his too-tight pants. Now that I lived in Los Angeles, I often asked myself: *Was this man gay, or was he just from California?* Ryan was eloquent, but if you took his elegant turns of phrase out of the equation, there was no new information, no brilliant intuition, no high-level reasoning. He was paid how many thousands of dollars with the money from *my* songs to utter such banality?

I stared at his $30,000 watch, furious and disgusted. His blond locks plastered down with gel made me want to hit him—I'd never trusted people whose hair was overly styled. Let Linda act as precedent here: At work, the less useful you are, the better groomed you are. Now I was giving him three minutes to add value. One hundred and eighty seconds to justify his salary and legitimize his presence in the room. In the meantime, I had to bite my cheek in order to let him finish speaking. His speech was nothing but a stream of foregone conclusions and absurd superlatives. Couldn't we get rid of all the embellishments and have a concrete exchange of ideas? *Sweetheart, religiously getting to the office at seven every morning doesn't make you competent. Your rhetoric cannot replace expertise: What do you have to teach me? Nothing. So be quiet.* This meeting was the antechamber of hell. Open the gates of purgatory for me; not interrupting this idiot was torturous. Only one minute left. Only thirty seconds left. Ten seconds. *Buddy, I regret to inform you that your allotted time is up.*

"Excuse me for interrupting, Ryan, but tell me something I didn't already know."

While I was at it, I was dying to suggest that he buy some clothes in the right size, but I forced myself not to. Ryan froze for a second, laid his pen on the table, drew upon his inexhaustible self-confidence to maintain his composure, then cleared his throat and continued to speak. Unfortunately, the meeting continued on as it had begun: Ryan had nothing wiser to say to us. I yawned openly three times. When was the last time that a *good idea* had come from someone other than me? Why was I always the smartest person in the room?

"Nice watch," I hissed to Ryan as I left.

Then I asked Stefani who I needed to talk to about getting him fired.

The good news was that in Aspen, there were more activities than there were on a yacht. At the end of February, I spent a week there skiing with John. Between runs we visited luxury boutiques and partied with other celebrities.

Unlike me, John knew how to maintain a network of powerful friends: He organized receptions in LA, jaunts to Cabo San Lucas, mountain getaways. At our first party in Aspen, I saw Natalie Holmes; I had no idea that in a year, she would be telling me about a mysterious desert island, inviting me to try the experience for myself, and that in the meantime, so many things would have changed. In a year, in a lifetime, in a century. If only I'd known. But we're never given glimpses into the future.

Sitting next to me in the back of an SUV with white leather seats, John was quiet. He looked good and was dressed well, but I hated his new backpack. His argument was that he found it practical, especially the side pockets, while I tried to make him understand the absurdity of this reasoning by using language he was likely to understand.

"John, when you're driving a Ferrari, you don't install a cargo carrier on the roof. This is the same thing. When you're wearing a Moncler jacket, you don't wear a backpack."

Before getting out of the car, I asked him to throw out his gum.

"And stand up straight. You're all hunched over."

John went around the side of the vehicle to open the door for me. We walked with our bodies semi-intertwined, my head nestled intimately against his shoulder. I slid my hand into the pocket of his coat before snuggling up even closer to him. We kissed amidst the fairyland of evergreens and snowy peaks. Suddenly the walk turned into a snowball fight, childlike and joyful. We bickered affectionately, grinning from ear to ear, and I packed my ammunition into my mitten before going on the attack again. John burst out laughing. Everything was perfect. Behind us, two photographers immortalized the scene.

Everyone knows by now that stars love to complain about being pursued by the paparazzi, but nonetheless, they willingly summon them for staged candid photos when they have a message they want to convey. This morning we'd arranged for Rick and Terry to wait for us at 3:00 p.m. on a walking path just steps from the city center. Right now tabloids were announcing that we'd broken up; stories were circulating that John had seen his ex, Lily Clayton, while I was having affairs with half of Hollywood; another rumor was that we'd secretly gotten married in the south of France before divorcing two days later. It was time to reassure the people: Our relationship was perfect.

We threw snowballs at each other four times, John took me in his arms three times, he lifted me up in the air twice, I kissed him on the mouth once. Five minutes of domestic bliss, just enough time for the paparazzi to do their jobs. The caption that would accompany these photos was crystal clear: I was madly in love with my boyfriend. If only I could clarify that I did not endorse his choice of backpack.

"*Cléo, sweetheart, you* never tell me that you love me anymore...."

"Stop pressuring me. The more you plead, the less I want to say it."

That night in the chalet we were renting for $15,000 per night, we had a heated discussion about our schedules. John refused to postpone the promotion for his show that summer; I refused to cancel my European music-festival tour. If neither one of us gave in, we wouldn't see each other for three months. My arguments were solid, and I was better at delivering them than he was. A goddess of rhetoric with the soul of a cutthroat lawyer, I wormed my way into the flaws in his logic, used his own words against him, pointed out all his contradictions. How could he demand that I put my career aside for him? In a power couple, it is always the women who end up fading away behind their partners—I wouldn't submit to a man. John clumsily retorted that he had always supported me, that it wasn't like he was asking me to give up music. He was getting annoyed; I wasn't letting him off the hook, pursuing him across the chalet, even when he begged me to allow him to go outside for some air so he could think. Where did he think he was going to go? I was in the middle of talking, I hadn't dismissed him, it wasn't my problem if stuff was happening in his head. John fell to his knees, bent over in pain, but I didn't give in, instead continuing to reproach him with my finger in the air, merciless. Completely exhausted, John threw a glass bottle across the kitchen—it shattered on the wall next to me. He apologized, mortified, trembling, uncomprehending. "What have I done . . . ?" I grabbed my phone to take a photo of the mess on the floor. John burst into tears. I'd never seen him like that, a real fountain of sorrow. On the bright side: For once, his beautiful blue eyes weren't lacking for moisture.

Fifteen minutes later, I was calmly reading the latest Sally Rooney novel in bed. Why was John still crying? Hadn't he had enough of playing the victim? We'd been arguing all evening; he wasn't going to prevent me from sleeping too. I needed eight hours to be able to perform on the slopes the next day. I turned my back to him and put in earplugs so that I didn't have to hear his sobs. If he weren't so famous, I would have banished him to sleep on the couch.

A week after we returned from Aspen, I was photographed in a children's clothing boutique in Beverly Hills. This time I hadn't arranged a fake paparazzi photo session. The media announced my pregnancy, and I received several congratulatory messages, including a phone call from my mother, who, once again, didn't understand anything at all. Even John seemed troubled by this nonrevelation, because he called me from Austin that day.

"So is it true? You're pregnant?"

"Of course not. I was looking for a gift for Juliette's daughter."

"That's too bad."

John kept talking, but I was no longer hearing him. "That's too bad?" How could he possibly hope that one day we would welcome a child together? Already our relationship was suffering from scheduling conflicts, and he wanted me to put my career in jeopardy to become a mother? It was out of the question for me to put a half-blind infant's needs before my own. That child would be famous from birth, an inherited gift it didn't need to fight for; a lazy and ignorant kid, too rich and too spoiled, conceited and wasteful, a privileged little brat, addicted to booze and coke, the kind to buy bottles of champagne with Daddy and Mommy's money in the VIP sections of nightclubs in Monaco. The baby didn't even exist, but I already hated it.

At the other end of the line, John was chatty and joyful as he continued telling me about his day.

"You talk too much, John."

"What?"

"I said that you talk too much. You're giving me a headache."

I need an account number, not a cure for cancer. Can you make your answer brief, please?"

Across from me, Linda was reeling off several muddled sentences that didn't solve my problem at all. Her inability to summarize was astounding. I got up to look at the sky and the ocean, equally blue and ever-changing. My office, which was on the third floor, had what was probably the best view of the house.

"Can you stick to the facts and not approximations?"

Linda's eyes were glued to her computer, and her investigations were taking forever. At that moment, I couldn't decide whether my assistant was unwilling or stupid.

"Are you capable of giving me the information I need, yes or no?"

"..."

"It's taking too long."

"..."

"You know, Linda, I don't like having to request it from you, but you see, I don't have a choice."

"..."

"Honestly, it's a pain."

"..."

That morning, when someone I worked with asked me for an account number for a wire transfer, I had to answer, quite seriously:

"Hold on, I have to ask three people." How had I gotten to that point? Of course, delegation is a luxury. But it is also a painful form of dependency. Powerless, I observed Linda. I wanted to bang my head against the wall. I'd been dispossessed of all control over the logistical aspects of my life—and now I was reliant on a permed assistant who looked like a cetacean.

"Can I have the account number, or does this request exceed your capabilities?"

"..."

"Go ahead."

"..."

"Skip to the important part."

"..."

"Spare me the details."

"..."

"Linda, I don't understand you when you talk. Articulate, please."

"..."

"I cannot hear you. Talk louder. I don't have supersonic ears."

"..."

"And stop rocking back and forth on your heels. You're making me seasick."

"..."

I was able to breathe again once Linda left the room—only to hear someone else's breath on my neck. John had witnessed the scene, standing behind me in the doorway.

"You're hard on her," he accused me.

"No, that girl is a dud."

"That's debatable."

"It's the truth."

"She's doing her best."

"It's not enough."

"Then why do you keep her?"

"Because everyone likes her."

"That's the only reason?"

"No, she's fairly reliable and effective. Is that what you wanted me to say? But the thing is, I've been wondering more and more whether her skills compensate for the frown lines she's given me on my forehead."

"You're exaggerating."

"That girl is slow."

"She's not slow, she's afraid of you."

"That's ridiculous."

"You don't realize how intimidating you can be."

"Linda couldn't care less."

"You're impossible to satisfy."

"I deserve an assistant who goes above and beyond for me."

"The girl is under your sway."

"No, she's under my command."

"Your insensitivity is freaking me out."

"Why are you defending her?"

"Because I can't stand unfairness. You're a tyrant."

"I'm not a tyrant, I just do what needs to be done."

"You're abusive."

"No, John. I'm strict."

The most important thing was not to let my distress show. I hadn't done anything wrong. Nothing. I was a hundred times easier on Linda than I was on myself. The girl was a pain in the ass. John saw only a tiny fragment of what our day-to-day together was like—he didn't know her the way I did. Plus, I was struggling to finish my third album; I needed support, not criticism and judgment. How could he turn his back on me like that?

"John, do you ever feel like killing everyone?"

"Well, I'd be a little more nuanced in my language ..." he said with a smile, softening again.

"And you're always so emotionally regulated. . . . It's unbearable."

That incident gave me the proof I was missing: Linda was a nasty, manipulative twat. She'd seen John standing behind me but had decided to set me up by not saying anything. This time I made sure she and I were alone before closing and locking the door to my office.

"Linda, I have a question for you."

"Yes?"

"What do you all say about me when I'm not around?"

"What do you mean?"

"You and the team. What do you think of me?"

Linda thought for a long time, then tried:

"We say that you're very charismatic."

"Charismatic ... That's a polite way of saying that I'm a bitch."

Good. I'd rather be mean in a real way than nice in a fake way. If I eased up, no one would work anymore. Did I have to remind them all that this whole impressive human pyramid rested solely on my shoulders? On my will? On my demandingness? On my talent? On my songs? If I were a man, people wouldn't resent me as much for being domineering—instead, I would be admired for my firmness and my ruthless decision-making. But I lived in a world where powerful women were seen as disturbing. So, yes, sometimes I was harsh, but you judge a tree by its fruit: Mine were successful albums, not a charity.

"Linda, kneel down."

"Excuse me?"

"You heard me. Kneel down and ask for my forgiveness."

". . ."

"There you go. Perfect. And now kiss my feet."

I was about to tell her she could leave when I realized that she'd wet herself.

Well, *it seems like I love him a little less every day.* John joined me on the terrace, a pack of Peeps in hand, mouth puckered happily in a kiss.

"Do you want any, babe?"

We talk so often about love at first sight that we forget to point out that it's a reversible process. Why does no one ever make art about falling out of love?

Romantic relationships might be the only area of my life in which I'm lacking in courage, so I tried to drive John away in order to spare myself from having to break up with him. I was horrible: I knew it, hated myself for it, kept doing it.

"Can you go eat somewhere else, please? You make noise when you chew. Thanks very much."

"No worries, my love," John answered, stroking my cheek.

Well, it seems like I have zero desire for you to touch me at this point. I was withdrawing from him, noting each of his physical flaws, despondent. I no longer felt any tenderness for his freckles, I resented him for not taking care of himself, I no longer dared look him in the eyes.

John walked away whistling, serene and confident, still holding his Peeps, while I wanted to demolish the rose-colored walls of his world. My favorite part of myself had always been my brain: I had a thousand intellectual strengths and very few emotional ones. How could I have ever imagined that I could be happy in a relationship? I didn't have a single quality that would make me a devoted girlfriend. And then there was the fact that we had no business being together. John was gentle, courteous, measured, affectionate. I was aggressive, blunt, curt, vicious. I had to face the facts: A bulldozer shouldn't be with a daisy.

John felt that he was truly worthy of love. When his first girlfriend had left him when he was sixteen, it took him two years to get over it. Flabbergasted, he couldn't understand how she'd gotten away; hadn't she realized that he was the perfect man, kind and generous? How unfair! How violent! Consoling, his mother had assured him, "She doesn't know what she's giving up. Her loss."

Around the same time in France, the boy I liked had stopped responding to my texts. I was sad for two hours. Deep down, I wasn't surprised that he wasn't interested anymore—I wasn't a good person, and he had finally discovered my true nature. When my mother found out, she told me, "It's not that surprising—you have a bad attitude."

No one doubted my self-assuredness; everything I did, I did forcefully. But having a very high opinion of oneself has never stopped anyone from hating themself.

"*Do you feel* like you deserve to be loved?" I asked Aria that evening on the phone.

"Of course I do, why?"

"No reason."

"Things aren't going well with John?"

"Everything he does annoys me. I want to strangle him some-times."

"My therapist always tells me that there are two choices: Either you embrace the other person's flaws tenderly, or you leave."

"I don't have much tenderness left to give."

"Well, then, you have your answer."

John and I have decided to go our separate ways. This was a mutual decision, and in no way does it take away from the love that we have for each other. I still respect John deeply and wish him nothing but the best, and I know he feels the same way about me. He will always have a special place in my heart. We may no longer be together romantically, but our love for one another as humans is more profound than ever. I would like to ask you all to please give us space and time at this difficult moment for both of us."

I posted the announcement on my social media one Sunday evening. I'd negotiated every word, demanded to be the first to break the news, chosen the exact time.

Linda ran a bath for me. Rose petals, Himalayan salt, sweet orange essential oil, coconut milk powder, and oatmeal. My inspiration: Cleopatra's donkey milk baths. I got into the creamy water, phone in hand, ready to browse the memories of my relationship with John on Google. Our smiles on the red carpet, the paparazzi shots from Capri, his declaration of love onstage at the Golden Globes. I could delete the photos of us from my phone but not from the World Wide Web.

The pain was real: I should start by saying that. Just because our breakup was public didn't mean I wasn't suffering—and just because I was the one who decided to leave him didn't mean I felt nothing.

John was in the middle of promoting his TV show, a comedic murder mystery set in an apartment building in New York. I didn't miss a single one of his interviews, because I knew that people would be asking him about me, and I wondered what his talking points would be. At night in bed, I learned what he'd been up to at the same time as the rest of the world. Behind my screen, I discovered one of the most acutely painful parts of a breakup: the loss of your privileged access to the other person.

With Vik, it had taken me one day to erase our four-month relationship. If I applied the same ratio for John, I would need 4.75 days to forget him. I rounded up to five. Perfect: Today was Monday. On Friday I'd be over him.

Breaking up is not unlike getting a tooth pulled; it is best not to dwell on it but instead to yank it out quickly. At the same time, you shouldn't rush the healing process, because you want to be sure that you've put it behind you for good. One week seemed like a reasonable amount of time: neither too long nor too short.

I called Celeste and Juliette regularly. Yet my recovery wasn't linear. I would wake up feeling light—obviously, I was getting better; a weight had been lifted off my chest; I was rediscovering the zest of joy. But then, around 11:00 a.m. or noon, I would fall back into melancholy; grief would twist my insides, and I'd be once again depressed and overcome with remorse, without knowing what had set off the painful regression. My two friends lived in different time zones, so I chose whether to send my anguish to Paris or New York based on how late it was in the day. Aria didn't pick up; she must have left her phone in a taxi again.

As soon as sadness took over, I'd wrap myself up in a cashmere sweater, slip on my white leather Hermès sandals, and take the narrow staircase that led directly to the beach. I'd be facing the ocean, tiny and alone, with the voice of one of my best friends in my ear.

We'd talk for twenty minutes or an hour. Sometimes I'd leave my shoes on the sand to dip my feet in the water. Sometimes the sun would be rising; other times it would be late at night.

When I was at my lowest, I'd pull out the king of kings of last resorts, the ultimate appeal to authority, and remind myself: If I'd survived the death of my father, I could survive anything. Anyway, heartbreak was very different from mourning: Mourning was a time of emotion, while heartbreak was a time of reason. I had to be rational, practical—efficient, even. It served no purpose to rehash the good memories, so instead I concentrated on John's faults. On the phone, Celeste and Juliette helped me remember why we weren't made to be together. The list of our incompatibilities was the most powerful remedy for the pain: In no world and under no circumstances would we have been a happy couple. Not now, not ever.

In the end, his big blue eyes just annoyed me. He didn't make me a better person. He settled for little. He wasn't all that good-looking, especially close-up. He was bad in bed. He was addicted to chick-shaped marshmallows as though he were a toddler. He was unsophisticated. He was gullible. He was completely useless when it came to doing anything practical. He didn't take care of himself. He was soft. He was incapable of seeing anything through (he'd taken five French lessons before giving up; he hadn't finished a single one of the novels I'd given him). He was an idiot. He was a messy eater. He wasn't a good conversationalist. He didn't teach me anything. I didn't like his friends.

I wanted to broadcast it, shout it from the rooftops, again and again: John wasn't as great as he seemed. *He doesn't deserve your admiration. You're just attached to him because you've watched him grow up, but there's nothing exceptional about him.* I was fooled too at first. He fascinated me, to say the least, and he did have a few good songs to his name. But he didn't work hard—sometimes he even slept in after 11:00 a.m.—and he never had to fight to get famous; he was just lucky. *I'm telling you on good authority: John is a nice person, but he doesn't have much in the way of intelligence or talent.*

Friday evening the necklace that John had given me for our first anniversary glittered around my neck. I caressed the pendant nostalgically as I looked in the mirror. Smiling, I remembered when we'd met, the first time we'd spent the night together, our first vacation. I didn't feel sad at all anymore, just an immense fondness for our love story. We'd been separated for seven days, and I was reminiscing as though it had been more than ten years.

I poured myself a glass of champagne to toast to my recovery. John had been forgotten. That was one good thing done.

I'm calling to see how you're doing."

"..."

"Is everything okay, sweetheart?"

"..."

"I learned about you and John."

"..."

"I'm sorry."

"..."

"Hello, can you hear me?"

"..."

"..."

"I don't care about that, Mom. It's just a breakup. No one's dead."

"..."

"Mom?"

"Yes?"

"Do you think that Dad would have been proud of me?"

"Excuse me?"

"You understood the question. Would Dad have been proud of me?"

"Of course he would have."

"You're just saying that to make me feel better."

"No, I'm saying it because it's true. You were the apple of his eye, how could you have any doubts about that? You were your dad's pride and joy. You always were."

"..."

"..."

"Mom, why didn't you say anything when my first album came out?"

"I didn't know that you wanted my opinion."

"A compliment wouldn't have hurt."

"You never needed us."

"..."

"Cléo, you never asked us for anything. You're so independent. You've always been so independent."

"That's not an excuse to never congratulate me."

"That's true. I'm sorry."

"It's not a big deal, Mom. You couldn't have known."

The outfits were so disappointing. A long fuchsia skirt with a slit, an emerald-green asymmetrical dress, a lavender lace jumpsuit. I raised an eyebrow, and five people sprang up to present me with new suggestions selected by my stylist. Every day Margot achieved the feat of being as slow as she was incompetent. She stood behind me now, biting her nails.

A powder-pink tweed ensemble, a blazer worn with nothing underneath, a black lace-up corset. Margot played her last card with a skater miniskirt and a sparkly bra that looked like shiny chain mail.

"It's like glamorous gladiatrix armor . . . the conqueror after her breakup," she argued as she adjusted the fabric on my shoulders.

I indicated my discontent with a shake of my head. My dissatisfaction filled the room, deadly and toxic. Why did Margot work for me again? I suggested she give my old stylist, Petra, a call. "Feel free to reach out. Petra Mackay is brilliant and incredibly talented, a real visionary. Go have coffee with her—she'll explain how to do the job."

My severity wasn't gratuitous. It matched the stakes: This would be my first public appearance since the breakup. If I wore something flashy, they'd say I wanted to win John back. If I wore something simple, they'd explain I was moping. If I sneezed, they'd snap a photo so they could report that I was crying. If I laughed, they'd maintain I was trying to provoke John. Every element would be seen as a sign, ripe for in-depth analysis; nothing would be able to stop the semiological frenzy. Fame never comes without a good dose of exegesis.

I pursed my lips when they brought me a green-and-red dress. "Were you also planning to have me wear Christmas ornaments and a garland around my neck?" Margot backed away, panicked. Meanwhile, I played idly with my tank top. When I was a kid, I often used to knot the bottom of my T-shirt to make a bralette. And it was there, in front of the mirror, as I raised the fabric up over my chest, that I was struck by a quasi-mystical revelation.

"I want a dress that shows the bottom of my breasts."

"What do you mean?"

"Instead of a plunging neckline, one that reveals the underside."

Once again all the good ideas came from me. And once again I wasn't wrong. That dress was the decision that the world was waiting for.

On the red carpet, I struck a pose just as I'd learned to do it, pushing my chin forward to elongate my neck. The photographers shouted my name; five more seconds in that position, then I turned my torso ten degrees, hands on my waist. The uninterrupted crackling of the camera shutters made me giggle with pleasure—I could sometimes hear it in my head still even once I was at home alone.

That night my sculptural black dress had only one eccentricity: its opening above my navel. The cutout allowed the bottoms of my breasts to peek out, round like two croissants.

My radical stance didn't go unnoticed. "Cléo Louvent flaunted a scandalous outfit after her breakup with John Cutler—her inverted neckline broke the internet." "The singer set the red carpet ablaze in a Miu Miu gown that revealed the underside of her perfect assets."

There I was, leader of the under-boob trend, which succeeded that of the side boob. It became sexier to expose the bottom of your breasts than the top or the side, which everyone had already seen a million times, from every angle. The style was adopted for all the dresses and bikinis of the following summer. The fashion industry could thank me once again.

My dress was groundbreaking, but it was also part of the long-standing historical tradition of revenge dresses. Everyone remembered the one Diana had worn after her 1994 split with Prince Charles. He'd just implicitly confessed to his affair with Camilla in front of all of England; Diana wasn't yet divorced, but she was free, and she held her head high through the torment. That was exactly the story that her little black dress with a plunging neckline told.

There was nothing I needed to seek revenge for after my breakup with John. However, it was crucial that I be the one to determine my own narrative. And at that point in my career—if I was honest with myself—my story was being told through the underside of my breasts more than through the depth of my songs.

I smiled at the photographers, perfect, strategic, warlike— unassailable in my iconic dress. I didn't know that a bomb was about to go off, a revelation that no neckline, even an inverse one, could protect me from. Because the bomb wasn't going to come from just anywhere. It had been planted within my own camp.

It was snowing in Malibu. The sticky California heat hadn't prepared me for the white flakes. My driver took me for a spin in the car; apparently, families were sledding a bit farther up the road. I needed air—I'd spent the last three weeks holed up at home, glued to my phone, shocked by the news. The saga of my breakup continued, and it was more entertaining than ever. The whole world was grabbing the popcorn. John and Aria were engaged.

Like every other celebrity, I used a burner account to keep tabs on my ex's social media. No followers, no photos: guaranteed anonymity. This profile allowed me to see John's posts without risking exposure by accidentally clicking on a story. So I scrolled back through the memories. Hey, John hadn't deleted the photo of me in my peach dress with my pearly nail polish and loving smile. In his most recent photo, he had hard-launched my replacement: The young couple was on their way back from a trip to Hawaii. Aria was posing in front of a waterfall wearing a mauve bikini, her left hand placed against her cheek—the Maui landscape was only a pretext for her to show off her engagement ring, a ten-carat oval diamond on a yellow-gold band. I sighed. *Sweetie, John had to spend $500,000 to make you believe that he prefers you to me. You're both pathetic.*

Three months. The speed with which John had entered this new relationship made me think that I was right to speed along our breakup. John and Aria had seen each other at a party at my house at the end of July; was that the moment when the transition had begun? Was that the reason why John had protested only weakly when I left him?

The world was vast. Choosing one of my best friends wasn't mere coincidence—Cupid's arrows don't strike that randomly. This relationship was the rotten fruit of vengeance. John wanted to get to me because I'd dropped him; Aria sought revenge because I'd surpassed her.

Come to that, had she already had this in mind when she advised me to leave John because I had no more tenderness to give him? I understood my friend—maybe I even understood her a little too well. If you want to be the star of the show, you have to be willing to appear selfish. Morality and glory rarely go hand in hand. Of course, I hadn't needed to use my body to advance my career, but I could imagine it was a tempting shortcut when you were lacking in talent.

On the phone, John denied everything entirely: *It has nothing to do with you.* He cried (no surprise there), asked for my forgiveness (begged, really), kept repeating that he'd done something wrong (no kidding), swore that he never wanted to hurt me (I didn't believe this). Aria had come into his life like a hurricane, and he had tried in good Christian fashion to resist her, but the pull was too strong to resist. I bombarded him with questions, reproaches, and accusations until he finally gave in, admitting breathlessly: "With her, I knew what I was never sure of with you." Bullshit.

Immediately afterward, Celeste called me and offered to visit as soon as possible. She was sorry for me. In a sickly-sweet voice, she explained, believing somehow that this would make me feel better, that Aria had *actually* fallen in love with John. The clarification was laughable. The two lovebirds had promised to spend the rest of their lives together. I couldn't wait to see that.

Aria and I had only one conversation. The call lasted two minutes and fourteen seconds. I didn't need more than that. My course of action was clear: wisdom, maturity, magnanimity. "I'm happy for you two, I really am. You have my blessing. I only want you to be happy—that's the most important thing. I never managed to love John the way he deserved, and I wasn't ready to be engaged to him. He knew it—he proposed to me a few weeks before we broke up, and I said no. John has so much love to give, so if you're feeling it, forge ahead. But be careful. You're my friend, and I want to be sure to warn you. John is still in love with me. That's to be expected; you don't forget your soulmate in three months. Try not to think about it too much. And honestly, Aria, if it's worrying you, know that I don't hold it against you at all. I've always wanted the best for you. How do you think you got your part in your show? Stefani called the director, that's how. By the way, just between us, since we're talking about careers, you're making a mistake by tying your name to John's. Of course you're world-famous now, so they'll give you parts in major franchises, popular big-budget movies—better start your diet now so that you can fit into a latex suit and play some random female superhero. You've always been a little tease. They'll all get hard when they see you in your costume—you just have to get your boobs done. By the way, you'll earn a nice wad of cash from these productions. Expect to be paid like a queen, which is a good thing, because it will mean John won't have to support you. Anyway, after that, good luck convincing a decent director to work with you. Say goodbye to complex roles. Goodbye, Cannes. Goodbye, Venice. But I'm sure that you're going to love Hollywood. Feel free to reach out if you need anything—we're almost neighbors now. Hello? Aria? Am I dreaming, or are you crying? Come on, dry your tears, it's not worth it. If the sadness becomes too much, there's always a solution. You could put a bullet through your head. I promise no one will miss you."

The fans reacted like children who couldn't accept their parents' separation: They plotted to get us back together. CléJo retrospectives proliferated on the internet, especially YouTube and TikTok—romantic music, photomontages, timelines of our relationship. Tens of thousands of videos of unprecedented kitsch. I couldn't believe my eyes.

In the comments posted below their Hawaii vacation photos, the attack on Aria was savage. "Aria is a bitch." "John and Aria shouldn't be together." "John will love Cléo his whole life." People uncovered the old photos of Aria and me on the beach in Ibiza. Aria had betrayed her best friend—she was a man-stealer, a home-wrecker, a slut. On social media she was inundated with hateful messages; she'd become the new woman to take down. I'd be lying if I said there wasn't a part of me rejoicing. Public opinion had chosen its side: mine.

Aria was harassed both online and in the street. The crowd shouted my name when she and John made their first appearance on the red carpet, and Aria broke down in tears in front of the photographers. Several days later, she was spotted with a long leopard-print coat that was strangely similar to one I'd recently worn. Fans spent hours studying the new tattoo on her ring finger: They claimed that it was a copy of the design of the pendant that John had given me for our first anniversary.

The story continued to write itself: Aria was obsessed with me, terrified of the thought that John still loved me. This narrative relied on the hackneyed refrain of so-called female rivalry, because everyone knows that two women have nothing better to do than fight over a man. It was misogynistic, and anyway, I had no intention of fighting.

My phone rang. Stefani was insistent that she be the first to tell me the news: John was about to release a song in which he talked about me. She shared the lyrics while I watched the snow falling on the ocean. "You were cold, I was unhappy / You were only an illusion, only a mirage / I found the one who could make my dreams come true." I couldn't blame John for using our relationship in his songs; I'd been profiting off it for a year and a half. And between us, I much preferred these predictable lyrics to ones that revealed I had bad breath or that I farted in my sleep.

Anyway, my strategy had remained unchanged since the beginning of the whole disaster: retreat into silence. In other words: *I was handling the situation with grace.* I kept well out of the public eye, refusing to rise to the bait. This major betrayal had made me the victim, a virtuous and valiant heroine, so beautiful in her pain. Alan, my image consultant, was thrilled—it was a godsend. Since I'd been the one to leave John, I could have easily been the bad guy, something for which women are rarely forgiven.

You always have to be at least two steps ahead, and I'd chosen mine. First, I would push back the release date of my third album by two months. Second, I would add three devastating breakup songs to it to ride the wave of momentum.

I looked at the photo of Aria in her mauve bikini one last time. Hawaii, the waterfall, the ring, her huge black eyes, her wet hair, her hips. She was enticing—I was all too familiar with the way she tasted like apricot. The most dizzying thing was that I'd licked her velvety skin; how could I not imagine what their nights were like?

When faced with the worst, you always have a choice. I could be floored by the news, wreck my career, gain thirty pounds, lose five years of my life rehashing what happened, argue with Celeste, deepen my frown lines prematurely. I refused to entertain this scenario. Depression was a choice, but it was the choice of the weak.

It was still snowing on the beach. I sat down to look at the sea while waiting for the sun to set. The waves deposited shells at my feet while a fine layer of powder slowly covered the sand. I turned off my phone.

All the world's woes stem from a forbidden fruit. For me the inevitable began with an apple. I gestured to Linda to bring me one: My assistant was in the kitchen, which meant—or so I thought—that my request could go without explanation.

"I don't understand. What is it that you want?" Linda asked.

Definitely not the brightest of people. I began miming the fruit's shape with my hands, bringing my palms together, but there was no spark of understanding on her face. Did she want me to draw her a picture? She stared at me with her sea-mammal face, unmoving and completely useless.

"Linda, you have to understand something. My voice is my instrument. I can't just use it for whatever and with whomever. When I motion with my hand, it means that you should take action. Try to use your own common sense to determine what that action should be. You are right next to a basket of fruit. What do you think I need? Some shampoo? A plane ticket? A pearl necklace? No, I want an apple. There you have it. It's not difficult."

"Sorry, I can't read your mind yet," she replied, bringing me the fruit.

"Yet that's exactly what I'm asking you to do."

"And again, that's too bad, because I can't peer into souls."

"Linda, I'm not paying you to be smart. Nor am I paying you to write my songs for me. You are here to make my life easier and to give me time to work creatively. So the least you could do would be to bring me an apple when you're near the fruit basket. Do you understand what I'm trying to explain to you? And stop this little rebellion right now. It's not cute at all."

Lying on my couch, facing the ocean, a guitar within reach, I bit into my apple. Then, without prompting, Linda spoke again:

"I don't understand why you're so mean."

"Your analysis is so simplistic, it's depressing."

"I don't agree."

"Stop answering, Linda. You're ridiculous."

"..."

"Seriously, I'm embarrassed for you."

"..."

"I feel sorry for you."

An hour later, Linda was blocking my way as I tried to go downstairs. When you're that low in the hierarchy, you should stay close to the wall. And not only that, but she was moving slowly. I sighed impatiently. The back of her head, with its curling-iron ringlets, aggravated me. *Step aside, goddamnit.*

It was pathological: The girl didn't know what to do with her body. Either she was walking too far behind or she was too close in front of me; right now, she was smack in the middle. *Keep to your right, goddamnit.*

But what was she doing now? I couldn't believe it. She was taking a granola bar out of her pocket. We were walking downstairs, not climbing Mount Everest. The physical exertion was minimal—there was no need for an extra carb supply. I could hear her munching on the superfluous calories. Absolute violence. She knew that it was inadvisable to eat in my presence. She knew that the sounds of the human body irritated me. Why was she inflicting this upon me? How could she attack me so directly in my own house? Descending slowly, blocking my way, chewing her energy bar, breathing heavily as though she were in the middle of a full-on workout—she spared me none of it.

And that was when she missed a step. She fell to the bottom of the stairs, her skull hitting the ground with a dull thud. I approached her; she was bleeding from the head and breathing with difficulty. A muddy, pleading, repulsive wheeze.

I had to go over the circumstances of the accident a hundred times. I explained that Linda had lost her balance on the stairs (false; I had shoved her, just a quick push on her shoulders), that I'd tried to grab on to her arms to keep her from falling (not at all; I was glad that I could now pass her and that she was no longer eating). I also said, through tears, that I'd rushed to call for help (false again; first I'd thrown away the remainder of the granola bar), and then described the blood flowing from her head and my growing panic (bullshit; I'd watched the puddle of blood spread over the kitchen-floor tiles while smoking calmly—it was very relaxing).

Looking serious, I asked the doctor: Was Linda going to make it? What were her chances of waking up from the coma? What would she remember about the fall? At this stage, he wasn't able to answer me. "With traumatic brain injuries, anything is possible. You have to keep up hope." So I hoped. I hoped with all my heart. *Please let her die.*

I went into the hospital chapel alone. No one had ever seen me pray, but the situation was critical: I needed her to give up the ghost, the sooner the better. I pressed my palms together, lifted my eyes heavenward. I appealed to my career, the good that I had brought to the world around me thanks to my songs, the value I'd added to the earth. I couldn't lose everything just because I'd pushed my assistant down the stairs. That was ridiculous. *Lord, if you'll permit me to say just one thing,* if Linda hadn't been eating, she definitely would have been able to grab the handrail and stop herself from falling. Likewise, if she had been on the side of the steps instead of in the *middle.* Really, I barely had anything to do with it.

A little farther away was a couple sitting in silence. Their daughter was seriously ill; after seeing me, they asked me to pray for her (and for a selfie). I lit a candle before leaving.

Where does a destiny come from? Mine was the logical result of my extraordinary personality and my strict work ethic. Now, for the first time, the remainder of my existence would be determined by a game of chance: prison for murder (if Linda woke up) or eternal glory (if Linda died). All my life, I'd fought to maintain control, and then Linda came along and caused me to let down my guard. I'd admit it, I'd made a mistake: I'd lost self-control. And I'd paid the price. My dazzling legacy no longer depended on my own genius but on the brain of an insignificant little girl.

Her condition deteriorated until, three days later, she died. Even on her deathbed, Linda was exhaustingly slow. The doctor threw some words around to describe the tragedy: severe traumatic brain injury, irreversible intracranial lesions. My translation: I was saved. There really was justice in this earthly existence.

A public tribute, an exclusive TV interview: It was time to trot out the violins and the melancholy refrain. I talked about how wonderful and irreplaceable Linda was (yeah, right), how she was a collaborator and a friend (as if!). I expressed my gratitude toward her, and more generally toward everyone on my team working away in the shadows, without whom I wouldn't be here (I paid their salary each month, and now I was supposed to thank them?

While I was at it, did they want anything else?). I continued with a soliloquy on accidents at home: Every year thousands of Americans die after falling down the stairs; if only I'd reacted faster, had the right reflexes. Solemnly, I announced that I'd decided to take a class in first aid techniques (false; I had plenty of other things to do with my time). I finished with tears in my eyes, quivering, overcome with emotion: Our lives could change at any moment, we were so fragile, we had to seize every moment. Thesis, antithesis, synthesis: the winning trifecta.

Now I was expected to give a generous check to Linda's family. Even in death, that girl continued to lose me time and money. Then my image consultant, Alan, suggested I write a song about her, to which I replied coldly that we shouldn't get carried away. What was going to be next? Was I supposed to build a church in her honor? Get her dolphin face tattooed on my lower back? I called on my team to *put things into perspective*. I had to find a new assistant, and Linda wouldn't even be there to train her. Plus, because of this whole thing, I'd started smoking again.

When I picked up my phone, I immediately recognized John's familiar voice. He was about to offer his condolences, to comfort me; in all likelihood, he would try to win me back. I could sense his pure heart beating on the other end of the line. I found a quiet spot away from all the commotion, my phone plastered against my ear.

"John, is that you?"

"What have you done?"

I stayed silent while John repeated, over and over, in shock: "You're crazy, you're crazy, you're crazy. . . ."

EPILOGUE

My favorite Agatha Christie novel taught me this a long time ago: When you isolate murderers on an island, chances are that they'll end up confessing their crimes.

I'm to blame for Linda's death. In the end, it took me months to be able to admit the truth to myself and to feel even a twinge of guilt. I went too far. Her cry of surprise when I pushed her down the stairs haunts me sometimes. For half a second, my own cruelty makes me shiver. I have to pull myself together. My assistant got only what she deserved. Fundamentally, Linda had no business being in my inner circle. I should have fired her at the first signs of her lack of dedication to the job. I sensed right away that she wasn't a good fit, and yet I had my heart set on training her, taking the trouble to explain things that should have gone without saying. My problem is that I'm too nice.

If only I could take a photo of this view—freeze in time the waves, the endless horizon, the sun rising over the Pacific, my little hut. On my island, alone, I've had the singular experience of living in an enclosed world facing an infinite ocean. I'll never forget the metaphysical exhilaration.

The seaplane will land in a few hours, and I've wrapped everything up. Faith, ascension, glory. The double betrayal of John and Aria, the death of Linda, the release of my third album. The dissatisfaction I'm no longer able to silence, the need for isolation, the desert island.

I'll come back from here rested and, most importantly, calmer and more clearheaded. Fame isn't just a sad passion. Success isn't just a desolate landscape. John, Aria, and Linda aren't the main characters; they're collateral damage. Like my grandmother always said: You can't make an omelet without breaking some eggs. Of course, fame can be a heavy costume to wear, but I'd avoided its two predictable pitfalls: oblivion and a downward spiral.

Everyone loves me. I have a wonderful life. I'm incredibly rich. I'm talented. I'm powerful. I bent the music industry to my will. I managed to last. I'm neither depressed nor addicted to drugs. Why do I forget all this so often? Why are women condemned to criticize themselves for all of eternity? I'm tired of being so hard on myself. I've received outpourings of acclaim; now it's time for me to congratulate myself. I'm rich and famous. I've won.

I clap louder and louder, whistle with my thumb and index finger; my insane laughter scares the birds. I finished another song this morning, and it's perfect—my work here is done. Soon I'll be back with a brilliant fourth album, the best pop of the decade, written on this island. The curtain falls, and I appear, triumphant. *Guess who's back?*

I'm giddy, overcome by euphoria. I take off all my clothes, jump with joy on the beach, run naked into the waves. My body is firm and golden from three weeks in the sun; I can't wait to see myself in a mirror again, irresistible, tan, slender. I lounge naked on the sand. I shout as loudly as my lungs will allow. I masturbate standing up, feet in the water, facing the ocean, while multicolored fish suck my toes.

Then I settle in for one last nap in the shade on the terrace. I've found the answers to my questions, and the magic has done its work: I've written an amazing album. My dear island has kept all its promises; I fall asleep satisfied.

I wake up in the pitch-black night, disoriented. I must have slept at least four or five hours. I put on a wool cardigan before scrutinizing the horizon. The seaplane didn't come to pick me up yesterday.

It doesn't come the next morning, either. Have I miscounted the days? I have faith in the knife notches in the wall that serve as my improvised calendar, but I also have to take into account the time difference, the Southern Hemisphere, the twenty-four-hour journey to get to the island. Did I lose track?

I still have water and provisions, but that's not the issue: The experience has lasted long enough. They told me three weeks, not four. I've learned the meaning of my life, atoned for my sins, and written a phenomenal album. It's time to go home.

I pace around the beach, chin raised toward the sky. My things are waiting on the terrace—my suitcase is zipped up, my guitar back in its case. My initials decorate the entrance to the hut, a memento of me for the future residents. Every time a bird calls, I think I hear the distant hum of a plane.

As the hours go by, I get angrier. I'd counted on coming back from this trip calmer, not furious with all of humanity. For $500,000, I would hope that the organizers of this merry expedition would be capable of coming to get me on schedule. But just like everywhere else, people are infinitely incompetent. I don't know why I'm shocked.

I scan the Pacific Ocean, easily visualizing the ten thousand private jets I could buy to get me out of here. I also think about buying my own airliner: an Airbus A380 or an Air Force One would do the trick. At this point, I'm so annoyed that I'd buy an entire airline and four airports. How much could that cost? I'm impatient, a fly trapped in a jar, powerless and frustrated. By the end of the day, I can't stand it anymore. I grab the phone with the antenna, the one I'm supposed to use only for emergencies, the one I'd promised myself I wouldn't touch. I've lost. What a bunch of idiots. They've managed to ruin the end of my trip.

I press on the receiver, but I don't hear anything at the other end of the line. Obviously it isn't connected; there's no electricity here. It must work via satellite. I point it toward the horizon; there isn't a cloud in the sky; if I punch all the buttons, it will eventually get a signal. Nothing happens. I brandish it, I shake it. It doesn't light up. So I smash it on the floor of the terrace, once, twice, ten times; I'm wild with rage, desperate, out of control; it opens at my feet; it's a plastic toy, an empty shell—and inside are yellow chick-shaped marshmallows.

REFERENCES

Some song lyrics slipped into this novel here and there: Angèle's "tout est devenu flou" ("everything became blurry") and "le secret, c'est qu'il n'y a pas de secret" ("the secret is that there is no secret") by the same singer in a duet with Orelsan. There are also references to Olivia Rodrigo's "ballad of a homeschooled girl" and Billie Eilish's "LUNCH."

You'll find words from Pascal's "Memorial" that refer to his "night of fire," when he had a mystical vision that changed the direction of his life. I quote from his *Pensées* (*Thoughts*), the dialectic between misery and grandeur (especially the fragment titled "Disproportion of Man," Brunschvicg 72, Sellier 230).

The following documentaries were particularly useful in describing the daily life of a celebrity and the torments of fame: *Billie Eilish: The World's a Little Blurry*, directed by R. J. Cutler; *Orelsan: Montre jamais ça à personne* (*Orelsan: Never Show This to*

Anyone), created by Clément Cotentin and Christophe Offenstein; and *Taylor Swift: Miss Americana*, directed by Lana Wilson.

And last, some people may have recognized two lines from the movie *(500) Days of Summer* (the bench scene), direct quotes from *The Devil Wears Prada*, the title of a book by Milan Kundera, the song "Malibu" by Miley Cyrus, the nail polish from the model Hailey Bieber, and the novel *And Then There Were None* by Agatha Christie.

The pages of Make Me Famous were inspired by songs, films, literature, philosophy—and life.

ACKNOWLEDGMENTS

This story was born amidst the joy of the publication of my first novel, *My Husband*. This book is dedicated to it, and to all those who read it, loved it, and supported it, both in France and abroad. Thank you, from the bottom of my heart, forever.

This novel is also dedicated to my husband—the real one. You are my greatest happiness.

Huge thanks to my French publisher, L'Iconoclaste, an extraordinary publishing house of shadows and light. To my editors Sylvie Gracia and Constance Beccaria: You gave me absolute freedom, time, solitude, confidence—are there any better conditions under which to create? Toiling away in pursuit of an "OK" in the margins is my favorite sport. Thank you as well to Laurent Beccaria, Alba Beccaria, Lise Chaton, Thomas Garet, Alice Huguet, Adèle Leproux, Alexandra Profizi, and Marie-Laure Walckenaer. With you I have found my clan. It's made of insane demands and beautiful feelings.

Lucky me: I also found a clan across the Atlantic, in New York, at HarperCollins and HarperVia. A big thank you to my editor, Rakesh Satyal, and to my international agent, Sophie Langlais, who stands by me every step of the way. And of course: Gretchen Schmid. Gretchen, you turned my world and my words into English with such precision and humor, I couldn't be more grateful.

I also want to thank the music professionals who agreed to answer my questions. Thank you for giving me a glimpse into the inner workings of French and international record labels.

To Marion, a great editor and tremendous friend: Thank you for being there—you're my compass. Thank you as well to my first readers: Noa, Éléonore, and Charlotte. And for your various perspectives on everything, from what it's like to be onstage, to stars' wardrobes, to ankle sprains, thank you to Valentin, Rosa, Léa, Jeanne, Dr. Le Guérinel, and Dr. Pesch.

Thank you also to my friends, so dear to my heart and my life. Zoé, Lucie, Nicolas, Clémence, Sarah, Pauline, Maud, Marianne, Jean-François, and Sophie . . . and above all to my beloved family: Sylvie, Serge, Damien, Marie-Lou, Léonard, Valentin, Louise. I'm lucky and grateful to be so well-surrounded.

And finally, my thoughts go out to the founder of L'Iconoclaste, Sophie de Sivry. Sophie, just a few hours from turning in my final draft, I can't seem to believe that I'm finishing this novel without you. I can't seem to believe that you didn't choose the cover, that we didn't squabble over the title, that you didn't reread the whole thing one last time. I hope that you would have been proud of this book, and of me. To give myself strength, I'm closing my eyes, and I can see your formidable smile.

A NOTE FROM THE TRANSLATOR

People often ask me how involved authors are in the translation process. The true—if unsatisfying—answer is "it depends." For *Make Me Famous*, it was uniquely collaborative, because Maud speaks fluent English and is a thoughtful, deliberate linguistic stylist. She read every word of this translation multiple times, offering feedback, suggestions, commentary, and context that helped me pinpoint exactly the phrasing she might have used if she'd originally written this book in English as a native speaker. These exchanges made the translation a hundred times better; I find myself wondering now how I could ever translate a book again without that level of author input.

If you've finished this novel, you have probably observed that one quirk of Maud's writing is that she is obsessed with details. An expensive Japanese dishwasher mentioned in a single sentence and never again isn't merely "an expensive Japanese dishwasher"—it's "elegant, silent, connected, with a heat exchanger drying system and an illuminated floor display." This level of exactitude led me down many research rabbit holes over the course of the novel: not just dishwasher drying systems but also taxpaying frameworks for performing artists in France, combed cotton vs. Egyptian cotton, slideshows of Karl Lagerfeld's former Hamburg villa, floor plans of the Naples Archaeological museum, classic children's dances in both France and the US, Greek etymology, Jungian philosophy, Heideggerian philosophy, Pascalian philosophy...

Once we'd gotten about one hundred pages into our work together, I was able to slip more easily into her brain—a gruesome image, but one that feels right for the work of a translator, where authorial intent is paramount. She pays careful attention to word echoes, so I did the same, suggesting small changes where necessary—revising "sailboat or pedal boat" to "ferry or pedal boat," for example, in the scene where a terrified Cléo is en route to the airport in a helicopter—to avoid introducing repetitions that weren't in the French.

Maud's specific imagery is also integral to her narrative voice. It took several back-and-forths to find the right translation for the metaphor she uses to describe the mind of Justin, Cléo's first producer, who's laughably fatalistic. In the original it's a "moulin," or mill, that transforms any piece of information into bad news, but when I tried translating that literally into English, the rhythm and evocativeness were gone— "the inner mill of his mind" just wasn't right, and "workings" and "machinery" were both deemed too vague. Finally, we settled on "paper shredder," and both of us were satisfied.

Our marginalia included arguments over whether a single banana could really cost $1.25, even at Whole Foods; exchanges of YouTube videos; lexicons of sexual terminology with vulgarity ratings; debates over washing one's hair Skeptically vs. Stoically vs. Pyrrhonianally; tugs-of-war over "ands" and various punctuation choices; playful insults about Americans looking ridiculous lugging around jugs of water (from her) and Europeans being chronically dehydrated (from me); and divulgences about which celebrities had inspired a given detail (but my lips are sealed on this front). Every one of these interactions was a joy. I hope your encounter with Maud's cheeky, surprising, *ludicrously* capacious imagination was at least half as much fun as mine was.

ABOUT THE AUTHOR

MAUD VENTURA lives in Paris. Before devoting herself to writing full-time, she led the podcast division of one of France's major radio stations. *My Husband*, her first novel, was a number one bestseller in France and has been translated into more than twenty languages.

ABOUT THE TRANSLATOR

GRETCHEN SCHMID is the translator of several novels and works of nonfiction for both children and adults from French into English, including *Kannjawou* by Lyonel Trouillot, nominated for an Albertine Prize, and *Suddenly* by Isabelle Autissier. She holds a degree in French literature from Columbia University and studied translation at New York University. She lives in New York and works in publishing, with a particular focus on literature in translation.

Here ends Maud Ventura's
Make Me Famous.

The first edition of this book was printed and bound
at LSC Communications in Harrisonburg, Virginia,
in DATE.

A NOTE ON THE TYPE

TK

HARPERVIA

An imprint dedicated to publishing international voices,
offering readers a chance to encounter other lives and other
points of view via the language of the imagination.